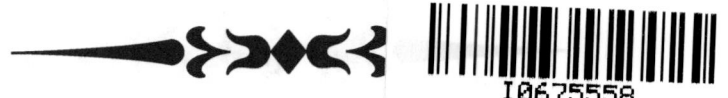

REDISCOVERING
CHARLIE

J.P. MAXIMUS

I

A man is a lion of his own cause.
—Scottish Proverb

REDISCOVERING
CHARLIE

PROLOGUE

Scotland 1563

 multitude of people were standing outside the courthouse awaiting the verdict. Inside, a man of gentle disposition and of esteemed rank was on trial by the highest court for a capital crime. For decades he had safeguarded the health and welfare of his nation. Rumours of his greatness had spread beyond the borders of the land, and for years, throngs of people had paid homage to the prospect of meeting this noble figure, that perchance there was an opportunity to heal their incurable ills. A magician, a wizard, and a healer he was called by the crowd of visitors that once adored this magnanimous figure. Their words of adoration had now turned to cries of abomination. The upheaval and agitation of the assemblage outside was intensifying to an increasing tempo. They were shouting 'traitor!' waving their sticks and screaming 'sorcerer!' towards the opening of the judicial building. The crescendo of their wailing unified to a chant for his execution.

Within the courthouse he was seen sitting calmly in a private room replying to the charges laid before him. The officials were orchestrating one last attempt to obtain a confession. He had been sleep deprived by force for three days to achieve this end: he was unwavering and peacefully countering their every accusation.

A new guard was ushered in to augment the persuasion of their claims. The crowd promptly parted on his arrival: he descended from his carriage and the officials quickly escorted his march towards the secluded chamber. Upon entry, he carefully studied the seated subject before opening his case to arrange his tools. He continued his preparation with the clanging of metal, pausing to look at the confined mortal who stared back without fear. Once finished, he slammed his fist on the table and demanded that the condemned prisoner state his name.

The captive quietly watched the guard tread towards him. He was neither perturbed nor disconcerted at his bellicose approach. He listened to him contemptuously repeat his question. The witnessing officials slowly turned, eagerly awaiting the prisoner to speak. After a long silence, he finally raised his head and confidently delivered his response:

'Charles MacKinnon I.'

I

Let me introduce myself: my name is Charles—Charles MacKinnon. My father is also named Charles, and my son, well, you may have guessed it, is Charles as well. For those of you who are keeping count, I'd be Charles XI; my eight great-grandfather from the 1500s would have been Charles I. You could say he's the one who started this all. Then again, that's not entirely true; this tradition was present even before his time. It dates back to about 700 years ago.

Thirteen names are circulated throughout the family tree if you're male and another thirteen if you're female—for a total of twenty-six names. James, Stewart, Harris, Duncan, Clyde, Abigail, and Fiona are a few names that come to mind right now, as these are the names of my uncles, aunts, and cousins.

If it weren't for this tradition I'm not sure I would ever

know that my cousin William was named after a great uncle that dates back to the Scottish Independence, or that our Great Uncle Murray had worked for King James VI. This was a way to keep order, and remember and honor the people who made you who you are.

I wouldn't expect everyone to understand this, just as I don't expect anyone to be sitting on a 400-year-old settee in their living room.

I received this settee on the Sunday afternoon before the advent of the most significant event of my life. My close friend John came to visit me that day, and I invited him inside for some tea.

"John, please make yourself comfortable," and gestured for him to take a seat.

Sarah and I had recently moved into our new home and had our furnishings transferred—some from my parents' residence and others archived at the MacKinnon cottage.

John hesitantly sat down on the settee and wondered where to put his cup. The tea table beside him, well, that was about 250 years old; it was the more modern piece in our household.

These items had been passed down from generation to generation. At first when people would come over with their children, my heart would stop when I'd see them jumping on chairs or playing around lamps. My father, who was never short on wise advice, put me at ease when he told me, "Take good care of these but don't be consumed by them." So I'm not. I also don't allow guests in certain rooms.

John had seen a few of these furnishings before and knew their history, but perhaps because of the significance of this day seemed to have a renewed interest.

"Who is this relative again?" John asked, standing to read

the inscription on the portrait.

"That's my Great Uncle William IX from 1792," I told him as I had a sip of my tea.

There are many portraits throughout our home. I don't yet have a portrait of my father, Charles X. Anyone who sees him comments on how much we look alike. Genes don't lie, and interestingly they always come back.

The painting on the right side of our living room is of Charles I. John was always enamored with this portrait.

"He looks familiar," he said. "I can't place it, but I definitely see his resemblance in all of your family."

Charles MacKinnon I was one of the founding fathers of neurosurgery in the world. He was born in 1513. They weren't called neurosurgeons then, and unfortunately after the passing of the Witchcraft Act of 1563 he was called by many other names.

Charles had been accused of witchcraft for his work as a neurosurgeon. He was burned at the stake by the hands of a jealous few for his talents—so too were his younger brothers and cousins. His home and belongings were ultimately set on fire. Every time I look at his portrait, I'm reminded of this grim episode.

"You can still see the burnt marks at the bottom edge of the painting near the arm handle," I told John, finally standing up to join him.

John examined the Renaissance-styled chair in the portrait before pausing to ask, "How many children did he have, if I may ask?"

"Just one; he was survived by his wife and son. They were the last remaining link to the MacKinnons."

"What did they do?" John said, still staring at the portrait.

"Their land was seized and they were left in destitute. For

the next eighty-nine years, the MacKinnons were neither allowed to be educated nor practice any trade for fear of recurrence and proliferation of their witchcraft."

Witchcraft prosecutions were commonplace then. However, greatness cannot be stopped, nor can it be contained.

John paused to reflect, shook his head and said, "It's amazing how it all turned out."

I silently nodded in agreement admiring the painting.

John slowly stepped back and asked, "I forgot; who again is entitled to a regnal name and number in your family tree?"

I looked at him and said, "It's only the first-born child of direct lineage, unless there is untimely passing in which case your next-born would also receive this distinction."

"What happens if a family wants to opt out of the naming scheme?" he asked.

"They can—just that nobody has."

Traditional families live by protocol, which is not limited to names. There is a protocol on how to act, how to eat, how to greet; there is even a protocol on how to resolve conflict. No one ever disobeys protocol as you're betraying not only tradition but the right and tested way of doing things. "There is the MacKinnon way, and then there is the other way," my father would say. There was always a family story about a person who chose to do things differently and how some awful tragedy happened to them. I have a whole library of those stories and they are always passed on.

Charles was a new name and maybe our forebears sensed the gleaning of something special. A new name is introduced every hundred years or so when some major epoch happens in our family history. Charles was the last name added to the family tree, and we've been stuck at thirteen names since. No one says why, but I'm venturing to guess that everyone cherishes the unlucky number 13, though they'll never admit it. Superstition is frowned upon with the MacKinnons, even though they're all superstitious; they merely call it by a different name.

Some days it's called magical, at other times you're simply jinxed; on a bad day it's a curse, on a good day it's an omen and on a great day, well, that's what you'd call a prophecy fulfilled. Of course, my personal favorite has always been karma—even though I believe karma is as much scientific as it is supernatural. Just don't call it superstition because the MacKinnons will shun any notion of that. "If thirteen is unlucky for everyone else, it's lucky for us," my Uncle Stewart would say.

Now, you're probably wondering why my father and I as well as my son are all named Charles. Is it that we love the name? No, this was destiny. There is a preset order to the naming for each gender, and we've drawn Charles three times. You don't have to be a mathematician to know how improbable that is. Was it luck? No, this was karma!

There is a general balance to the universe; when something is taken away, the balance is restored somewhere else. This, by the way, is another MacKinnon universal theory.

John had slowly drifted to the other side of the room and was now admiring the swan quill pen on the desk.

"That's the pen Charles II used to depict the life story of

Charles I that is recited by every generation."

"Fascinating," he whispered as he bent down to look at it closely.

Charles II decided to move his family to England in 1652 for a new start. He chose to study medicine and followed in the footsteps of Charles I in his neurosurgical pursuits, and that's not even the part that's karma. There have been over 300 neurosurgeons in the family since Charles I. Everyone did their training at Oxford to keep with tradition even after we migrated to Chicago.

With all the gifted members in the family, there has always been something special in our history with the name Charles. That was where everything started, that was where everything was renewed, and each consecutive Charles since then has pushed the innovation and MacKinnon potential to a higher level than previously imagined. It's for this reason when a Charles is born the entire family looks forward with anticipation.

You can say there have been many special "Charleses" in the family that predate me. That's true, but the Charles that I always like to speak of is the fine gentleman that came after me. It's my son, Charlie—Charles MacKinnon XII.

That Sunday afternoon opened the start of a new chapter, not just for me—but also for MacKinnon history.

"Are you ready for this?" John asked as he sat down again on the settee.

It was the day before the birth of my son Charlie. I don't think words can adequately describe the complete impact of what was to come. It's like walking into a realm that you've never seen before, like a man walking on the moon; everyone can tell you what the lack of gravity and the complete darkness of space can feel like—you really don't know until you experience it.

Walking on the moon was exactly what it felt like when I was with Charlie. Time stopped and nothing mattered. He was born on April 22nd. It was a beautiful sunny day in Wilmette, a suburb of Chicago, 73° with no wind and just the light cool air that leaves you breathless. That spring just seemed different; everything felt right that day. I can't remember the last time I heard so many birds singing like they were trying to prompt you a message. The birds were right; it felt as though there were celebrations around us.

My connection with Charlie was unlike anything I've ever seen before. If you are wondering, the connection was there from the moment of his birth.

The labor had been a complicated one—a breech delivery. Just before rushing for a C-section he decided to make a turn with a little bit of help from the good doctor, and just like that, before I knew it, he was in my arms.

As I held him, he stopped crying and our eyes locked. He was reading my soul and I his. There was a conversation, though there were no words spoken. That penetrating look must have lasted a few minutes, but it felt like eternity. Most people in my shoes would give anything to know what exactly he was thinking, though my instincts already knew. Even holding him, there was a connection in the touch I'm at a loss to describe. This isn't something a man can explain as not many are privileged to have experienced this. I don't expect you to even understand, but that's where it all started.

II

Let me first go over a few things I need to tell you. For starters, let me say a few words about my wife Sarah. We met and became best friends when we were thirteen years old at a summer camp. My mother had many reservations about her, but that was the least of my worries. It my grandparents' opposition that had the most influence and echoed the loudest.

Sarah, by all accounts, was not considered worthy of a MacKinnon. She lived in the wrong part of town. She was two grades below me even though we were the same age. She had never met her father, and her mother worked hard to support Sarah and her sister, by singing at bars.

"Charles, sit down," my grandfather once said. "When I was your age my own grandfather gave this advice that was given to him by his grandfather and his grandfather before that. You can trust that these words are tried and tested over centuries."

I didn't like where this was going, but "go on."

"The early MacKinnons from seven hundred years ago did not acquire their wealth from the practice of medicine. They owned land and were in the trade of agriculture. That's where their wealth came from."

"I understand," but I wasn't sure where he was going next.

"Charles, in order to build a home or start a farm, you have to pay careful attention to the quality of its soil. The foundation of any building even today is built on a strong and stable soil."

He paused to let me catch up on what he was about to tell me next.

"You cannot just take any soil and make it stable, nor can you take any soil and make it strong. Its stability and strength depends on its inherent properties." He looked at me more intently before saying, "Charles, I love you and want to support you, but a relationship also depends on some intrinsic characteristics. You're building your home on swampland. The foundation just isn't there to support this long term."

I wanted to be respectful but I also felt I had to say something: "I know what you're saying, Grandpa, but you don't know Sarah the way I do. You'll have to trust me on this one. There is no swampland here. The soil is strong and stable."

My grandfather shook his head. "I hope you're right, but I think you'll look back and regret this."

I guess when your family is close you have to appease

everyone, especially the grandparents. It took a lot of convincing and diplomacy from my father, a gift he had that I unfortunately didn't inherit.

Sarah and I were practically inseparable since meeting at camp. Our favorite activity was watching the sun rise and then watching it set all in one day.

We would sit there on the grass overlooking the beautiful lake in front of us. We'd have two sandwiches, two sodas, one big bag of chips, and nothing but a view. We'd talk for fifteen hours.

There was never a dull moment; even the silent moments felt packed with an exchange of dialogue. I had calculated that we had twenty-one minutes of light after sundown. I would hesitantly look at my watch, and she would ask me, "Is it time?"

I'd count the seconds before finally making that dreaded call, "We have to go," and we'd cheerlessly ride back on our bicycles.

When did I know I want to marry her? I'd like to say the day I met her, but I was too clueless to know what marriage was then. I just knew I wanted to spend the rest of my life with her, and that feeling never wavered.

I proposed to her when I was eighteen. She didn't hesitate to accept even though she still had two years of secondary school left; we'd also be living in separate continents while I attended Oxford for my medical training and PhD in neuroscience.

We both knew we were eternally meant for one another and that trust is something one doesn't always have a chance to experience.

We were married just before we turned twenty, but it wasn't without a stern warning that I will tarnish the MacKinnon name and Sarah will betray me. Sarah understood and in her own unique way never held a grudge. Not once was she perturbed by my family's disfavor, never did she complain about it, and at no time did she hesitate in her commitment. It was always about us.

Even though she came from a very different background, Sarah seemed to understand the nuances of my family's tradition. She seemed to grasp it, or maybe she just pretended and respected it. Either way, it was something that I appreciated and I wished my grandparents would take note of, but unfortunately, stubbornness is also a MacKinnon trait. This trait I regrettably did inherit.

Sarah deferred on starting her university education and joined me in England nine months after we were married. It was during this time we had James, our firstborn. Jesse, as we called him, had beautiful golden brown hair at birth. It was light colored just like his mother's hair. Sadly, he had also been born with a rare congenital lung disease. He lived all but eighteen days.

It was amazing to see that even after a few days of life there was a personality, an identity, and deep connection between parent and child. We spent as much time with Jesse as we possibly could. We had been told he wouldn't last a week.

It was challenging for both of us, but especially for Sarah. She continually spoke and whispered in Jesse's ear every day, showering him with motherly advice. We took as many pictures as we could, and Sarah even saved some of Jesse's hair and clothes to remember him.

In the end, I decided to return home to complete my medical training. My grandparents weren't too happy about me leaving Oxford as this was breaking with tradition; they blamed Sarah even though it was my decision.

Sarah was in England only for me, and in many respects, coming home was a medical necessity. After several months, we decided to conceive again. It was my idea, and I thought it would be good for her. In view of the challenges we had with Jesse, it was prudent to have genetic testing as there was a possibility of a similar occurrence happening again.

My father owned a facility at the time, Genomica Hospital, a world-class research institute in genetics and neuroscience research. No other center had the breakthrough services that Genomica offered, which is one of the reasons we turned to my father's hospital to have the genetic testing and screening done.

Unfortunately, the federal government had been closely monitoring the activities of any genetic center and our facility had been under strict scrutiny during those times; despite the concerns, the physician who treated Sarah was a family friend, and nine months later, Charlie was born.

As wonderful an experience as Charlie was, having one child never erases the memory of another. Sarah continued to keep pictures of Jesse, and other memorabilia, in and around the house. It was when Charlie turned three when I noticed a sudden transformation. I'm not sure what it was, but one day I came home and she had packed all of Jesse's items in a small wooden treasure chest and stored them in the basement. I never asked her why, but figured Charlie was now older and asking questions.

II

Sarah never opened that treasure chest even in later years. This was something we didn't often talk about, and it wasn't the type of wound I wanted to reopen. We had other challenges on the way.

III

It was the day before Charlie's fifth birthday. I was sitting in my study room when my father arrived. I wasn't sure if I heard the sound of the doorbell as Sarah was playing the piano. I stepped out in the hallway and saw Charlie running to open the door. My father was an avid baseball fan and wanted to take Charlie to the ballpark to experience his first game; this was an early birthday present.

Unfortunately, it was spring and one of the MacKinnon-inherited traits is we all have asthma. Springtime is not our friend with the number of seasonal allergies we have. My father was already coughing at the door.

"Where is my Charlie?" he asked.

"Grandpa!" Charlie screamed, excited, leaping into his arms.

"Are you feeling okay," I asked him.

"I'll be fine," he said and laughed. I have asthma myself and wasn't too concerned with his symptoms.

He brought Charlie his first baseball cap, placed it on his head, and shortly after, they departed for the game. Sadly, the fresh outdoors only made his symptoms worse; near the end of the seventh inning, failing his inhalers, he wanted to leave early commenting to Charlie with a smile and pointing to the puffer, "Hopefully in the future you won't need this."

Considering our long, tortuous journey, one would think everything would go more smoothly in our lives. "This is the most important lesson I can teach you," my father would always say. "Where there is struggle there is development." At least one would hope things would turn for the better at some point. The universal balance on this day didn't quite make a turn as expected.

I received a call later that afternoon. There had been an accident: My father had died. I can only assume the rest from the police report. The bystanders had said he had lost control of his vehicle, probably from having trouble breathing, and was hit by an oncoming truck. The firemen who helped extract him out of his car observed that his lips were blue with his inhaler in hand. He died shortly on route to the hospital.

Charlie had been in the back seat, which is why his life was spared. When I later saw the insurance photos, I'm not sure how anyone could have survived.

There are days in your life when you're left with the realization that life had just lost its innocence. This was that day. I can recount the events of that afternoon as though it was yesterday, and Charlie later told me the rest of the details.

As for Charlie's fifth birthday—he was on a ventilator in the intensive care unit, unable to breathe on his own. He had significant injuries and was left quadriplegic retaining only partial use of his arms. I hadn't even considered what the future might hold for us; it was all about making it till tomorrow. This was also the day we were busy preparing my father's funeral.

I never had an opportunity to mourn my father's death. The only thought occupying my mind: *am I going to have a call at any moment with some bad news about Charlie?* I didn't have a chance to thank my father—for his love, his support, and everything he had done for me in my life, especially with Sarah. I never had the opportunity to listen to him tell me a few last words of wisdom.

I returned from time to time to take flowers to my father's burial site. Each time I was haunted by the fact that I didn't have a chance to say goodbye—not even at his funeral.

As for Charlie, he was in the hospital for the next five months. Ironically, knowing he was never going to walk again didn't upset me as much as I thought. Every day I was fighting the battle of whether he'd live. When he was eventually weaned off his ventilator, simply breathing on his own was one of the greatest moments of triumph.

I guess pain and joy are all a matter of perspective. It all depends on your starting point. Knock a man down to the bottom of an empty well and he'd be celebrating when there are a few drops of rain even though he's sitting in mud now.

Suffering also does a few things to a man's brain, both psychologically and physiologically. One discovery neuroscience has shown is that we tend to dream more when we suffer. So I can assume that would somewhat explain why over the years I'd have recurrent dreams of my father enjoying a beautiful spring day playing on a baseball field—except there was never really much conversation in those dreams, though it sure was comforting.

Lost in the turbulence was the karma of the first Charles of 1513. There were, at last count, 317 neurosurgeons in the MacKinnon family since Charles I amongst both the men and women members. That's a high number but it's worth mentioning that not all members of the family necessarily became neurosurgeons; however, every "Charles" had become one and went on to become a great neurosurgeon. In my humble opinion, my Charlie was going to be the best.

You can see a child's talents and inclinations in the early years. I know my own parents always raved about my eye-hand coordination when I was a child. Let me tell you, whatever talent I had paled in comparison to what I witnessed in Charlie.

When he was three years old, Sarah had asked him to draw a picture of what he experienced that day when they had visited Sarah's mother and sister in a small city called Galena west of Chicago. Sarah provided Charlie some supplies with the hope of keeping him busy. After few hours when she stopped to look at what he had made, she was astonished. She saved it for me to see later that day, and it would sit beside our grand piano for the next few years.

Charlie didn't just draw a picture. He had cut out a three-dimensional model of the entire city core with a meticulous recall of every building, street, and sign.

"This is incredible," I almost shouted.

"Did you notice the tree?"

"What tree?" I asked.

"The tree!" Sarah reiterated, tilting her head toward it.

I guess this probably wasn't a good time to forget that I had proposed to Sarah under a tree overlooking the river in Galena. "Wow. You showed him the tree," I told her and admired that he even had the bench beside it.

"Actually, I hadn't shown him," Sarah said. "We were all so busy talking in the car that I didn't even realize we had passed by it."

I stood there baffled and marveled at what Charlie had accomplished.

"Charles," Sarah continued, "I looked at all the pictures I took today. I think Charlie has every tree and lamppost we passed in its perfect place and orientation."

The attention to detail, the precision, the creativity and coordination in making such a brilliant design—well, this was the stuff legends were made of. He wasn't just going to be a great neurosurgeon, he was going to be the best one of us all; but after his accident, that was all gone. God had given him a gift and the universe had taken it away.

The truth is, right now we had a multitude of problems. I had just finished my medical training. With my father gone, many of the family responsibilities were upon my shoulders, so I decided to work at Genomica. This wasn't what I had ever intended. Sometimes in life you can't take the path that you chose, but rather the path that is chosen for you.

To be honest, I wasn't even certain who I was doing this for—was it to continue my father's legacy? I'm not sure. Or, did I want to help my mother in relieving the burden of putting the company's affairs in order? Again, I don't know. I did know one thing: Genomica was a leading research hospital and we had a whole department dedicated to gene therapy research for nerve regeneration; if for no other reason, I had to do this for Charlie. It offered me hope, and hope for Charlie.

There are many simple things in life we take for granted: going for a walk, standing up to shake someone's hand; Charlie was denied these simple rights, amongst other things.

The summer I started working at Genomica was also when Charlie finally came home from the hospital. Sarah also decided to leave school, where she was striving toward her music degree. This time she wasn't leaving school for me, it was for Charlie. His condition initially called for continuous and ceaseless care. Even with hired workers and me helping, this wasn't sufficient to meet our needs.

After a period of adjustment, I believe it's fair to say the next ten years were the finest years of my life. Charlie's condition provided me a sense of purpose.

I was working for the hospital that was on the leading edge of gene therapy and spinal cord research. The cure was not only possible—it was just a matter of time. Somehow, everything was now starting to make sense. The karma not only wasn't broken, but in a roundabout way was being pushed to new heights.

Once I was sober from the pain, I could start connecting the dots that I hadn't seen before. Perhaps the universal karma that every Charles MacKinnon would push the innovation in neurosurgery needed a new catalyst. "Where there is struggle there is development." Maybe this was the crisis needed for ultimate victory. My father had left me a legacy and had an arrow pointed for his desired direction.

As for Charlie, he was my best friend. Though he could not use his legs and had limited use of his arms, his brain shined ever so brightly as time went on. By the time Charlie was eight, he was studying at the secondary school level.

He was home schooled at that time, and his teachers were in awe at his brilliance. Mrs. Alice Spencer, one of his teachers throughout those years, once said: "Sir, your son's like a sponge. Whatever I teach him gets absorbed, and by the end of the session if you give a squeeze he's teaching me a thing or two." We tried to reassure her, but she went on, "Sometimes I'm not sure who the teacher is here. Just letting you know, pretty soon I'll have nothing left to teach him."

It was about this time when I came home one evening and saw Charlie in my library reading my neurosurgery textbooks and avidly studying the journals I had left on my desk. A father knows his son; he knows exactly what he's thinking and what's running though his mind. I just watched and didn't say anything. Charlie was starting his own escape plan and figuring out a cure for his condition. I don't think there was ever a Charles MacKinnon with this kind of tenacity and thirst for knowledge. He would not only make our legacy proud, but true to the MacKinnon way, he would have to overcome an obstacle to achieve his ultimate destiny.

In later years, when Charlie was twelve, he was on par with most graduating neurosurgical residents. In fact, if I wanted to gauge how to examine my residents I would first test and run it by Charlie. This is how it went: I'd provide him with a three-hour test and say, "Here, Charlie; take your time."

I'd sit there with my stopwatch, read a journal, and occasionally ask him, "Any questions?"

He would silently glance up, shake his head, and look back down. Then when he was finally ready, with a serious expression he'd put his pen down and say, "Done."

If Charlie could complete the test in less than one hour, it was too easy. If he could complete it in one and a half hours, it was fair. Anything close to two hours then you might as well forget about it; that would be too difficult for even the sharpest resident. One thing was for sure: Charlie seemed to enjoy these tests much more than the residents did.

Those were happy days, though no one seemed to understand our joy except for us. I relished coming home to Sarah and Charlie; I cherished our time together. There was a sense of purpose in our lives. We had an aim, and that aim was always us, together. What people perceived as a challenge was the central point that united us, and now seemed like an acceptable part of life.

Turn the page and move forward and enjoy every moment was our collective mindset. It is times like these when you ask yourself the question, *what do I need in life to be happy?* I need Sarah, I need Charlie, I love my job and if you push me, maybe a good friend or two. Everything else for me was just a mirage.

Unfortunately, others didn't see it that way. There was that time when Sarah saw Mrs. Jenny Backer. She told me about this episode later when I spoke to her that night almost laughing at the absurdity of people's ignorance.

Mrs. Backer was one of our neighbors who lived down the street. We had heard that her daughter was in a drug rehabilitation program and her son had quit school, left home, and was not on speaking terms with the family.

We always pitied Mrs. Backer, so it came as a surprise to see she actually pitied us. Sarah had seen her at the local grocery store. I know Mrs. Backer had meant well but people have an interesting manner in providing support.

"Sarah, it is horrible what happened to Charlie! Poor girl, what you must be going through." She said this not once but three times over the course of that conversation.

"Actually, we are well and enjoying life. Why, have you heard differently?" Sarah asked.

"When they told me about Charlie, I cried so much. I wept for you and Dr. MacKinnon. It's horrible what you had to endure."

Sarah patiently listened before saying, "There were some challenging times—that's for sure; but everything is back to normal now and we're happy. So not to worry, all is good."

Unfortunately, it didn't end there. Mrs. Backer wanted to reiterate her support by showering Sarah with more pity. These episodes would occur from time to time. It was uncomfortable but comical as it was also far from the truth. These were, as I said, the happiest days of our lives, and the outside perceptions didn't matter to us.

IV

When Charlie was nine, Sarah made a plea for Charlie to be integrated back into a regular school. She was concerned about his need to become socially adjusted and wished to see him around other children.

I didn't entirely disagree. I was Charlie's only friend. My only hesitation in all this was not being sure what Charlie could possibly learn from a traditional school. I reluctantly agreed, but Sarah fortunately met me halfway and we placed Charlie at the Montgomery School for the Gifted. He was also entered two grades above his age group; two years was all I could negotiate with Sarah. This school had a long tradition with the MacKinnon family. Charlie had to pass an exam in order to be admitted. Although the scores are usually kept confidential, I was eventually told by the principal, Mr. Jones, that on the creativity scale his scores were off the charts, and his general score was the highest ever in the 93 years of the school's existence.

I couldn't hold back my pleasure and marvel at Charlie, so I remarked, "You'll have to send my apologies to the kid who held the previous record."

Mr. Jones was silent. He waited and then hesitantly uttered, "Well that's interesting, because the name of that previous student was also Charles MacKinnon."

I was stunned. "Wow," I said. "That's amazing...I didn't know I had the record."

Mr. Jones looked at me before saying in a restrained voice, "Actually...it was your father."

"Oh." I was speechless and realized my dad had never mentioned anything about this. Then again, should I even be surprised? He was never one to talk about his accomplishments; this was exactly how we'd always find out.

The school was divided into sections and each child's education could be tailored to their talents if desired. Charlie was naturally placed in the science section of the school. Unfortunately, he didn't like his experience very much. He was always a step ahead of any of the so-called "gifted" students and that aroused nothing but jealousy. Adding to the hurdle was his shy personality and being much younger in age than his peers. Sarah had advised me this might happen. All of these factors along with his disability became an obstacle for Charlie to adjust and make new friends.

That being the case, I was still perplexed when I was called to his school by the principal to discuss Charlie's detention. His teacher, Mrs. Crouch, was present there along with the principal and she explained with slight agitation, "Today is the fifth time I have caught Charlie reading comics under his desk."

I said, "Ma'am, I'm not sure I understand; as far as I know Charlie has never owned a comic book."

"Well, Dr. MacKinnon," she said, "then you don't know everything your son does. He has a whole stack of them in his bag with his superhero weapons."

"Did you say weapons?"

"Yes," said the principal. "This is why he's been in my office and why we called you."

I opened the bag and there it was. A variety of comics on the outside, but as I flipped the pages on the inside it was a completely different story. The teacher couldn't see as I was looking through the pages inside, but Charlie could see me, and the look in his blue eyes was priceless. He had hid several different neurosurgery journals within the comic book covers. I guess he didn't want to attract additional attention at school and just wanted to fit in. The "superhero" tools they talked about, well, they were just neurosurgical instruments. State-of-the-art tools I might add. They weren't mine, nor were any of these journals. Although, as I could see on the label, all these journals were addressed to my name, or perhaps I should say our name. This is where I found out I had apparently been subscribing to five additional journals I didn't even know about. I would venture to guess Charlie had been emailing all the medical supply companies and journals, giving his name and address, which he cleverly shared with mine; the companies, assuming it was me, were sending him free samples of everything. Knowing my son, he was enjoying all this. To be fair, he hadn't exactly lied in using my identity as we shared the same name. He simply outsmarted the system. Charlie was looking at me very intently as I was browsing through his comic books. I would look at him from time to time as I flipped through the pages. I could tell he wasn't so worried what his teacher or his principal was thinking. He knew the moment I looked into his bag I had figured out what he was up to and his schemes had finally caught up with him.

I looked at his teacher and said, "You're probably right. I may not know all the sorts of things my son has been doing; definitely not as well as I thought."

The school principal then said, "Dr. MacKinnon, you realize Charlie would have to be expelled from school for carrying a knife in his bag."

"Mr. Jones," I said, "Charlie has limited use of his hands, what could he have possibly done with these so-called 'superhero' tools?"

"Yes...but these are the school regulations."

"Was he a threat to anybody?" I asked.

"But the rules clearly state, Dr. MacKin—"

"Sir, has he shown any violent behavior?"

"No, but..."

"Would he be physically capable of showing violent behavior?"

"No, but the rules..."

"Mr. Jones, the rules are there to protect the students, not to persecute them. It's clear Charlie was not a threat to anyone so why are you victimizing him?"

I didn't care for Charlie to stay home for a week; he might actually learn more than where he was. I knew Charlie probably didn't mind it either; he was never really happy at school. The only thing I cared about in this equation was that I didn't want for any of this to be stamped on Charlie's record—so I plea-bargained with the principal. Charlie would come home for a week as punishment, but this would not be marked on his school record.

If you're wondering why I didn't mention these were neurosurgical tools, it's because it would place the burden of responsibility on me as to why he was even playing with these to begin with. I would have to prove that they were not mine, and that was not an easy task given that each item was addressed to my name. So it was simpler to keep it as Charlie's "superhero" weapons and negotiate from that end. In all fairness, their version, while imaginative, was probably not too far from the truth. I fully expected Charlie to use these instruments one day and perform super-human acts.

The drive home was an interesting one to say the least. I was never prouder of Charlie, yet I felt impelled to punish him. I always knew he was different; even in a gifted school he was steps ahead of not just the students but the teacher and the principal as well. In truth, he was steps ahead of me on most days. He had the prototypes of the most modern surgical tools that I didn't have, and he did this all without lying. So I quietly said the only thing that came to mind after a long silence.

"Son, do you like comic books?"

"I don't know, Dad. I guess."

"If you like them we can buy you some more for you to read at home?"

"Sure, Dad," he said with a nod, desperately hoping to change the conversation.

"What about those superhero weapons? Do you want to tell me how you got those?"

Charlie was silent.

"You know, I'd like to see you use those one day, but, Charlie, these aren't toys; they are to be used responsibly in the right place—not at home, not on the playground, and definitely not at school. Do you understand, son?"

He nodded his head again and said, "Sorry, Dad."

Our drive home was about finished; I gave Charlie a big hug and stopped myself short of telling him how pleased I was with him. Then I looked him in the eye and said, "C'mon, son, let's go in—this was the easy part; now we have to explain to your mother why you're not going to school."

The week Charlie stayed home was part destiny and part luck as Charlie would have a chance in changing his own future and fortunes. For years, researchers including myself had been perplexed on how to foster spinal cord regeneration. Using a combination of stem cells and gene therapy, the nerve could be regenerated but would slowly degenerate over time. I brought Charlie with me to our hospital grand rounds for my presentation on this subject. We could never work our heads around why the regeneration worked in animals but not in humans.

After my presentation, Charlie, later musing over the ornaments on my desk, asked the obvious, "Dad, why don't you just inject them with the protective enzymes, analogous to the monkey?"

"Well, that's because the human body would soon reject that. The patients would become ill."

"Yes, but if you used the recombinant DNA strategy along with the modifications you talked about in your presentation; they wouldn't get sick, would they?"

Charlie was alluding to the select use of genetic material from multiple sources to express a desired protein. I told him,

"Well no, but their condition wouldn't improve either."

"So, they wouldn't get sick?" he repeated with a smile.

"No, but what would be the point?" I knew he was up to something; I just couldn't figure out what it was. So I continued, "If you're thinking of administering this to maintain viability in their nerves long enough for them to gain strength, it's been tried and it doesn't work."

"Dad, what if you're looking for the wrong enzymes in humans?"

"Not sure I understand, Charlie."

"Couldn't you just use different algorithms of the tested enzymes pre and posttreatment only to help you identify which enzymes it inhibits and activates in humans? This might help you identify the right ones."

Then it dawned on me where he was heading with this. When I sat down and he showed me the full scale of his thoughts—it was brilliant. He was using a common strategy to look for something completely different. The idea was right in front of my eyes for all these years, but it was Charlie, who was able to connect the dots. The final algorithm took another year to put together, but its inception was that day, and Charlie was the catalyst to solve this final puzzle.

Greatness cannot be stopped, nor can it be contained. Even with Charlie's challenges, it was easy to see that he would be one of the greatest neurosurgeons that would have ever lived, even though he wasn't yet a neurosurgeon.

Charlie helped see the study through; every day I'd come home and talk to him about it. I had quickly discovered my rabbit's foot. When I published the paper, it was a landmark study—a breakthrough that had long stymied researchers.

V

We were now ready to move to our Phase III trials. I had the option to have Charlie included as a patient in this study. Sarah had actually wanted this. "I just want him to be playing and enjoying his youth like the other children," she said. We went back and forth debating this. I wasn't enthusiastic about the idea.

I had my reasons. First, it would seem selfish to include Charlie in the study when there were people who had suffered longer than he had. Optics was everything, and selecting your own son didn't send the right message. Not to mention the GSA, Genetic Safety Administration—a federal agency specifically dealing with biologics and gene therapy—would question the integrity of your selection process. Second, there were benefits in being enrolled later for these treatment trials. If Charlie wanted to be a neurosurgeon, he would need to have the finest motor skills. So it would serve him better to do this at a time when some of the techniques and methods had been improved.

Sarah finally understood and accepted to delay the treatment. I wasn't really asking us to wait too long. We agreed for Charlie to do this in one year when he would be fifteen.

The early results from our clinical trials were outstanding. Mark Simpson, who was a patient of mine, had become paraplegic when he was eighteen after falling off a horse during an equestrian competition. You'd never know looking at him that he was once an athlete. He was forty-seven now, 40 pounds overweight and hadn't walked for nearly thirty years. It was impossible to know what effect the surgery would have on his nerves and muscles having been dormant for so long. He was one of the first few to enter the trials. It was unbelievable watching him walk again. Mark Simpson was now jogging every day, and at his last visit, he was hoping to prepare for a marathon.

There were many cases like this, each with their own story and each with their own miracle on returning to normal function. With such positive results, we quickly increased the number of patients we were treating in the trial.

Of course, there were limitations in how many of these we could do. Few surgeons were skilled in this technique and our hospital was by far the only one with the proper technology to perform it. We also didn't know too much about the long-term outcome, which is why the GSA wanted a more reserved approach. While the argument had its merits, it was hard to accept with so many patients demanding this treatment.

It was about this time that I met the lead agent from the

GSA. With the many spinal regeneration procedures we were completing, the agency wanted to ensure all regulations were being followed. This agent was a young man, smart, motivated, and looking to make a name for himself in the industry. He dropped by the company for the first time when I was in the office with Charlie.

"Dr. MacKinnon, may I come in? My name is Mr. Dawson from the GSA."

Of course, those last three letters would perk up the ears of anyone in my field. "Good afternoon, Mr. Dawson, nice to meet you," I greeted.

"We're doing a random inspection," he said sternly. "Do you mind accompanying me to your labs and procedure rooms?"

Charlie didn't like Dawson on seeing him that first day. That should have been my first clue for what to expect. Charlie was a "feeling person" and had a great ability to distinguish the sincere from the deceiver just from the way he felt from their interaction. Rarely was he wrong, and I attributed this to his creative nature. He didn't have to tell me what he thought of Dawson—I could read it from his expression as he gingerly observed him looking around from lab to lab and room to room. Charlie quietly followed along but kept a safe distance as he watched him cautiously.

Unfortunately, when the GSA comes to your office they are not looking to pat you on the back or to congratulate you for all the services you've provided. Our technology was so superior to anyone else's—their agency was simply scared of its implications. They were specifically looking to understand it. The GSA always felt a need to be ahead of the people they were monitoring. Genomica's technology was built in-house; there was no copy and no rival. It was not only the best, but nobody else understood it or had access to it. That frightened the GSA and they were always looking for any excuse to spy and replicate it in order to monitor us.

It was then, on that first meeting, when Dawson delivered his first blow—a blow that still reverberates in my thoughts today.

"Dr. MacKinnon, we'll need to take this machine for testing and inspection."

The device he was referring to was our GEMA, Genetic Engineering Medical Apparatus. He sure knew where to look and what to ask for. GEMA was where all the magic happened and allowed us to do what we did. No company had such a thing. My father worked on building GEMA for over thirty years. I knew Dawson didn't want to inspect it for safety, but rather so that their agency could duplicate it.

We had anticipated such an occurrence, and had built codes and modifications so that the replication of GEMA would be impossible. We also had a backup machine in case of such an event. The fallback device was no GEMA, but our operations wouldn't come to a complete halt either. Our machines could not be understood by their team of engineers, but didn't stop the GSA from trying. After quickly realizing they couldn't decrypt the code, they asked if they could also inspect our backup machine and collect our research.

"What! Why? Is there a problem?" I asked.

"Sorry, Dr. MacKinnon, we're just following protocol," Dawson told me.

"Why do you need our research?" I pleaded. I wasn't sure what protocol he was referring to. They were simply trying to slow us down. The research data they were collecting were not even from our current treatments but for our planned future treatments. It bothered the GSA that our research was miles ahead of any other research institute. Where other facilities had failed, we had succeeded. Where others had stumbled, we had forged ahead. Our research along with GEMA was what distinguished us. Then Dawson asked the question, which never did sit well with me: "Dr. MacKinnon, your son—you're not planning to treat him, are you?"

I was actually planning to treat Charlie at the conclusion of our Phase III trials, but now that he mentioned it, "No, why do you ask?"

"It would be a conflict of interest to treat him at this time."

Technically, there isn't one when there are no other alternatives. I wasn't about to debate this with him—not at that moment. I was fully aware what this was all about; it was backdoor punishment for not supplying them with what they had wanted. Dawson also needed to win somewhere. I was only beginning to understand his psychology; if I knew one thing, it was that Charlie's treatment hinged on his clearance. Until then, I had to be patient and yield to everything he requested.

They held our machines for nearly six months and that had ramifications for Charlie. This setback also backed up our ability to treat people by the same length of time.

Charlie wasn't happy about having his therapy delayed, but I think he always had a good sense of what Dawson was up to from the day he walked into my office. I reassured him once we were approved and the Phase III trials were over that there was nothing that could stop us.

V

Those were difficult times, yet encircled within those challenges were some of my fondest memories. My days consisted of spending time in the lab, treating patients, and going home to Sarah and Charlie.

VI

One afternoon, John, came over to my office. He was wearing his baseball uniform with gym bag in hand. "Charles, me and the guys are going to play baseball this evening at Finnegan's Field. I thought you might want to join us."

"Thanks, John, but I actually have plans tonight."

"Does it have to do with Charlie?" he said with a concerned voice.

"Yes it does."

"Well, we thought you might need a break. You haven't played with us for years."

"Thanks, but I'm watching the baseball game on television tonight with Charlie."

"Oh, okay. I know how tough this must be on you with the challenges and all. I hope you don't mind me bringing up this subject; I just wanted to let you know I'm here for you."

"Thank you, John. I appreciate the sentiment, but I'm happy and I don't mind what you're referring to. I enjoy going home to Charlie, I like taking care of him, and I know nobody really gets this, but you don't have to worry about me. I wouldn't trade what I have for anything else that's out there."

"Sure. No problem, Charles. I understand, but if you ever need me, I'm here."

"Thank you, John," I said, appreciating his sincerity, "but I have to run now."

I raced home and Charlie was waiting by the window in his usual spot. I enjoyed going for a jog every day and Charlie liked accompanying me. He loved the outdoors but was shy to venture out on his own, so he would wait patiently for me to come home so we'd go together. It was during these runs that we'd have the most quality time to talk and have our usual father-son chat. When I walked in I asked him, "Are you ready, son?"

"Dad, have you forgotten?"

"Forgot what?"

"It's haircut day!"

It had slipped my mind. Charlie was very particular about his hair. Being a neurosurgeon I would be required to partially shave people's heads from time to time, so Charlie didn't trust his hair to anyone but me, and as he put it, "you practically do this for a living."

I would trim Charlie's hair frequently, as he preferred his hair short ever since his accident. In the early years he had spent a lot of time initially in bed and also in a wheelchair that provided a headrest. The shorter hair just felt more comfortable. He didn't have to worry about it being disheveled and he didn't perspire as much either.

"Okay, Charlie, you know the drill."

We went into the elevator to go downstairs. Our basement was our palace. I spent many hours here with Charlie. It opened to a beautiful garden, and in its main hall there was a large open area decorated with Edwardian-style furniture. The elevator and spiral staircase both opened to this grand hall. On the right side of this main area was one large storage room. On the left and opening to the outside was a beautiful room we called our "hideout." Here it was customary for us to meet and cut Charlie's hair every two weeks.

"Your hair already looks short; are you sure you want me to trim it more?"

"Yes, Dad, it makes me more aerodynamic," he said, beaming with joy.

"Okay, then I'll have to run faster to keep up with you."

Charlie's wheelchair was not your ordinary ready-made wheelchair. As I was cutting his hair, I couldn't help but think back to the episode when he had received this incredible device.

Charlie himself had sent the manufacturer a design to produce a working prototype without our knowledge, using well, my name—again! He had provided his own specifications as to what he wanted and had the functional prototype delivered right to my office. As one would expect, I was a little surprised when it arrived with the agent knocking on the office door.

"Dr. MacKinnon, it's nice to finally meet you. I'm Andrea Miller. You are a busy man. I have tried calling you many times," she said as she struggled to carry the prototype inside.

I didn't know who she was and what she was doing here

until she remarked, "In our emails you had mentioned wanting speeds up to 40 miles per hour. I'm afraid our engineers had safety concerns so we limited the speed to 20 miles per hour."

"...our emails?" I muttered with a blank face. It didn't take me long to figure it out this time—who and what was up to this.

"Thank you. Umm, this is actually more than what I expected," I said, trying to hold back my thoughts. Yet, I was clearly dumbfounded at what I was viewing.

"Great. We were worried you might be disappointed. We weren't sure how to incorporate the buoyancy specifications for the water floatation either. So we—"

"No, this is wonderful," I said in a hurry. "Thank you for this. It's more than enough. I'll test it out and give you my feedback."

When I finally arrived home and took the robotic wheelchair out of my car, Charlie was waiting and immediately rushed outside; he knew what was coming.

"Charlie, do you know what this is?"

"It's my birthday present. I was wondering when you'd come home with it!"

"Your birthday isn't for another six months..."

"Thanks, Dad. You're the best."

"I'm not sure how to operate this, do you?"

"Don't worry, I got this."

He sure did. Charlie opened the package and started assembling it. He knew exactly how all the configurations worked and which buttons to push.

I asked him as he was swiftly putting it all together, "Charlie, it looks like you approve the design?"

He just nodded in his frantic state of excitement and

didn't stop to even catch his breath. It was actually my hope for Charlie to no longer need the wheelchair in the near future, if only Dawson would hurry up with his meddling. I wasn't sure how to tell the poor agent that soon these wheelchairs would become obsolete. I didn't want to worry about it though. Seeing the thrill on Charlie's face was worth the trouble that my son had managed to put me in once again.

This newly designed wheelchair had some pretty interesting features. To begin with, it could go as fast as a person sprinting and had built-in countermeasures to avoid collisions. It also came with a protective vest that resembled a suit of armor, and would seamlessly synchronize with the device to safeguard the operator. To provide a more natural movement it could wrap safety supports to help the person stand upright. Using the same upright technology it could rotate and tilt to roll up any staircase. There was no activity that Charlie wouldn't be able to do with this device; he had thought of every situation. It was made of titanium alloy and was so small and polished you'd think it was made for a spacecraft.

Charlie was finishing setting up the configuration for the fingerprint sensors so he could have sole operation of the machine. He had his fingers pressing on the instrument and then finally looked up and said, "How do I look, Dad?" with a grin on his face.

I was looking at him and smiling in awe. Charlie had the device in the standing position, and did another spin around and asked again, "How do I look?"

This was the first time I'd seen Charlie standing. "You look great. I can barely recognize you."

"Why, what do you mean, Dad?"

VI

"You've grown up!" It had never dawned on me how tall Charlie had grown.

That momentous occasion was just a few months ago. Although, he quickly discovered they hadn't followed all his specifications. "Why is it going so slow?" he would say in a glum voice even though it could move at the same speed as an athlete sprinting.

As I was cutting Charlie's hair and reflecting on that episode, he asked, "Dad, why don't you cut your hair short? We looked so much alike the last time you did it."

"I know, but how else will people know who is the father and who is the son?" I teased as I brushed the hair off his face.

Once I finished Charlie's military haircut, his beautiful dark brown hair was all but gone. He looked at me with a glow on his face and asked, "Are you ready to run?"

I replied, "How aerodynamic do you feel now?"

That's when Charlie pressed a button on the chair's remote control. One could set up and synchronize passwords for the door to automatically open with the push of a button. Charlie had the door burst open as he sprang out shouting, "Catch me if you can!"

"Wait, let me clean up. Your mom will get angry if…"

That's when I heard Sarah yell, "Don't forget to sweep the hair off the floor."

I quickly picked up whatever hair I could grab before asking, "Where is the wastebasket?" It was gone. I desperately looked around and finally opened the desk drawer with my elbow and placed the hair inside before running outside.

We took our usual route and Charlie knew I'd know where to find him. We'd always run along Linden Avenue, up Sheridan, and then back down Central Avenue. It was a beautiful day and Charlie was enjoying its every moment. When I was finally able to catch up to him he asked, "Any news from the GSA?"

"No, not yet; but hopefully soon."

"And the clinical trials—are the tests still indicating normal nerve function?"

I was starting to run out of air. "Charlie, stop here—your puffer!"

We stopped on the beautiful bridge overlooking the Wilmette Harbor. I borrowed Charlie's inhaler and took a few deep puffs. Charlie himself looked slightly out of breath so I offered the puffer back to him to take a couple of puffs as well. Once I was breathing more comfortably I said, "Well, so far all the test results have been great. I was hoping to have you ready and set for this by now; we just have to wait a little longer, that's all, son."

Charlie was gazing at the harbor with all its sailboats; he was deep in thought. "Charlie, would you like to tell me what you're thinking?"

"Dad, if they built this robotic wheelchair as I had wanted them to, we'd be sailing on this harbor right now."

We laughed and turned to the other side to enjoy the beautiful view. Charlie admired the sunset, and looked at it peacefully.

"Dad, I love it when the sky is red like this."

"Me too, Charlie. Me too."

"Why do you think it's red?"

I said the only thing that came to mind, "Probably because it's sad to say goodbye."

Charlie smiled. "No, why is it really red?"

I enjoyed the view a while longer before telling him: "It has to do with the refraction of light by the atmosphere particles. Light has to travel more at sunset so most of the light is scattered except for the red ones."

"Why not the red ones?"

"They have a longer wavelength."

Charlie thought about it for a moment before saying, "Dad, I liked your first answer more."

We returned home to watch the baseball game. Charlie put on his Chicago baseball hat, outfit and glove, as did I; this was the same cap my father had given him, but it fit a little better now. It had Charlie's own elegant handwriting inside the hat. He had written his name while he had been at that baseball game with my father on that tragic day. That also was the last time Charlie had full use of his hands. I was never sure whether he wore the cap to remember his grandpa or whether seeing his own name written inside was his last connection to who he was before his injury. In either case, the memento meant a lot to him and there was no way Charlie was going to watch a baseball game without it; this had become a ritual and he considered it bad luck not to wear his hat.

"Watch, Dad, curve ball coming up—and strike out!"

"Good call, Charlie. How did you know that?"

"He's a lefty; he threw him two changeups and set him up for that curveball."

"What is he going to throw now?" I asked.

"It's a lefty on lefty. Normally he'd pitch him inside, but this guy is weak on the outside pitches. He'll throw a sharp fastball inside to pull him back a little, and then he'll throw a breaking ball outside to get him to pop fly."

Sure enough, that next batter had a fly out on the second pitch just as Charlie had predicted. Charlie enjoyed calling the play-by-play during the game and saw it a challenge to announce the outcome before it actually happened. In baseball, if you're batting over .300, which translates to hitting the ball in the field less than one out of three tries, you're considered a hero and paid millions; not bad for being right only 30 percent of the time. If I had to guess, Charlie was batting close to .700 when it came to calling the plays. He knew every player, all their strengths and weaknesses. He had studied their every strategy and knew the sequence in which they were deployed. It might sound ridiculous to say this, but if in an alternative reality I ever owned a baseball team, I'd feel very comfortable having Charlie as one of my managers. He was that good.

"Watch this next throw, Dad; it's going to be a base hit down the third-base line."

It was actually a home run, but just as Charlie called it—a home run down the third-base line.

VII

The first weekend of every month, it's a MacKinnon tradition to gather at a cottage 50 miles north of Chicago. The cottage was bought by our great-grandparents more than 125 years ago. When it was purchased, they had said it reminded them of Scotland and wanted something for the family to retreat to. It measured to about 6,000 acres of land with a large green hill in the center facing a beautiful lake.

We've retained the tradition of meeting there on the first Saturday of the month, and every so often all the family and relatives would come to stay for the weekend. There would be over one hundred of us there at any one time. This was for everyone to maintain their ties and for the cousins to identify their sense of belonging to the family.

Uncle Stewart was my dad's first cousin. He valued and cherished our family traditions and was often heard telling the stories of our past. "How else are they going to remember where they came from unless we tell them these stories?" he'd frequently tell us. During the gatherings, he'd have the children circle around him and would recite a story of a particular MacKinnon. We had more than 700 years of family history so there was a lot to share. In recent years, he had gathered a compilation of stories and was planning on putting them together for a book as a means to ensure these stories were never lost. Every anecdote had a pearl, and each one was a guided lesson on how to live our lives according to the MacKinnon standard. Still, everyone's favorite story was always of Charles I. I didn't mind hearing it over again. It had been a while, so it was refreshing to hear Uncle Stewart pick that stirring account to share with the kids today.

"Children, come here. James, Alison, Agatha—everyone, gather around. It's storytelling time."

There was a resounding cheer as this was one of their favorite parts of the day trip.

"Are we going to hear the story of William VI?" asked Agatha.

"No, we said that last time," Uncle Stewart told her. "I'm going to tell you about Charles I today."

I enjoyed listening to this story, as did Charlie.

"Once upon a time in Scotland, there was a king."

James put his hands up. "Yes, James?" asked Uncle Stewart, wondering why he was interrupted so soon.

"It was King James!" said James with a glow on his face.

"Indeed, it was," continued Uncle Stewart, "you remember that king's name quite well, don't you?"

James nodded boldly in agreement.

Uncle Stewart then continued: "There were in fact two kings in 1513 in that auspicious year when Charles I was born. Do you know what the second one was called?"

"It was also King James!" said James with conviction.

"You are correct again!" clamored Uncle Stewart.

I wanted to listen but my mind was drifting to my worries at work. What had been in my thoughts and everyone else's was the state of Genomica. My cousin Harris was the first to approach me.

"Charles, why is the GSA troubling you so much?"

"I don't know, Harry. It's a mystery to me. They have nothing on us, they know it, and so they'll have come around soon. This is more about saving face."

When story time finished, we all went inside, and that's when I noticed Charlie admiring the scroll of Charles II. This manuscript was the handwritten story of Charles I, penned on the centenary of his persecution; it had been beautifully preserved and placed on display in the living room. After hearing the story of Charles I, it was natural for anyone to want to view the story in its original text. Charlie noticed my presence as I stepped toward him; he slightly turned his head and asked, "Dad, do you know what is really beautiful?" He slowly scanned the writing and gradually continued his thought, "This calligraphy is absolutely stunning. It's matchless."

"I know," I said with a smile, "it's worth the price of admission all on its own."

"Who could write like this? It's mysterious!" he gasped.

The only thing more fascinating and enigmatic as the story of Charles I was the calligraphy in which it had been written. Uncle Stewart had also wanted his MacKinnon history book to have the same calligraphy when describing the story of Charles I. As he once told me, "It would only feel right if it was presented in the same spirit as it was first delivered." Unfortunately, neither he nor any calligrapher he had searched for came close to matching this original penmanship.

It took many more months than we had anticipated but the GSA finally did finish their inspection. Charlie, meanwhile, had come up with a coded method of writing his research that only he and I could understand. This was to hide our data from the meddling of the GSA. He also liked the idea of us having our own unique coded language. He had acquired the inspiration for this from a presentation I had done in Beijing, China. Charlie accompanied me on that trip and spent six weeks prior studying the language. You have to understand that six weeks for Charlie was about three years for everyone else. My secretary, Wendy Wen, was from Xian, China; Charlie spent every day studying with her on how to read, write, or receive clarification of an expression he didn't understand. On our trip, he was completely fluent and spoke as though it was his native tongue. He was ordering food, joking with people, and comfortably navigating us throughout the city. He was also my official interpreter when I did my presentation.

When Charlie finished writing the code he would tell me, "The effectiveness of a code is in its simplicity, not its complexity." The simplicity of its structure also had to come with a clever diversion and Charlie didn't miss a beat on that either. I didn't speak Mandarin and Charlie wanted to appear as a young teen learning a new language. So he built a system using Chinese characters, except it was coded and its translations weren't always Mandarin; so you could say it was a code within a code with a shrewd deflection. If anyone wondered what this was, we had many Asian staff so it could be attributed to any of them. If anyone inquired further and realized the writing was a little unsophisticated, well Charlie was learning a new language and my secretary could testify to that. Charlie had cleverly designed it so if they ever obtained a Chinese interpreter it would appear as if a non-native speaker, a child, was attempting to learn their language.

Every time Dr. Li passed by Charlie in the cafeteria he would stop to admire what he was writing before saying, "Isn't that cute?" and correcting a few of the characters.

"Thank you, Dr. Li."

Charlie would wisely wait until he had left his presence before changing it back. One of the benefits of this code was that you could write several pages of information in a very small space. It was extremely efficient not just in writing but in memorizing and recalling information. It was the most effective way of storing information that I continued to use for many more years.

Understanding the code, of course, was extremely simple once Charlie explained it, but impossible to figure out otherwise. More importantly, this allowed us to hide our evolving research from the GSA.

A few times even Dawson himself personally came to look for our research data. If it were up to me, I'd hide all our documents and take sanctuary with the code Charlie had devised. Charlie convinced me otherwise. He knew exactly where Dawson would come searching for his gold and as he once pointed out, "Sometimes it's better to let the mouse know where the cheese is than to leave it to his imagination to find it."

Clever boy, quoting his mother; that's a line Sarah often used. Charlie also rationalized it would deflect attention away from the Mandarin code and keep it safe, so I hesitantly agreed. Charlie provided Dawson parallel research documents that had nothing more than what other research facilities had with their flawed methodology. We weren't entirely dishonest as we had actually done that research simply to verify it didn't work. Dawson didn't know that and he didn't need to. I just asked Charlie to "dress it up a little bit" so they wouldn't question its integrity. After all, we were Genomica; they would expect a certain standard.

Charlie had an excellent sense for what Dawson was looking for, how he wanted it to be presented, and how much he needed to feel satisfied. In the end, Charlie not only provided the cheese, he also provided the grapes to go with it. We just ensured Dawson wouldn't see any of our current research for no other reason than with knowledge comes fear.

Some months later, when Dr. Li was passing by Charlie he took note that Charlie had been making the exact same mistake in his Chinese characters as when he had first started. He knew Charlie quite well and must have suspected that he was simply too smart to repeat the same error. He paused to reflect before smiling and saying, "Charlie, I want to teach you a word you'll never forget."

Charlie listened carefully as Dr. Li wrote down at the top of his sheet how to write the name "Charlie" using Chinese characters: 查里.

Then he said, "This character—查—is the sound of the first part of your name, and this one—里—represents the sound for the last part of your name."

"Thank you, Dr. Li," said Charlie gratefully.

Then Dr. Li continued, "But wait—there is more. This first part also has a meaning when used in a sentence. It means 'to search.' The last half of your name sounds like my name 'Li.' It could also be used as a word in a sentence—it means 'inside.'

"See, this is how you write to 'search inside.'"

Charlie watched as Dr. Li wrote this sentence at the top of his page, and then circled the central characters and said, "Notice, if you look at it carefully, at the heart of it there is a 'Charlie.'"

He paused and smiled before Charlie told him, "Thank you, Dr. Li. It's really nice. I like it."

"You're welcome, Charlie. It's beautiful, isn't it?" and with a twinkle in his eye he said, "You wear every part of your name well."

Dr. Li, of course, knew that Charlie was aware of all this information; he was only trying to kindly convey that after observing him for so long, he was only now starting to get a glimmer of what was running through his brilliant mind.

VIII

Dawson finally concluded his investigation and had GEMA begrudgingly returned to us. Our Phase III trials were complete, and the GSA had approved our standards of care. It was now time to push forward not only with our treatments but also to restore Charlie's destiny.

To be sure there was no turning back we decided to have a press conference announcing our revolutionary treatments. Every media outlet both national and international had been invited. We redesigned the layout in the lobby to fit the multitude of journalists and reporters.

Unfortunately, our public support was also met with some resistance. Our invitation was not only heard by media sources but also by the many people who opposed the ethical aspects of gene therapy. We regrettably had an equal number of petitioners outside the building. Nonetheless, there was some anticipation in the leading weeks, and most knew this breakthrough was not only of colossal importance to spinal cord research but to other diseases as well.

"Welcome, everybody. Thank you all for coming today. I am here to announce that Genomica has completed its Phase III trials on gene therapy for spinal cord regeneration. All our studies to date have shown our treatments to be both safe and curative for spinal cord injuries. It is our intention now to move forward and make this treatment available for all patients.

"This milestone is only the beginning. We have had concurrent studies on treatments for cerebrovascular accidents, Alzheimer's, multiple sclerosis, diabetes as well as colon, breast, and prostate cancer. There will be many more applications of this treatment modality to be utilized in the coming years. I will now receive your questions."

Reporter #1: "How long after therapy can people expect to walk?"

"Thank you for that question. It depends on how long it has been since their injury. If the injury had occurred recently, then perhaps one week before signs of recovery can be noted. Otherwise they will need extensive therapy to help recover from all the atrophy of their muscles. Those patients will have some progress in a few days, but it may take two or three months before they are walking again."

Reporter #2: "Many people are concerned about ethical issues regarding gene therapy. Can you please comment on that?"

"Thank you. We're very conscious of all the ethical concerns and have taken measures to meet those needs. We do not have any unethical practices. All of our treatment methods have been screened by the GSA and accepted as safe and in line with the current ethical standards."

Reporter #3: "You had said that Genomica had many more applications for this treatment in the future. Can you please clarify what you're referring to?"

"Yes. The application of this treatment modality is quite broad. We anticipate successful clinical outcomes not only in the areas that we're currently studying, but we're cautiously optimistic that using this technology we have the foundation for the cure of all diseases."

The questions continued for some twenty-five minutes. Charlie was watching from home. He knew with this announcement that his turn had finally come.

John came to meet me after the press conference.

"Charles, congratulations! You finally did it."

"Thanks, buddy! We did it," I told him as I put a hand on his shoulder. "It's a great day."

"You know, there were times when I was worried about you. Everything that happened with Charlie, your father and all that you went through."

"Thanks, John. Yes, those were challenging times."

"Well, it is inspiring to see everything going your way finally—your work being acknowledged, you've got the perfect family, the perfect home, and Charlie will finally be walking again."

"Thank you, that's nice of you to say, John. I appreciate your support."

"You finally have peace of mind. Boy, the security must sure feel nice after all you've been through."

"Thank you, John, it is satisfying, but the security and tranquility that you speak of is really just an illusion; that's a lesson I learned a long time ago. We're all hanging by a thread. You can build yourself the largest safety net—nice house, good career, great family; then in one instant, it's all gone! I'll enjoy the moment, but trust me, there are no guarantees."

John was silent before he finally smiled and said, "Okay then, let's go celebrate."

"I'd love to, but Sarah and Charlie are waiting for me at home. We've got a small dinner planned for tonight."

"Sure, Charles, no problem," he said in a subdued voice.

"John, why don't you join us?" I asked him and also invited his wife. "We can call Sandra and have you both over tonight."

"That's okay; you guys have your family time. We'll catch up and make up for this another day."

"Please. I insist, come over."

"No, really Charles; I'm fine but I'll take a rain check on that."

"Are you sure?" I asked, hoping he'd change his mind.

"Absolutely! Enjoy this; you deserve it."

"Thank you, John."

It certainly was a day to celebrate. Charlie was waiting for me looking out the window in his usual spot. He was standing in his robotic wheelchair. This was the first time he was in the upright stance waiting for me when I came home. It sure was odd seeing him in that posture, but it made me reflect—this is how I'd see Charlie from now on. Sarah was also standing behind him, and what a sight it was, seeing them both together. I embraced them when I came home, and to be sure this was a celebration, I had brought dessert.

"Dad, are we having rhubarb pie? That's my favorite!"

"Mine too," Sarah quickly affirmed.

I could see the candlelight dinner ready in the corner so I wasn't sure if it was okay to ask this but I did anyway, "Do we have time for me to go for a jog before dinner?"

Sarah looked at me perplexed. Charlie was all excited; he loved going out and started cheering. "Mom, we'll be back soon. I swear!"

Seeing his animated expression brought a smile to her face. "Sure, I'll put the food back in the oven—be back soon!"

I sprinted upstairs to change, and came back down to see Charlie all ready to go.

The door sprang open and Charlie screamed, "Catch me if you can."

I don't think I ever enjoyed jogging as much as I did that day. Everything we had worked for, all the suffering we had gone through, somehow they seemed to have washed away at that very moment; it was gone—no bitterness, no anger, no resentment. I just felt pure joy and gratitude. What's more is that I could now see the meaning for all the pain we had endured and appreciated we were that much better for it. It's sort of like looking at a bunch of random stars, and now you can finally see the patterns and admire the beautiful constellation. At last, it all had meaning.

Charlie let me catch up to him this time; he had a lot on his mind and wanted to talk.

"Dad, do you think I could play for the college baseball team next year when I start?"

I had to pause and think about that one. "Sure! We'll have you started on an accelerated rehab program. Your coordination may take some time to catch up, but your muscle bulk should be built up in time for next year. I don't see why not."

"How about practicing as a neurosurgeon? Will my fine motor skills be where it needs to be to perform surgeries one day?"

Charlie was asking about his ability to coordinate sophisticated hand movements. The truth is I didn't know, but right now I was a father, not a doctor, so I said what felt right, "All I know is, destiny didn't bring us this far to turn us back, so yes, why not."

We were passing over our favorite bridge on Sheridan and I was running out of breath. "Charlie, your…" I didn't get a chance to finish my sentence. He had the inhaler ready in his hand this time and was stretching his arm toward me as I asked the question. We had to stop at our usual bridge.

"Besides, do you know for sure you want to be a neurosurgeon?"

"Of course, Dad, why would you even question it?"

"Well, there are many successful blueprints in life and any one of them can lead to your happiness; there isn't just one. The important thing is for you to find your own blueprint and not live someone else's. This is what my dad told me and what his father told him; this is what I want for you too."

"Dad, not sure what you mean. I love neurosurgery; this is what I've always wanted."

"Are you sure? Your well-being is what's important to me."

"I couldn't be more certain. This is what I feel I was born to do. You know that."

"Okay, son, I know, let's get back before your mom becomes worried."

Sarah had prepared the most delicious appetizer: a cullen skink soup. Even though Sarah was not of Scottish heritage, you'd never know it if you tasted this appetizer. The creamy thick taste was exactly the right texture you'd find back in Scotland. This was my favorite soup and Charlie's as well.

For dinner, we had roasted chicken with vegetables. Charlie was starting his high-protein diet with the hope of building his muscle bulk after his surgery. Chicken was all he was requesting these days. He had limited movements of his hands and arms, but he was moving what he could in the hope of taking part in some exercise. You can't blame him for having hope and for trying.

"Thanks, Mom, the chicken was great! Can I have more?"

"Son, go easy on the protein, if you get any more muscular I may not recognize you."

I had to feel his marginally flexed upper arm that was still pencil-thin as I joked with him. That sure brought a glow to his face.

"You're funny, Dad," he said, grinning ear to ear.

Today was a celebration of the past and the future. Then Sarah made a plea: "Can we all go and see the sunset?"

"Perfect! That's a great idea, what do you think, Charlie?"

Charlie liked any excuse to leave the house. "Yes!" he said with excitement.

Sarah's favorite walk was just a few minutes from our house. We walked along together to Gillson Park. Charlie was happy and roamed free by himself ahead of us. He was finally feeling his independence and asserting it as he knew this was just the start. I don't know if it was seeing Charlie so autonomous that triggered the discussion, but Sarah asked me a surprising question.

"Are you ready for the changes that will come when

Charlie has his surgery?"

"What exactly are you referring to? I've been waiting for this for a long time—too long!"

"Well, Charlie has never really expressed himself to others—certainly not the way he does with us. That may change after his surgery. He might show himself in a way that may even surprise you."

I knew where Sarah was treading with this—I did. "I am actually looking forward to that. It will be nice to see him spread out his wings and assert himself in whichever way he was meant to. There is so much he has to offer."

"I know," she said, "but he is fifteen and will be going to college next year. There will be changes ahead. I know we're both excited, but are you prepared for it?"

I couldn't help but admire watching Charlie as we were speaking. He was perplexed to move passed the dog that was blocking his way. At age three Charlie had an incident with a dog at a friend's home. There were no major injuries, but the incident had terrified him. The dog had leaped to stop Charlie from opening the door. It caught him off guard and resulted in a bite wound on his hand. I think the shock of that incident always remained with Charlie, and he was never too enthusiastic to be around animals, especially dogs.

"Don't worry, he won't bite. Just move past him," I told him.

Charlie was standing there frozen and completely mute at the golden retriever in front of him. "He's friendly; don't worry," said Sarah as we caught up to him. "Come, just follow us," she continued. Charlie placed his hands on the fingerprint sensors and slowly backed up to maneuver past the dog.

We walked in the park along the beach. The sunset was

magnificent that evening. We had enjoyed many moments such as these, but this time it felt different. I was overjoyed about where we were heading. It all seemed worth it. I wouldn't be the person I was today if it hadn't been for those challenges. I wouldn't trade who I am now for who I was back then.

Sarah said, "The sky in this sunset is beautiful. We should take a picture."

"Good idea; leave it to me." I looked around and found a large rock to put my camera on. "Are you ready?" I asked.

"All set, Dad!" Charlie said with a smile. I put the timer on, ran next to Charlie and Sarah, and took what would be my favorite photo of the three of us.

We walked home shortly after sunset where we enjoyed the rhubarb pie. We had sand on our clothes, but even if it had been mud, nothing was going to stop us from enjoying this evening.

Sarah was playing the piano, Beethoven's *Moonlight Sonata*. Charlie was watching her and was deep in thought. He was overwhelmed with emotion and had tears in his eyes. I too felt his sentiment, and reached over to hug him. "We did it, son; we finally pulled through!"

Wiping his tears, I gave him a kiss on the head. I think his repressed feelings had finally caught up to him. The melancholic music had also stirred and intensified his mood. I could only imagine the emotions he had bottled within—all the suffering and every agony. He had conveyed some of it to us, but Sarah was right: we were just beginning to see the gleanings of his desires, thoughts, and expressions.

IX

School started the next week, and Charlie's surgery was scheduled in a few months prior to Thanksgiving in the fall. We had planned for an accelerated rehabilitation program to be started prior to his surgery. The outcomes were much better when they were initiated on a therapeutic regimen to help stimulate their nerves and promote muscle growth in the preceding months.

A few weeks into the school year, I was informed by Sarah that the school psychologist, Ms. Carrigan, wanted to meet us; so we arranged the appointment for Friday when I finished work early.

"Mrs. MacKinnon and Dr. MacKinnon, thank you for stopping in."

"It's no trouble. We are just a little curious as to what this meeting is for?" I asked.

We didn't think Charlie would be in any trouble. I had a long talk after the last time he was called to the principal's office, and knew Charlie was too smart to ever make the same mistake twice. This though wasn't the principal calling us, it was the school psychologist. Charlie was happy these days and looking forward to his surgery. In truth, things could not have been better, so we were confused as to what she wanted to talk to us about.

"Well, it's about Charlie," she said. "I am little concerned about the fact that he is shy. He doesn't seem interested in integrating with his peers."

"I'm not sure why that's a problem?" I questioned.

"Does it not concern you at all that he's introverted and doesn't enjoy interacting with his own classmates?"

"Ms. Carrigan, I don't view his introversion as a weakness as you are suggesting. I am sure you're familiar with the history that when introversion was originally defined, it was used to identify the strength of an individual in finding more meaning in an introspective activity rather than yielding one's will to accommodate the likes of others."

"I don't entirely disagree."

"So, you'd agree that viewed from that perspective we're really talking about modifying Charlie's strength here, are we not?"

"Well, that's a matter of perspective. What is concerning me is that he has such an aversion for his peers that he spends his lunch hour at the other side of the school hiding from his classmates behind the music halls."

"Ms. Carrigan, do you know what Charlie's SAT scores were?"

"Yes, but I'm not sure I'm seeing the connection."

"This is a school that prides itself on having gifted

children. When was the last time someone had Charlie's scores?" I paused for her response before saying: "The connection here is, never. His peers can clearly see that even if they tried their hardest and did everything in their power, even if they got lucky, they could never accomplish what Charlie could do on a bad day."

"Dr. MacKinnon, I see what you mean but I'm not convinced that's all there is to it."

Sarah finally interjected, "Ms. Carrigan, we appreciate your feedback and I don't mind you raising your concern with us. Charlie was home schooled until a few years ago and we knew there would be some adjustments once he went back to school. Charlie has surgery in less than two months to help correct his underlying disability."

"I didn't know he had surgery scheduled, sorry," Ms. Carrigan said with a surprised look.

"Yes, so it might be fair to wait and see how everything turns out after the surgery before we react to this," Sarah suggested.

"I agree, Mrs. MacKinnon. We'll keep an eye on this and perhaps we can touch base again in the winter."

Sarah said, "Agreed," before I had a chance to interject one last comment. Then again, it probably didn't matter. Charlie would have his surgery soon and everything would change. I rationalized that this was a transitory stage; when he goes to university next year, there will be new faces, new teachers, and new friends. I just know with a renewed confidence he will begin an exciting chapter in his life.

Charlie had started the application process, and had applied to Oxford as well as many reputable schools here at home. He would be faced with a difficult decision. Charlie had wanted to go to Oxford to keep with the MacKinnon tradition, but it would be the first time away from home. He also had hopes of playing for the baseball team one day; this wasn't a MacKinnon tradition, but it was something that was important to him personally. Playing baseball would imply staying back home—unless of course I could convince him to play cricket. To me this was entirely Charlie's decision and I was resigned to whatever he wanted. That didn't stop him though from asking my opinion.

"Dad, if I get accepted, do you think I should go to Oxford or stay closer to home?"

"Well, whatever you feel is best for you, Charlie."

"I just don't know what the right decision is," he said, probing my thoughts.

"Well, sometimes in life when we are left with two good choices, we look more at what we're losing with one selection than what we're gaining with the other. If you pick one, you wonder what you surrendered with the option you turned away from, and had you picked the other, you also lament your lost opportunity with the alternative you had to forego. Sometimes, son, it's not so much about making the right choice, but about making the choice with the least regrets."

Most students would love to have this dilemma. I never dreamed ten years ago we'd be sitting here having this conversation. I don't think he was too caught up in the decision as it was a few months away, and he had his important surgery coming up. This was a nice diversion for him to think about something other than his surgery, which probably was a good thing.

Our research and treatment program had gained popularity, and had received a plentitude of media coverage and was a constant point of conversation on the news and talk shows. As is always the case with anything new—the reviews are sensationalized and all the initial comments are positive. Then when they run out of things to say, the rhetoric turns into looking for controversies. Misery loves company and controversies love attention. If you're miserable and controversial, well then, I guess you'll have plenty of company and plenty of attention.

In the coming weeks the weather was becoming colder and we were advancing closer to Charlie's surgery. I think Dawson must have known this was coming up; they had accessed all our records and scheduling. If he was aware, he certainly wasn't letting us know it was in his thoughts.

A week before Charlie's surgery the GSA requested having a routine audit done. This was a rare request considering we had been approved only five months before. Unfortunately, this wasn't just an audit; there was clearly an agenda.

The agents from the GSA walked in very politely and asked to do their general review. We complied with their wishes and tried not to worry even though we knew something didn't seem right.

It was about this time when Ms. Andrea Miller stopped by to follow up on her initial visit.

"Dr. MacKinnon, I was wondering if you had a chance to review the wheelchair prototype we had sent."

"It's excellent," I said. "Thank you."

"At the time you had sent us the request for this device, we weren't aware that your program was on the verge of a cure. Do you think there will be a demand for this product when everyone is treated?"

I knew what she was alluding to; she had a valid point and I really didn't know what to say. These are the variables Charlie hadn't thought through when he had requested them to build this. He was smart, but he was also fifteen; the idea of costs and savings was a foreign concept to him. He could solve the most intricate problem that would stymie the most intelligent scientists, but present him with a practical cost analysis of day-to-day living and you'd remember he was still teenager. There is a subtle virtue to that period of life and their way of thinking. I wanted him to be responsible, but I didn't want to entirely rob him of that innocence either; so in some ways this mistake was also on me.

"Ms. Miller, even with our treatment, candidates need to go through an extensive period of rehabilitation. I would be happy to work with your team to make certain redesigns to not only make this a device that helps the patient's mobility, but also to assist in rehabilitating their neuromuscular function. Would that work for you?"

That sure brought a smile to her face.

"That would! Thank you."

"Great. Let me work on this and I'll send you my thoughts. I have your card."

"Thank you, Dr. MacKinnon."

X

It was now November 24th. The day had finally arrived for Charlie's treatment. We all woke up at 6am in preparation to drive to the hospital for his 8am surgery. The entire process would be roughly five hours from start to finish. My close friend, Dr. John Jennings, was the only non-MacKinnon in the neurosurgical group and had kindly accepted to do this surgery. To me he was like family, but legally he was the only one not binding to any family ties. Considering the scrutiny we were under, this decision was our only option. I also felt very comfortable leaving Charlie in John's hands.

This day, however, could not have been a colder day. You could feel as if winds were talking to you. That didn't stop us from being hopeful. It was, after all, a big day for Charlie. As optimistic as we were, before any operation you are always anxious. This is where you forget you're a surgeon, and all that medical knowledge dissipates and you start worrying like a parent. I had done this procedure hundreds of times and not once was I concerned about the outcome. If there is ever a battle between fear and knowledge, fear wins every time. Sarah was her positive self, never displaying any worry.

It was close to dawn when we were preparing to leave for the hospital.

"Are you excited, Charlie?" I asked.

"I guess," he said in a reserved tone.

"What do you mean? It will be a piece of cake." That was my best effort to mask my feelings.

Sarah must have known we were both nervous so she offered to drive and did what Sarah does best: in her own gentle way, she put us all at ease. "Sometimes it helps to sing a song when we're a little tense."

"Mom, I'm not really in the mood."

"Come on, it will be fun," she said.

Well maybe it was fun for Sarah; after a minute, it certainly had Charlie in a cheerful mood; he was singing along. I was beginning to enjoy the moment as well until we arrived at the hospital.

Sarah dropped us off at the front door and went to park the car. When we stepped inside, there were men in black suits everywhere, which was not a promising sign. One of them finally walked in our direction.

"What's going on?" I asked, baffled at the spectacle in front of us.

"Dr. MacKinnon, can you please step here to the side, we'd like to have a word with you."

The agent who approached me to explain their curious presence was Mr. Devon Jackson. He was a man of gentle temperament. He looked familiar and I definitely recognized

X

his name. I remembered as we spoke that his mother had
been my patient ten years ago and he would often accompany
her while in college. She had been doing well, but I had not
seen her after she had started treatment for her kidney
disease. Prior to working at the GSA, Mr. Jackson had done
excellent research at the Woodlands State Penitentiary on the
correlation of anger and genetics. No one knew the details of
what had happened for him to leave, but I'm venturing to
guess the large scar on the side of his neck might have had
something to do with it. I could tell that it was from a
penetrating wound from a sharp object such as a knife.

Mr. Jackson approached me respectfully that day and said,
"Our office has done an evaluation and we are putting all
treatments with regard to biologics and gene therapy on hold
until a thorough review."

"We've been through this already. Why now?"

"Sorry, Dr. MacKinnon, this is all the information I have
at the moment."

"When does this take effect?" I asked.

"I'm afraid this will be enforced immediately."

"But we have patients booked; they have driven from out
of town and sacrificed considerable resources to be here. Can
this not wait till the weekend so we can adequately warn
them?"

"We realize the inconvenience and unfortunately that's
not an option right now."

"Can't we at least honor the appointments we have
scheduled today?"

"I'm afraid not."

In the back corridor, I could see Dawson walking and
inspecting, pretending as though he actually knew what he
was looking for. "He is responsible for this, isn't he?"

With a stoic face Mr. Jackson replied, "There are many people that contribute to any decision—it's never just one person."

"I wish I could believe you, but I think we both know this is his doing."

I wasn't going to debate this any further with Mr. Jackson. I knew he was only reiterating his orders and providing me rehearsed clichés. I stormed toward Dawson.

"Can you please explain what this is all about?"

"I don't have time to talk about this right now. If you like, you can discuss this with Mr. Martell and he'll be happy to answer your questions." Dawson directed me to the person standing a few feet away from him.

"This is ridiculous!" I said.

I saw John approach me and he intervened before things escalated any further. I could see Charlie a few feet away with his head down. There was a quiet dejection in his posture and disappointment was all over his face. This was something he had waited for almost his entire life, and now it was being taken away.

John tried to calm me down. "Sorry, Charles, I did my best to talk to them this morning. I did everything to have them delay this till the end of today just to get Charlie in, but they wouldn't budge. Everything I threw at them with the costs and preparation, they didn't care."

"But why? We did everything according to their protocols. We played entirely by their standards. They couldn't find a single thing wrong. What more could we do?"

"I know. I'm sure this is nothing. It will only delay Charlie's surgery for a few weeks. Don't worry, we'll be alright."

Charlie was more concerned about me than he was about

himself. I knew he was disappointed, but as usual, he was putting aside his own needs for mine. "Dad, it's okay. If we did this during the winter holidays, it might even work better than now. It would allow me a longer time to recuperated and miss less school."

He had a point. There are those who look at the cup half empty and those who look at it half full. Charlie would simply see the cup full when it was empty and find a way to convince everyone else to see it that way too. That's not something you can teach a man. You're either born with your brain wired that way or you're just not. Right now I just wanted to see Dawson and say a few parting words that was on my mind. John knew this, which is why he insisted I take the day off.

"Charles, go home. I've got this. Let me speak to them."

As much as I wanted to stay, I knew it would disappoint Charlie even more if he saw me engaging in an argument with Dawson.

"Okay, son, let's find your mom and give her the news."

We met Sarah just as she was stepping out of the parking elevator.

"Mom, we're going back, stay inside."

We both joined her and pressed the button to go down to Parking Level 3.

"What happened? Why are we going back?"

"The surgery is canceled, Mom."

I was too upset to speak, so Charlie did all the talking.

"We're just going to postpone it until December."

Well, I hoped that was all it was going to be. As much as I wanted to be optimistic and hoped this audit wouldn't be an impediment, I couldn't help but feel as though our destiny was thwarted.

The next week I went to and fro from the hospital and meeting with the auditors. They were elusive about what this audit was concerning. Unfortunately, there is very little legal recourse to prevent any investigation on their part. All you can do is be patient and hope for the best.

It was close to the winter break and Charlie knew the window of opportunity for a surgery during the holiday season was passing. If he was upset he wasn't saying anything, but you could see it in his eyes. He approached me one day and asked if I had any updates.

"No, Charlie. I have nothing yet, but hopefully soon. They will be coming to inspect this week."

"It's Dawson, isn't it? Why doesn't he like us?"

"I don't know, son, I don't know."

Seeing the glum look on his face, I decided this was a good time for me to unveil my surprise. "Charlie, I got you something today that I think you'll like."

"What's that?"

I reached across, picked up his gift, and handed it over to him. The gold 15 x 11.5-inch envelope was addressed to his name and had come in the mail today. Charlie had a difficult time opening it, so he passed it back to me, which I unsealed with a paper knife.

He looked inside and saw a large beautiful picture of the three of us by the water that we took a few months earlier. I had the photograph ordered and sent to our home. It certainly was a majestic sunset.

"With you going away next year, I figured you might

enjoy something like this to take with you as a nice memento from home."

"Thanks, Dad. I love this. It's my favorite photo."

"We'll now have to find you a nice frame for it."

"Dad, I've decided I'm going to go to Oxford if I'm accepted there."

"Well, what brought about this decision?" I asked.

"Oxford was where you started and you left there partly because of me. It only feels right to complete what you started, and in some ways what we started."

"What about playing for the baseball team here?" I had a hunch that a part of Charlie's decision was that he knew this delay would take longer than expected; he wouldn't be ready in time to play. Right now, that was an unrealistic dream, and even Charlie wasn't going to fool himself with the chimera of optimism.

"I'll worry about baseball later. I can join some of the summer league teams when I visit during my holidays."

"Are you sure?"

"I think so."

"Well, you still have time to decide; let's see what next week brings. We can have your surgery scheduled within twenty-four hours of them clearing us. You can always change your mind."

"Dad, I wouldn't be able to play baseball even if I had the treatment done today."

"What do you mean, son, of course you could. Who is better than you?"

"It's not that, Dad. I've reviewed some our data; if you look closely at all the study outcomes, after six months they start regressing 0.52 percent per month."

"Well, that's because we're stopping the treatment

program. That's an expected drop-off."

"Perhaps, but I don't think that's it."

"Why, what do you mean, Charlie?"

"I've looked at the growth factor levels; they're also dropping off after six months."

"Well, that's part of the same logic; we'd expect that result too with the discontinuation of their treatment."

"I'm not convinced that's the reason."

"What are you suggesting, Charlie?"

"I think the treatment algorithm we have right now works for them to walk, not for them to run. Not long term anyway; they'll regress."

"I don't know, Charlie. Everything will be fine."

"I'm not sure; I've been working on a supplementary treatment algorithm to complement their current therapy. We'll have to test it first, but I know it will fix the problem. They'll be able to sustain complete function afterwards."

"Sure, Charlie. Where is it?"

He pointed to his forehead, "Well, right now it's just here. It's actually quite simple."

I smiled and leaned over to kiss that same side of the forehead he pointed to and said, "Have you thought about putting what's up here to use here?" I pointed to his finger.

"I know. I don't like writing much; I just think it's safer up here," he said with a mischievous grin. It was nice finally seeing Charlie smile again.

"I'll tell you what I believe. I have a hunch you're over-thinking this. I know the treatment will work. Have some faith. In fact, I am so sure that I'm willing to make you a bet. I think in six months you'll be running around, and in a year you'll be playing baseball. How does that sound?"

"Sounds good I guess," he said, feeling noticeably better.

X

"Here, let's shake on it." And just like that, we made an agreement and shook hands.

XI

The GSA was coming this week and we both knew that with a little bit of luck we could resume normal operations. We were prepared and methodical; I had already talked to John about our plan. Once we were back to normal practice, Charlie would be first on the treatment list, and he'd be scheduled the next day. I was not leaving anything to chance this time.

If I took a moment and thought with my head and not my heart, did they actually have any case against us? No, they did not. Had I done anything wrong? No, I had not. Did they have any reason to be concerned about this type of treatment? Maybe, but not any more concerned than five months ago when they had approved us. The GSA's main mission was to ensure your genes were not manipulated to make you something more than human and to follow their ethical standards. Did I agree with that? Of course I did. I just wanted our patients to reach their normal potential, that's all. The GSA had strict guidelines as to where, when, and for what conditions any treatment could be used for. Did I comply? Absolutely! So our strict adherence to their rules should put their mind at ease, right? One would think so, but these decisions become intertwined with personalities and regrettably become somewhat personal. That's what this had become for Dawson.

We were in December and it was a chilly month. The holidays were around the corner and we started to wonder if we were going to miss another deadline. Charlie would not be able to attend university by himself next year. While he would have mobility in a few months, he would need six months of rehabilitation before we could practically have him live on his own. Every day became a marathon waiting for some news. Sometimes knowing it's not going to happen is easier than sitting on the fence wondering your fate. I think the stress of this must have overwhelmed Charlie. He suffered a cold and asked to stay home one day.

"Do you have a fever?" Sarah asked him, putting her hand on his forehead.

"No, I think I'm okay."

"You don't look alright."

"I'm fine. Just need some rest from everything, that's all," he said, trying to downplay his emotions.

"Don't worry—I'm sure your dad will come home with some good news tonight. Even if you don't do your surgery before the holidays there is still plenty of time; we've talked to your teachers and they will find a way to make up your classes."

"I know, Mom."

"So don't let it concern you too much."

He waited by the window for me to arrive. I came home that night and unfortunately, I didn't have the news he wanted to hear. He didn't look happy.

"Charlie, did you start your puffers?" I asked, noticing him coughing.

"No, Dad, I'm breathing okay."

With severe asthma, someone's condition can change in an instant. One moment they are fine, the next minute they are in the infirmary. We had many bouts of hospital visits when Charlie was young but things were different now. Charlie was older and his asthma was under better control. Regrettably, things took a turn for the worse the next day. I didn't think his symptoms warranted too much concern when I received a call from Sarah.

"Charlie doesn't look well, so I've brought him to the hospital," she said with a concerned voice.

"Why, what's wrong?"

"He was breathing heavy so I wanted his lungs to be checked."

"How is he doing now?" I asked.

"He seems to be doing better, but the doctors still want to do some tests."

If I had thought for a moment that it was serious, I would have immediately been on my way. Sadly, I was in the middle of my workday.

"Which hospital are you at?" I inquired, as we had been to a few in the past.

"We came to the closest one: Westlake Children's Hospital."

"Okay, let me finish up here and I'll join you after."

I completed work early that evening and went to the

hospital with the hope of picking up Sarah and Charlie. I thought they would have concluded his treatment by the time I arrived. Let me tell you, when you walk into a hospital department and everyone has their head down or just looking away, it's not a good sign. You could hear a pin drop in a hospital that has over 479 beds.

I walked into the emergency room thinking I'd see Dr. Wilcox, his pediatrician, who is typically called down to attend to Charlie when he's in the emergency room. There was no trace of him, nor any sign of Sarah or Charlie. Everyone was keeping a safe distance from me while occupying their time with some other activity. I knew they were aware of my presence, which felt strange. I finally caught the attention of one of the nurses, Janice, whom I recognized from our previous visits.

"Ms. Janice, do you know where Charlie and my wife are? I thought they would be here."

"I believe they were transferred to the pediatric ICU on the fifth floor," she told me as she slowly looked away to attend to her work.

"Pediatric ICU?" I said, not certain if I heard her correctly. Janice glanced back and didn't say any more, and I really didn't like the worried look on her face.

I quickly ran to the elevator and started thinking, *how did this happen? Could this be serious?* My heart was racing and there really are no words to describe the state of being in the dark and the feeling of impending doom. I think the only thing that provided me solace was that I hadn't heard anything from Sarah, and this offered me hope. Just as that thought ran through my head, I reached for my phone in my pocket and noticed I had five missed calls from Sarah and one voice message.

My heart was now galloping faster than I could count. I tried calling her but being in the elevator, I had no reception, so I tried redialing several times before realizing it was best to wait and see her in a few moments. Those four floors the elevator went up must have felt like forty; I can recount every thought that went through my mind floor by floor, second by second. I was nauseated and lightheaded, but too furious and scared to worry about it.

I stormed out of those elevators like I was ready to run a track race; as I ran toward the intensive care unit I had to slow down; I saw a curious sight I was too familiar with, but in that moment I wasn't a physician—I was a patient's father and completely in denial. I pushed open the doors to the ICU and witnessed a sea of green shirts: doctors, nurses, and staff leaning against the hallway wall with their heads down. None of them were facing each other; none of them were making eye contact, and none of them were talking. I have been on the other end of this a few times in my career. I guess I fooled myself into believing this wasn't what I was actually seeing; there had to be some other explanation. Then you start negotiating that maybe, just maybe, this was all for somebody else. The brain can do a good job of tricking oneself into believing whatever it wants when it wants to.

"Where is Charlie MacKinnon?" I demanded from one of the staff standing at the counter.

"If you can wait here, Dr. Wilcox would like to speak to you."

I had no desire to stand still. I ran down the hallway looking into each room and behind each door, hoping to see Charlie and Sarah in one of them. Each one gave me more of an empty feeling. With each passing room, I felt a wave of fear surge that I cannot begin to describe. I'm not sure why I did this but thinking rationally was not my strength at that moment, so I finally yelled, "Charlie? Sarah?"

That's when Sarah emerged from a room a few feet away from me with eyes filled with tears and hands covering her face. She was trembling and I embraced her as she spoke. It really didn't register for me at that moment what had actually transpired. My instinct was to protect Sarah and all I could feel was emptiness.

The pain of what happened next is something I will carry with me for the rest of my life. I have tried many times to block out of my mind the events of that day, but my dreams remind me.

I walked into the room and saw Charlie for the last time. The ICU physician came over to tell me how sorry he was for my loss and what had happened. Not a single word penetrated. I was numb. Charlie had pneumonia, which exacerbated his asthma to the point where his inhalers were simply not working. His asthma had taken a sharp turn for the worse around 3:00pm, which is when they called the ICU team to admit him to their unit. They had tried to intubate him but the swelling in his airway was so tight that multiple attempts had failed. Their team then tried to open a surgical airway in the ICU but they were too late. Just like that, he was gone. My life was gone. I had lost him, my son, my treasure, the focal point of my life.

The pain of losing a child is not something one can describe. This is the one loss a person doesn't recover from; this is the one time you fall off that horse and you're not getting back on. There is no pain in the universe that even compare. We can talk about it, hear about it, but when it happens to you—the range of anger one feels, the fury in your veins, leaves you thinking, I didn't believe I could ever have those levels of emotions. It's like hitting a black hole in the galaxy; you're now floating in a dimension that you've never seen before and cannot compare to.

I heard the voice message Sarah had left me that same night and carried it with me for a long time. Why? I'm not sure. Was it a reminder that I failed to be there for my son? I don't know. Was it to remember everything I had lost? Again, I don't know. In times like these, it isn't so much about rational behavior—it's the emotional behavior that rules. I do know one thing: I could hear Charlie's voice in the background of that message and that's what I wanted to keep.

Sarah's message was at 3:02pm and it was thirty-seven seconds long. His condition was not as serious then, but her voice was tremulous and she sounded concerned.

"Hi, it's me, they're moving Charlie upstairs; they're worried about his breathing. Please come soon." I could hear Charlie in the background speaking while struggling to catch his breath: "Mom, is it Dad? Can I speak to him?"

Those were Charlie's last words. He was calling for me, and I couldn't be there for him; those were words I never wanted to forget. I listened to that message every day to remember him. I knew it wasn't healthy to do this, but healthy or not, living or dead, nothing mattered. Charlie had died, and on that day, a part of me died too.

I have been present at many funerals in my life, including those for family members, relatives, and friends. The feeling is sad but there is also a resigned feeling to the situation. Perhaps it was the person's time to depart. They lived a good life. Maybe this was meant to be. You might even say there is a feeling of hope. Attending the funeral of a young child had a completely different undertone. The feeling is anger. You could probably cut the tension in the atmosphere with a knife. The vexed emotions permeate the room like a collective conscience.

It was snowing on that ominous day with a hard northern wind. The weather did nothing to add to my grief. My cup was already full. We had asked for a limited number of guests to attend. This wasn't just any funeral, and what we experienced didn't feel normal. I wanted to cry but all I felt was rage in my heart. The resentment made me unable to express any other emotion. To be direct, this was Dawson's fault; if I could charge him for murder, I would have. If Charlie had his surgery as scheduled last month, he would be walking right now. He'd also have better use of his lungs.

When Charlie had his spinal cord injury, I had already mentioned that he needed to be weaned off a ventilator for injuring the nervous tissue that helped him breathe. Even though he eventually regained function, his breathing was weakened and certainly not where it would have been had he had his operation.

The what if's were the only thing occupying my thoughts. Charlie could be doing his rehabilitation right now. Sarah and I would be planning our trip to visit him while at school next year. I could watch him throw his first pitch playing baseball. I would see Charlie married one day. Charlie and I could ultimately be working together. I could spend days thinking about the possibilities only to return to the current reality: Charlie was gone.

This is exactly what Dawson had wanted. Charlie always

had a keen sixth sense. He knew from that first moment we met Dawson that he didn't have a single sincere intention and was just looking to make trouble. In life, you sometimes choose your battles and then sometimes they choose you. This wasn't a battle we'd wanted. *If Dawson wanted to hurt someone then why not just hurt me? Why did he have to involve Charlie?*

Sarah was visibly torn and emotionally distraught, and was by my side the entire funeral. This was the second time we had lost a child. Children are supposed to bury their parents in this world, not the other way around. What had we done to deserve this? When bad luck happens to you once, there is an acceptance of your fate. The second time and you're wondering why the universe is begrudging you. For me this was not just about chances of the universe; it was about the malice of one person—but still, I was awfully unlucky to have crossed paths with that person.

"Charles, I can't begin to tell you how sorry I am for your loss. We're all devastated!" John said as he embraced us.

He was there that fateful day when the GSA declined Charlie's surgery despite our pleadings. John knew, having witnessed it all, the fury that was boiling in my heart. He persuaded me to not attend work for a few weeks; what he hadn't expected was for my absence to evolve into many months. I entrusted the hospital and all its affairs to the care of John and Dr. Li, and I was gone.

When I returned home from the funeral, I madly went downstairs and in an agitated frenzy picked up my own baseball hat, outfit and glove, and furiously stormed out of the house and threw them in the trash can. I knew the days where I would derive any joy from these had expired.

The next few weeks after Charlie's passing, I'd sit idle in my basement and listen to his recorded message asking to speak to me. That was Charlie's last wish—one that I didn't fulfill and would carry with me forever.

Three days after the funeral I heard in the news that the GSA's review of our hospital had been over and we could resume normal activities. I was despondent. The truth is—did it even matter anymore?

I guess on a sober day, the answer would be yes. Even though I didn't drink, this wasn't a sober day. I had done all of this for Charlie. Could other people benefit from this? Yes, they could. Did I want others to benefit from this? Yes, I did; but like a driver looking into the horizon, my vision was always Charlie. He himself contributed to its cure and wasn't here now to benefit from it.

John never bothered to call to inform me of the announcement. He knew it would just be adding insult to injury and would infuriate me more.

Every day I wondered if I had been there, if there was something I could have done to intervene. No one was more familiar with Charlie's health as much as I was.

This was a long winter. Several months passed and John started to call me every day. Most days I would let the calls go directly to my answering machine.

Today's message was, "Hi, Charles, I haven't heard from you in a while. Some of your patients are asking about you. I wanted to see how you're doing and when I'm going to see you again? Call me when you can."

I didn't—so I heard a knock on my door the next day. It was John. He had come to visit. We talked about how I was doing, some work-related matters, and he had some personal suggestions on how to help with the healing process.

When John left that morning, I went to pick up the mail and there was a letter addressed to Charlie from Oxford

University. I stared at the envelope unsure how to feel. After a few minutes of reflection, I finally opened it with an excitement I wasn't sure I even understood.

"Dear Charles MacKinnon XII,

"Congratulations on your acceptance for admission to Oxford University…"

I felt a joy reading the letter, a delight I only felt when Charlie was around. I could have closed my eyes and forgotten everything, and pretended life was back to normal. Then the brain starts retracing your steps, and you remember exactly where you are and how you got there, and "who am I kidding?" I muttered. "There is no fooling anyone here."

Every success was now a reminder of failure. I was always good at using every obstacle in life to my advantage. That was my talent. Not anymore—not this time.

All I knew was that I couldn't continue living like this; so I grabbed my coat. I didn't know where I was going, just that I needed to leave. It started to rain during my walk, which was fine by me as I was indifferent to being wet. In a strange way the wet weather was actually nice as I sensed it speak to me. I could discern the cry of the drizzle sympathizing with my plight. As the storm up-surged, I heard screams of thunder and winds howling around me; it felt as though the universe had finally understood my sorrow and was reaffirming it in a way more powerful than words.

I walked until finally arriving at a neighborhood village with small picturesque shops. There I saw a sign I had seen a million times before but it had never caught my attention. This time there was a different aura of connection with its message, "Psychic Open"—it was a glowing red-lit sign above an antique shop. There was a small printed message underneath: "Commune with loved ones in other worlds." I knew of friends who had been to these sorts of places when their loved ones had passed away as a medium to speak to them. It was quite common amongst those who had lost a loved one prematurely; we all need closure. They would swear that they were told things that only their loved ones would have known. Surely, the psychic couldn't have made it up. Still the idea seemed strange. The science part of me just felt plain awkward believing in such things. Although right now I wasn't a man of science; I was desperate. I was a father who wanted to speak to his son.

I stood there across the street for thirty minutes staring at the sign in the rain. Did I want to speak to Charlie? Yes. Did I believe he's somewhere? Yes. Yet I couldn't bring myself to do it. I wasn't sure how to feel about this. Ultimately, was any of this going to bring me more or less pain? I don't know. My pride prevented me, and I moved on and continued to walk, and went by the waters where I would always go with Charlie.

We had a lot of memories here. The rain didn't bother me; more and more it felt like a friend. Still, it was cold and I had to go back home at some point.

XII

Sarah felt that resuming my work schedule might help me adjust back to a normal routine—so I eventually returned, but it took another five months. The GSA was no longer lurking, and when I came back, John brought me up to speed on everything that had happened. The hospital was doing well; we were curing people for spinal cord injuries, strokes, and Alzheimer's. We were now expanding our treatments to include a whole host of other illnesses, including diabetes, asthma, and various cancers.

"Charles, there is one last bit of news I need to tell you," he said with hesitation.

"What is it, John?"

"Your research on DNA activated transfer is up for an award," he said in an uneasy tone. "It's the Sir Lawrence Roswell Award."

XII

Under normal conditions, this would have been great news as it was the highest-standing scientific award in the country. He paused before he continued, "I wanted you to return to work before sharing this with you."

"Let me see it," I requested.

He gently handed me the envelope and said, "The deadline for your acceptance was yesterday. I spoke to Sarah and we felt it would be good if you could attend the ceremony."

I looked up at him in surprise and wondered why he looked so intimidated. He then put his head down, rubbed his forehead, and timidly said, "So I took the liberty of accepting the invitation on your behalf. The ceremony is in three weeks."

He let me read the letter by myself and quietly left the room.

"Call me if you need me," he said, slowly closing the door.

Charlie and I had been co-authors on this study. He had worked on this project a couple of summers ago and deserved most of the credit. The award was addressed to both of us.

I sat there and thought about this. I understood what John and Sarah were trying to do and I appreciated it, but the award had no meaning for me without Charlie being there to share it. I didn't want to go, but Sarah talked me into attending the ceremony and I ultimately went for her. "I can't help you, if you're not willing to help yourself," she kept saying. Those, by the way, were my words that she was now cleverly using on me. I had my acceptance speech ready and Sarah didn't tell me this directly, but I knew she had called them in advance to let them know of Charlie's untimely passing. Unfortunately, someone didn't get the memo when the awards were being called out.

"…and this year's winner of the Sir Lawrence Roswell Award is the TACT study on DNA activated transfer. I'd like to congratulate and invite Charles MacKinnon XI and Charles MacKinnon XII in accepting this award."

I can't explain it, but when I heard Charlie's name something clicked in my mind. I didn't feel right to go up and was lost in my thoughts; I sat there as they called out our names repeatedly. I couldn't do it.

I expected Sarah to nudge me to move toward the stage, but other than putting a hand on my shoulder and ask how I felt about going up, she didn't do anything else. She too was caught off guard when they called out Charlie's name and must have known how difficult it would be for me.

Time is supposed to heal all wounds; a year later and the cuts were as fresh as the day it had happened. In the coming months, my mother also decided to move to San Francisco where she was originally from. She too had many agonies dating back to my father's passing and now wanted to be closer to her parents and sister. We would speak on the phone but I could feel the loneliness of my predicament.

I returned home one day after a walk in the park where I would usually go with Charlie. Sarah knew exactly where I had been from the wet sand on my clothes but she deferred to comment. I went downstairs to where we had our laundry area. I needed to clean up and have a change of attire. I was embarrassed to go back upstairs so I took solace in sitting on the couch in the "hideout" room.

Sarah finally came down and I knew she wanted to talk. She sat beside me and waited a few moments before gently saying, "I know nothing can ever bring back Charlie; I'm feeling this loss as much as anyone." She continued, "When we lost Jesse, I thought nothing could ever replace him, and in some ways nothing ever does. I thought this pain would never go away and—"

"This is different than Jesse," I remarked.

"They were both our sons. It's different only in that we had Charlie to ease the pain of the loss of Jesse."

I knew where she was going with this so I quickly retorted, "Are you saying we should have another child just to forget Charlie?"

"Did we have Charlie just to forget Jesse?"

Okay, she made a good point.

She pressed on, "We'll never forget Charlie, just as we'll never forget Jesse." She paused for me to look at her before continuing, "I just think it will be good for us to have a family again. That's all."

"I know what you're trying to do and I'm grateful. I really am, but it's different this time."

"How is it different?" she appealed.

"I don't know...it just is."

"Charles, will you stop and listen to yourself; you're making excuses."

"...but?" I said, feeling a need to say something.

"...but what?" she asked.

I had to take a moment and gather my thoughts on this. "I don't want just another child," I said in frustration. "...I just want Charlie!"

My heart really wasn't in it. I can't remember what Sarah was talking about next. I was in a fog. She was offering me her loving advice and my attention was beginning to drift. I was looking down and away when she was speaking. I was focused on the corner of the room where I could remember the number of countless hours I spent with Charlie. As I was thinking back to those warm memories, I could see outside the drawer of the desk a little bit of Charlie's hair sticking out. It was from one of the last times I'd cut his hair.

"Charles, hear me out," Sarah said, gesturing, redirecting my attention.

"Sorry, I'm listening," although my thoughts were still clearly distracted.

"I think bringing another child will be good for us. I know you may have concerns that it's too soon, but give it some thought."

I wanted to focus more attention to Sarah's words but all I could think of at that time was how Charlie's DNA was actually in that hair. He was there. The genetic code and every biological matrix pertaining to Charlie were in that drawer.

"Charles! Charles!" Sarah kept repeating as she could see me drifting into fantasy land.

"Sorry—sure, let me think this over," I proposed.

Sarah embraced me with a hug, but my thoughts were still Charlie. While I am no expert in matters of the heart, there was definitely a shift in direction of the compass of my feelings from that moment onward. I wasn't entirely sure what it was or where it would lead, but I had a new lease on life.

I spent a number of days mulling over this idea. That weekend we decided to travel to the MacKinnon Saturday retreat. We hadn't attended one of these outings since Charlie had passed away.

We had family visit from time to time, but avoided large gatherings. All of the family were supportive and understood why we had lost touch. Uncle Stewart was the first to greet me. "Charles, it is great to see you. It's nice having you back. You're looking good."

"Thanks, Uncle Stew."

Although each member was welcoming, it caught a few of the relatives off guard; no one was more uncomfortable than Harris and Margaret. I can't blame them. They had planned to disclose their good news at this gathering, but seemed a bit apprehensive when they saw us. Ultimately, they shared their recent glad tidings.

"Everyone, Margaret and I have an announcement to make," said Harris. "We had wanted to tell you about this for a while now." After a pause, he completed. "We will be starting a family and have a baby coming next spring."

There was a loud cheer in the room. I was the first to congratulate him, "I am very happy for you, Harry." I didn't want anyone to think I was going to sulk on someone else's good news. Harris is a good man.

"Thanks, Charles. That means a lot to me." He shook my hand and hugged me before saying, "You know I'm always here for you."

"I know."

Everyone then took a turn to congratulate and embrace them. The only thing that remained to be seen was the gender of the child. That would, of course, also determine the name.

"Do we know if it's a boy or girl?" my cousin Fiona curiously asked.

"The doctor wasn't sure, but said it looks like a boy," Margaret told us with a smile.

"Clyde MacKinnon," shouted Uncle Stewart. "Clyde is the next heir in the MacKinnon family of names."

"Wow, have we moved up to Clyde that quickly?" my cousin Bruce remarked.

"That's what happens when the last five have been boys, and all first born! Count them six now."

I hadn't realized it either, but we really were up to "Clyde."

I could hear in the background Annabel speaking quietly, though I pretended not to have heard as I was sipping on my soda. She whispered, "You realize the next boy will be a Charles."

I had done the math too in my head as I was hearing those words uttered. I really wasn't prepared to see another Charles unless it was my own Charlie. I guess you could say that was when the idea really became consolidated in my head.

All I could think about from that moment on was that I had Charlie's DNA sample sitting in a drawer right at home. By my estimation there would be approximately 125,000 hairs in that drawer representing an average sample of a full set of hair. In order to extract his DNA there would need to be some hairs with their roots attached. The hair shaft is way too tricky and unreliable to extract the DNA even with GEMA. Charlie had a complete military haircut; the closer you go to the scalp the higher the probability of a few hairs being pulled out from their root. Even if I took a conservative number of 0.01 percent, that would leave me with approximately 1250 hair roots. Still, many of these wouldn't provide an adequate sample, but I just needed one to be viable in the lab. The more I thought about it, the more it seemed plausible. I kept running these numbers in my head over and over again that evening. All I could think about was, when I arrived home I needed access to my microscope to look at those hairs more closely.

Ultimately, I figured that without Charlie my existence had no meaning; my life was aimless. His life was taken away unjustly and in the process, they also robbed me of any joy in life. This was not a case of bad circumstances, a universal plan or, for that matter, the Will of God. This was the malice of one person—Dawson—plain and simple. If there is to be any equity in this world, we should at least be able to undo the wrongs of others, should we not? If there is to be fairness in this world, we should at least be able to compensate the losses of the innocent, should we not? So why was I having an ethical dilemma about this? I don't know.

I was running the ethical checklist through my head:

Would Charlie be born of the love of two people? He definitely was. Would Charlie be naturally created? I guess that all depends on your definition of natural. Initially he certainly was. Would I be harming anyone by recreating Charlie? I wouldn't. So why then would it be wrong?

I could hear my father's voice now saying "it's because you're playing God!"

Okay, if that's the case then how is this any different than doing in vitro fertilization? The principle in theory was the same. Really, using that line of logic you can argue that any significant medical intervention is playing God. To me this argument just didn't pass the litmus test and was too subjective. Although I'm sure if my father was here he'd come up with another astute explanation, but he wasn't here. That, by the way, was another universal injustice that I will not attempt to comprehend.

The more I circled on this subject the more I came back to the original starting point. While I could argue the merits of the right and wrong of this, I knew one thing for sure: Charlie was unequivocally taken away from me by Dawson. He was too precious to lose. I couldn't justify the universal balance on this one; wrong or right, I wanted Charlie back.

XIII

On my drive home, I realized that for the first time in a year I felt a renewed feeling of optimism. Sarah even noticed too. I guess whistling while driving was a clear signal. Not only could I have Charlie back, but he'd be named Charlie as well. To me this part just felt like destiny. This was the one element of the equation I could not control. Sometimes you have a sense the universe is prompting you with a sign; for me this was it. If I didn't act swiftly, the opportunity would be lost and the next Charles could be as much as a full generation away.

When I looked back at our family history, a Charles was born anywhere from 117 to 21 years apart. This, of course, depended on circumstances and the ever-changing size of our family, which varied over the centuries because of persecution and from various diseases such as the smallpox outbreak in the 1800s. The next Charles would be a new record of close to seventeen years if it were to happen. I couldn't let this pass. The more I thought about it, the more it felt right.

"You seem pretty cheerful," Sarah said.

"I'm really happy for Harry and Margaret. They are the nicest couple. This couldn't have happened to better people."

"Yes, Margaret was sure excited," she said.

"It was nice, wasn't it?"

When we arrived home, the curiosity of this had me anxious and it was unbearable. I had to run downstairs to see if any of Charlie's hair was retained with its roots.

Sarah asked, "Where are you going?"

"I'm just checking on some things downstairs. Go on up; I'll be up soon to join you."

The exhilaration I felt was something I hadn't sensed in a long time, walking down those steps. I had an old microscope stored from my university days, and just had to find the box where I had placed it. I searched inside the closet; the first box I opened had some books in it, I knew that wasn't it. The next box had some old clothes. Then I opened another box and couldn't believe what I saw. I sat down to appreciate what I was witnessing: it was my baseball hat, glove, and outfit nicely cleaned and folded. I knew Sarah must have retrieved it when I had thrown it away and stored it here. After a moment's reflection, I continued my search and finally found the box I was looking for. The microscope was old and it had collected some dust, but it sure worked.

I quickly realized I needed to be careful. This was not just any cut hair now; I was working with specimen samples that would serve as Charlie's DNA. I dusted the microscope and wiped it clean with alcohol. I then grabbed a pair of surgical gloves from a box I had in one of the drawers. Charlie's condition always required us to keep a fair amount of medical supplies at home.

Once prepared, I carefully brought the hairs from the drawer into a clean sheet. I had to turn the lights off in the room to see the hairs more clearly under the microscope. I looked at several hairs at a time, moving from batch to batch. I couldn't hold my emotions back. I just knew I'd find it.

"Cut hair," I muttered to myself as I moved to the next cluster of hair.

"Some more cut hair," I mumbled.

"No root." Next batch of hair.

"Nothing in this one either." Next batch.

"For heaven's sake!" I lamented. Next batch.

"No hair roots!"

And wait, I took a close look and breathlessly froze in excitement—there it was! Unbelievable! There under that bright microscope light, I could see its shape. It left me speechless—it was beautiful. The hair not only had its root, but also the protective layer around it. Usually it's not much of a sight to look at a stand of hair, but under those dimmed room lights that hair could not have shone more majestically as it did at that moment. I had to pause to take this all in. My face could feel the rush of blood, and my eyes were filled with tears of joy. All I could do in that moment was utter one word: "Charlie!"

I continued to search, carefully gathering the viable hair

samples and putting them in a specimen container.

I couldn't sleep that night; I was too excited. I wasn't tired the next day either. I came home straight from work and decided to prepare for a run. This was my first time jogging since Charlie had died. To me Charlie was coming back. It wasn't a question of if—it was a question of when. The more I thought about it, the more I became confirmed in the idea.

When I walked into the kitchen after my run, Sarah couldn't help but comment, "It's been a while since you've been jogging; are you sure your heart can take it?"

I laughed as I was drinking my juice. She was probably right, but I was so contented that I couldn't feel any fatigue even after not having slept the night before.

"I think I'm alright!" I said, searching for my next words. "I have given some thought to what you mentioned a few days ago."

"Oh, what's that?" Sarah asked.

"You know, about having another child."

"Oh yes, and?"

"Well, I know nothing will ever bring back our Charlie. There are certain wounds that don't like to heal. All the experiences, the memories, the love that we shared with him: we can never have those back. That's something we just have to learn to accept and cope with as best as we can."

Sarah was looking at me intently wondering where I was going with this.

I continued, "Having one child never replaces another; nothing can, but Charlie filled our lives with so much love that it flooded and overwhelmed whatever pain we felt." Sarah looked at me more optimistically now.

"I know adjusting won't be easy. I also know there is no painless way for us to turn the page and move forward with our lives after what we've been through—but I'm willing to give it a try. I agree, Sarah; it might be a good idea for us to have another child."

"Aww, Charles, I'm so happy!" Sarah embraced me tightly and didn't want to let go. I know this whole ordeal was as hard on her as it was on me; she just didn't outwardly show it as much as I did. Then I made one additional request,

"But, on one condition."

"What's that?" Sarah asked.

"I lost Charlie to asthma. I also lost my father to asthma. I just can't psychologically endure another loss to this."

"Go on," Sarah said.

"Well asthma is one of the listed conditions we can actually do gene therapy for at our lab. The GSA has approved this. We can cure this once and for all."

Sarah was a bit apprehensive. "What are you saying, Charles? What does that involve?"

"Well, we would apply the therapy before the implantation of the embryo," I explained.

Sarah was quiet. "I don't know, Charles. I'm not certain if…"

"Sarah, after everything we've been through I can't handle another setback."

She looked at me more tenderly now and realized I really needed this.

"Please do this; do it for me," I pleaded.

She took a moment to gather her thoughts and nodded gently in agreement.

XIV

Gene therapy for asthma was a new treatment. Fortunately, we were the only hospital in the world that provided this specific service and since there were no other alternatives, there were also no conflicts of interest.

The GSA had strict criteria for all therapies including treatment of internal staff and family members. For special circumstances where it wasn't clear, you'd have to fill out a GS-1 application for approval. This case technically was clear because their rules had already stated that a treatment could be "provided on any patient in the absence of any alternative therapy or substitute source for treatment."

"Severe asthma" was also included on the approved list of conditions. One of the criteria to qualify as "severe" was a family history in which there was a death in the family. We had two—so checkmarks on all counts.

XIV

That being said, our physician, Dr. Oliver Li, felt slightly uncomfortable in view of the turbulent past we had with the GSA. He wanted the GS-1 application filled regardless.

There was no way I would consent to that. I didn't want Dawson probing around us; it was too risky. In the end, I persuaded Dr. Li to agree. We were following their rules, and according to their by-laws, we were in the clear to go ahead without seeking any specific permission.

The arrangements didn't take long. GEMA allowed us to accomplish almost anything we wanted in the highest quality in a very short amount of time; had this been the 1500s, they probably would have blamed GEMA for witchcraft. Thankfully, it was not, but when I think about the current regime's interrogations, was it really all that different?

Sarah and I met with the genetics team, an extension of my team but under direction of Dr. Li for this case. They would first attempt to select for an embryo with a genetic combination that was free of asthma. For this reason they needed to acquire and review as many samples as possible; considering the frequency of asthma in my family history, there were no guarantees they would find this. If unsuccessful, using GEMA, they would determine the most appropriate sample to minimize risk, and gene therapy would then be applied before embryo implantation.

The only thing that remained was setting a date. "When would you like to go ahead with the embryo transfer?" Dr. Li asked.

"How is your schedule next Monday or the following one?" I intentionally asked for a Monday appointment. In some ways it didn't matter as I had access to every lock and room in the hospital—but still, I had to mitigate risk. What if Dr. Li or one of our technicians had decided to work late every day that week? I would have a difficult time making the necessary preparations. It would also be much less complicated for me to switch the samples during the weekend where our lab tends to be empty. There were a few other reasons that I desired the Monday schedule—more on that later.

Dr. Li finished reviewing his appointments, looked up, and said, "This coming Monday is good. I have a cancellation at 1pm if that works with your timetable?"

It did; this almost seemed too good to be true and perhaps too easy. Every time I was faced with the question, "Why do this?" I kept replying to my own conscience, "Why not!" Charlie was the perfect child. He had a gift. His life was worth reliving. No gift should ever be wasted.

I had thought this through, analyzed it backward and forward, inside and out, and every dot seemed to connect. Questions like, "What if people start noticing he looks the same as the previous Charlie?"

First and foremost, there would be an almost seventeen-year gap between this Charlie and the last one; people's memories aren't that sharp. The two Charlies would not be synchronized within the same time period. No one clearly remembers what Charlie looked like when he was five or ten years old, and trust me, in seventeen years they'll have faint memories at best for what he looked like just before his untimely passing.

Secondly, many siblings appear similar. Sarah and Hannah looked like twins if you observed pictures of them at the same age. In general, resemblance of siblings was nothing new.

The third reason and this one was the decisive factor for me: this Charlie would actually look very different from my last one. My Charlie endured his best years of growth and development in a wheelchair. Had he been able to have full use of his arms and legs, his musculature and body morphology would be shaped completely differently. Take any person, add or subtract fifty pounds of muscle, and you have a completely different-looking person.

Lastly, not too many people recognized how tall Charlie had grown. When Charlie was seated, he was about 4 feet tall. If you've never seen a person stand, you just don't have a feel for their height.

I can go on analyzing this: the new Charlie would have a different hairstyle, he would probably wear different clothes, and every genre has its own unique style and so on. All of these aspects would contribute to a different look and feel. I could keep rationalizing with the reasons, but for me it was a non-issue; this Charlie would not be confused with the last one, and no one would suspect that it's the same person genetically—not even Sarah.

Monday was just six days away. I couldn't believe all this suffering would be washed away in just a few days. I'd have Charlie back. There is one thing I would miss though: the new Charlie would have no memory of the last. Those recollections were something I'd never want to let go. That, unfortunately, was a sacrifice I didn't have a choice in. I'd have to keep those memories locked in my head and in my heart. Altogether, it wasn't too bad; this was, after all, Charlie—the same genes, the same brain wired the same way, the same parents, the same upbringing, and the same circumstances. The only thing different would be that he'd now have a chance to complete the dreams we had always aspired for him.

I had already purified Charlie's genetic sample in the lab

that week using GEMA. The DNA had been transferred from the donor cell to its recipient site, and its development had been prepared by GEMA for implantation. I had secured the specimen it in a safe place and would make the switch on Sunday.

Were there video cameras in the lab? Yes, there were. Could they see what I was doing? Absolutely. Did I care? No. Of course, you may ask why I wouldn't be concerned about some compromising evidence that could incriminate me. What was relevant here was time. The security guards would not be able to comprehend looking at any videos as to where I was going and what I was doing. They would not know which rooms I should be in and which ones I shouldn't. I was the hospital owner, after all; why would they speculate something was off. They didn't know we were conceiving a child, nobody knew that. This is where patient confidentiality is your best friend.

The only person who might suspect something is if Dr. Li happened to be sitting behind that video in the security room, and that wasn't happening—not on a Sunday, and quite frankly, not on any day.

That brings us to the original question of time. Videos are wiped clear and recycled every six months. That's pretty much the industry standard. Let's say someone in the future were to raise a question; could that person go back and look at the videos? Well, if it happened in the next six months, then sure they could, but why would anyone be suspicious to pursue that in the next six months? Not much would happen in that span to raise any questions. I've long learned that there is no such thing as risk free. However, the risk here was almost negligible, so I was not worried.

On Friday when I came home, Sarah and Hannah were in

the living room talking.

"Hannah, it is nice to see you!" I said.

"You look good, Charles," she noted. "Sarah told me about your plans."

"...plans?" I asked.

Sarah then interjected to explain: "Hannah and Mike will be moving this Monday, and since you seem so reinvigorated by jogging every day, I thought you might want to help them?"

There wasn't much that Sarah didn't tell Hannah, but surprisingly she hadn't told her anything about our arrangement on Monday.

"Hannah and Mike are moving?" I questioned. Sarah had mentioned this a few months ago; I hadn't anticipated the time to have passed so quickly. From the expression on Hannah's face, I realized she had been led to believe I had planned to take Monday off to help them.

"You mean he didn't know?" Hannah was looking at me apologetically. "Sorry, you don't have to come, we'll be fine."

"Well, I'd love to, but I can't this Monday," I said, shrugging my shoulders.

Hannah and Michael were moving closer from the city of Galena to Rockford, about 85 miles from where we lived.

"You've taken Monday off; you'll have plenty of time," Sarah said. "Mike has a broken wrist, so they'll need your help to drive the trailer."

"Really? How did that happen?" I asked in disbelief.

"Michael was painting the garage door of our new home; he slipped off the ladder and landed on his arm," Hannah said.

Fortunately, a broken wrist was all it was. In our family, helping with a move is considered an important tradition. In some ways, I'm all for movers, but it is for "the spirit, not the material gain" as Sarah always framed it. After all, it's a new start, the home is our sanctuary, and it builds bonds of friendship that will last a lifetime.

Yes, it was true; I had taken Monday off work, but it was to accompany Sarah for the procedure. Hannah and Michael were both in their twenties and starting a new life together. I knew helping them would be important to Sarah so I told Hannah, "In that case, consider it done! I'll be more than happy to help. Tell Mike not to worry; I don't want him lifting anything."

"Charles, I'm so sorry, you don't have to come. We'll find another way. Mike is also looking into hiring movers," Hannah sorrowfully explained.

"No need for that. I will be there. What is family for? It will be fun. I don't mind the exercise either."

I waited for Hannah to leave before talking about this further with Sarah. It was obvious she had her mind made up, so there was no point raising the issue in front of Hannah without making a scene.

"What was that all about?" I mentioned once we were alone.

"What do you mean?" she said.

"You know Monday is a big day for us. I want to be there that day."

"Charles, I don't need anyone to hold my hand; the deed is done. You've made your contribution. Besides, it just a fifteen-minute procedure; you said it yourself."

"Still, it would be nice if I was there when it all happens."

"Charles, did you know when it happened when it was a natural conception?"

Okay, I wish she wouldn't be so logical about this; that's

supposed to be my department. "Well, you've got a point, but who is going to drive you home from the hospital?"

"I'll take a cab. It's just a ten-minute drive."

I hesitantly agreed to Sarah's suggestion. Right now, being there was the least of my worries. The procedure is painless and most of the work is done prior to the patient's arrival.

I had already prepared the specimen from Charlie's hair. I also knew Dr. Li's lab would have had their work done by Friday as they only have a seventy-two-hour window to complete their task.

In general, the GSA has very strict criteria for the storage of genetic material and they can only be stored for a brief time. Nonetheless, there are a few exceptions to this rule. The first is if your condition is ongoing, in which case you could apply for an exemption to store stem cells for future use. The second is umbilical cord samples. These can be frozen at birth and preserved for life; at Genomica, we universally store these for all our newborns. We had saved these for Charlie too, but John had asked when visiting eight months ago if I'd consider donating them to the public blood bank.

The strictest GSA policy is reserved for the genetic modification of a fertilized egg as this has the highest ramifications. As a rule, specimens have to be genetically prepared within seventy-two hours prior to embryo transfer. They simply don't want facilities retaining genetically modified embryos long term for fear of additional manipulation and all its implications. So with the procedure being done on Monday, it was imperative that it be prepared by Friday to be safely within the allowed timeframe. This is why I had specifically asked for that Monday appointment.

To be true and fair to what we were doing, the only modification I made was to cure Charlie's asthma as I had promised Sarah; this was also the only alteration Dr. Li and his team were planning to do if necessary. I could do other refinements: making Charlie taller, altering the hair or eye color, but that wouldn't be in the spirit of what I wanted. I just wanted Charlie the way he was.

Even though I never technically lied to Sarah, I hadn't been entirely honest with her either about everything I was planning. This perhaps was my only dilemma in the process. Everything else, as far as I was concerned, was perfectly legitimate. For this reason, I wanted to satisfy her wishes in every other way. I had agreed with Sarah that asthma would be the only genetic modification: done. She wanted me to help her sister on Monday: done. This is how I negotiated my conscience to a resolution. Still, I felt like a thief who donates a portion of his wealth to charity to appease his conscience. Not sharing what I was doing with Sarah was something that haunted me every day, and I figured I would deal with it at some point in the future.

On Sunday, I went to the lab early. Most people were either asleep at this time or attending religious services. Mornings on Sunday tended to be lightly staffed with less surveillance personnel; there was also a change of shift for the security guards at 9am. During that change of shift, there would be a ten-minute window when one security is handing over all the evening events to the next guard coming on duty. In the course of that period, they would be occupied and not paying particular attention to the cameras.

It was still possible that the security guards would see my presence in the wrong lab as an unusual event. That's why I preferred distracted eyes on me than ones that were focused on what I was doing. While the risk of them being suspicious was low, it was not zero. It was a well-known fact that I didn't work on Sundays. There was always that off chance they could make a comment to the wrong person that they saw me in hospital on this particular day, at this lab, which would raise an eyebrow or two. I decided it was best to play it safe.

I waited in my car until 9:02 am. I could access all the security cameras from my mobile phone. This was another benefit of being the owner. I was simply looking for two things: first, making sure nobody was in the lab that I was entering, and second, making my move when the handover of shift of security guards was taking place. The ultimate task was a simple one: walk upstairs, take the specimen that I had prepared, and switch it with the one in Dr. Li's lab. I estimated this venture to take approximately seven minutes from my car to the lab and back. This would put me well within the ten-minute security handover of shift.

When the oncoming security guard Phillip arrived, that was my cue to put on my baseball cap and move. I kept a close eye on when the security left the table for their change of shift, and that's when I proceeded through the back door of the hospital to where the elevators were. I could see from my mobile, there was no one there in the south side of the hospital that I personally knew. The object here was risk management. While I couldn't avoid being seen by everyone—after all, many of my patients and their families were in the hospital—I could at least negate being seen by someone who was staff. I navigated the floors and elevators in order to elude being spotted. After a quick scan, I calculated there were three people in the hospital to keep a close eye on, aside from the security guards.

Dr. Zeeman, a workaholic who worked seven days a week, and a close friend of Dr. Li, was coming down the south elevators, so I comfortably switched routes and walked to the central ones. The central elevators took slightly longer than expected to arrive, and that was when my first hiccup happened.

Phillip, the security guard, came to the desk to get his notepad and looked right at the security monitors. To evade being identified, I just turned my back to the camera, flexed my head down, stared at my phone and pretended to read something. Of course, I was watching them watching me. When the elevator doors opened, I couldn't just walk in as they would recognize me from the elevator cameras. I had to wait until Phillip had finally left the desk; then I stepped into the elevator and angled my back to the camera in case he returned to his station.

Finally, I went up and that's when I noticed John on my mobile view of the security cameras on the eighth floor. What John was doing there? I had no clue. He never worked on Sundays. He had walked up the corridor and was now waiting for the central elevators that I was situated on. I quickly pressed the seventh floor to get off earlier but it was too late, it was going to the eighth.

The doors opened and my heart stopped. I stood on the side where he couldn't see me and just thought about what I was going to say. *How am I going to explain this? He knows me too well and would detect if I were up to something coming to work on a Sunday wearing a baseball cap.* This is where you need to think quickly so it all looks natural. Fortunately, another elevator arrived at the same time. It might have been a couple of seconds, but it felt like eternity for John to decide which one to choose. Luckily, it was the other elevator. I took a deep breath and finally arrived on the twelfth floor.

I went into my lab like a man on a mission. The specimen was nicely prepared and labeled. I quickly took it down the hall. I entered Dr. Li's lab, walked in and opened the specimen storage door; I looked at their prepped specimen and couldn't believe what I saw. The sample had some initial preparations with GEMA, but it was not yet fertilized.

This was supposed to have been completed by Friday. It wasn't done. Either someone forgot or something had happened. There were so many specimen preparations this past week; it was probably an oversight. I stood there frozen, not sure what to do; I was ever conscious that the clock was ticking. There were no second chances; my time was short and the impact of the decision life-long. The only thing that kept running through my mind was *if I don't do this, it won't be Charlie...it just won't be him.* I didn't have a choice; it was now or never. I took a deep breath and replaced it with the specimen labeled C.S. MacKinnon 720023.

There, I had finally done it. I can't explain how or why, but I felt an incredible relief that I'm lost to describe. There was now a defined clarity in my thoughts and a complete tranquility in my heart. I was finally at ease. I knew there was no turning back and I didn't mind. All I would have to do is wait another nine months and Charlie would be with me once again. He'd be running in our home, playing practical jokes like he used to, we'd have our chats, and he would join me for my jogs every day. I would once again hear his voice and work side by side with him. A lot went through my mind. I was melancholic—sad that one chapter had closed and yet exhilarated to start a new one.

I grabbed the other specimen and quickly closed the storage door. I looked at my mobile phone and the security cameras showed that the guards were continuing their exchange of notes. I still had time. I stepped out, locked the door shut and hurried into my own lab when suddenly I heard a knock on the door.

"Charles, is that you?"

"John! How is it going? What are you doing here?" I was clearly stunned to see him.

"Well, I was about to ask you the same question!"

I had to hide the specimen behind my back. If John saw me with this, he'd know exactly what I was up to. "Oh...I was in the neighborhood and just wanted to come in and catch up on some things," I said, gasping for an explanation.

"On a Sunday, Charles? You never work Sundays!" John grimaced.

"I know, but there's a lot on my table these days and I just needed the time. I wasn't planning on being here long."

John could sense that I had an awkward posture from the way I was holding my arm. I couldn't let him catch me with this. To make matters worse the specimen storage door in my own lab hadn't been properly shut; I could see that it was opening wider and wider from the periphery of my vision.

"Charles, is everything okay?"

"Everything is great, why would you ask?"

"You're wearing the same baseball cap you'd only wear when you were with Charlie," he said, visibly concerned. "Look, it's me you're talking to. I know you. I recognize when something is off and you're not yourself. If you need somebody or just want to talk—"

"John, really, you have nothing to worry about. I'm

well...couldn't be better these days."

"Are you sure?"

I nodded.

He didn't seem convinced. "If you need me, I'll always be here for you—even if I have to protect you from yourself."

"Thank you, John. I appreciate it."

Then he motioned with his hand and said, "Charles, come here, I want to show you something."

As John turned around to head toward his office, I quickly put the specimen in the back end of the storage where it couldn't be seen, and swiftly closed and locked its door. I then promptly walked out behind him and followed John to his room.

He then opened a folder and said, "A couple of days ago I was clearing my desk at home and found this!" It was a photo of the two of us when we were eight years old playing on a baseball team together. We were both posing in full gear with our baseball bats in hand, grinning from cheek to cheek.

"John, where did you find this? This is amazing. Wow, those were great times."

"They definitely were. Your dad was our coach. I'd never seen him so excited and involved in the game."

"He sure was. Our moms had to hold him back from running on the field and catching the ball for us."

We laughed before John gestured toward the picture and said, "Keep it! I found a couple more. I thought you'd like this one."

"Thank you. This means a lot." And it did; except my time was running out and I had to dart out.

"John, Sarah is waiting for me at home."

"Oh sorry, I don't want to keep you."

"No problem. We'll have to get together sometime soon.

Call me and we'll arrange something."

I ran to the elevator. I looked at my phone to see where the security guards were. They were just finishing their exchange when I walked into the elevator. I turned my back to the camera once again. As it reached the main floor, I had to wait a few seconds. When the security finally looked away from his screen to pick up a package, I quickly stepped out and walked down the hall and out toward my car. The total time was fourteen minutes but I was sweating as if it was a full hour's workout.

When I arrived home, Sarah was awake and had just come downstairs.

"There you are. Where were you?" she politely inquired.

"I was just running around and doing some errands."

"On a Sunday morning?" she asked. "Who is open on Sunday?"

I hadn't exactly planned on her being awake and having this conversation. "It really was nothing important. Just some run-of-the-mill stuff," I answered.

"Okay," she said softly as she walked away to the kitchen.

"Would you like some orange juice?" she said and turned back to complete, "You look like you're thirsty."

"Sure, that would be great." I had sweated more than I usually did when I went for a ten-mile jog.

"What time did Mike and Hannah ask for me to come to their place?"

"It's up to you. Anytime in the morning should be fine. By the way, Charles, thank you for doing this. You helping my sister and Mike, well, it means a lot to me."

"Don't mention it. It's nothing," I said.

"I wish I could join you all, but I'm having your baby tomorrow."

"Yes. I've heard. You're getting pregnant while I'm out of town—how could you?"

She laughed and I couldn't help but smile. We both knew our lives would be different after tomorrow. We'd be parents again.

That night, despite my excitement, I slept well. I had my recurrent dream that I had over and over again for many years. However, the dream was a little different this time—it marked the first occasion that I also saw Charlie in this dream. Superstitious or not, I took it all in as a good omen.

I dreamt that my father was on an open baseball field playing catch with Charlie. It was a beautiful spring day, sunny with no wind and not a single cloud in the sky. They were both in full gear wearing their baseball uniforms. My father was younger than I remembered him: healthy and vibrant, throwing that baseball with a velocity and strength that I had never seen him throw in his living years. Charlie was about the same age as before his death. He was not in a wheelchair and had an athletic physique. He was running and throwing as I always imagined he would. What caught my eye was just how happy they were, how free they felt, and how beautiful the setting was. Neither of them seemed to have any asthma symptoms or difficulty breathing, and considering it was spring, you can say it was definitely a dream. There was no conversation or words spoken. I was simply a silent observer and just enjoyed the scenery.

XV

The alarm woke me that morning. I wish I could have slept longer but I wanted to leave before the traffic. Sarah was already up and preparing breakfast.

"We both have a big day today," she said when I came downstairs.

"Yes, but it's a big day in a good way!"

"Is there such thing as a big day in a bad way?" Sarah remarked. She was the ultimate optimist.

"Yes. We've had our share of a few of those. Have we not had enough?" I retorted, looking for my key fob remote.

"Be positive!" Sarah said. "I'll call you when I'm done. Are you not having breakfast?"

"I want to beat the traffic before it gets bad," I told her as I grabbed my tape measure and working gloves.

"Here, I've packed you something for your journey."

Sarah had made me small breakfast bag of fruits, sandwiches as well as a cup of coffee.

"Thanks, you didn't have to do this," I said, and kissed her at the door to say goodbye.

Sarah then waved. "I'll call you when I'm done. My appointment, by the way, has been moved back to 3pm. Dr. Li called this morning to let me know."

"Why, what happened?" I asked, stopping to ascertain the details.

"Not sure," Sarah said, "I think he was having problems at work and just asked to change the schedule to be safe."

"What problems could he have?"

"Don't worry, it's probably nothing."

"Okay!" I said before leaving.

I tried to call Dr. Li several times as I was driving but each time I was directed to his voicemail. I finally reached him before arriving at Rockford. "Oliver, it's me, Charles. I received the message from my wife that—"

"Hi, Charles, not to worry, everything is okay. I'm in the middle of something right now. I'll see you at 3pm?"

"Actually, I won't be there; I'm in Rockford on some family matter."

"Oh! I hope everything is alright?" he said.

"It's all fine. I'm just helping my in-laws with their move."

"That's nice. I'll know who to call then when we're moving," he said laughingly. "Not to be concerned, Charles, she's in good hands. I'll see you then at work tomorrow."

"For sure; thanks, Oliver."

Hannah and Michael were apologetic and appreciative of me coming when I saw them. "How is your wrist coming along there?" I asked.

"I have no pain. The cast is coming off in a few weeks,"

Michael told me.

"Okay. Let's get to work then."

We started to pack everything inside the trailer. That day my thoughts were with my dream and Charlie. In the afternoon, we arrived at Michael and Hannah's new home. At 3 o'clock, I found a moment alone, sat down and took a break. I pulled a picture from my wallet of Sarah, Charlie, and myself, and stared at it for a few minutes before whispering, "I miss you, kid." I could have stayed in my thoughts for another few hours, but my phone rang. It was Sarah.

"Hi, Charles."

"Hi, Sarah, how is everything?"

"It's all done. I'm officially pregnant."

"How are you feeling?"

"Great. Everything went very smooth. Dr. Li was very pleased and reassured me that all went as expected."

"That's wonderful," I replied, feeling exhilarated.

"I'll be leaving soon to go home. How is everything coming along with the move?" Sarah asked.

"Great. We should be done in a couple of hours and I'll be home before supper. Maybe we could go out for dinner?"

"Actually, they've asked me to rest tonight."

"Oh yes, you're right." I had forgotten our protocol in my own excitement.

"Maybe tomorrow?" she appealed.

"Sounds like a plan. I'll pick up dinner then on my way home."

After that phone call, I realized Charlie was officially back. He was alive and growing. He was now part of the living. Everything in my life just felt different from that moment—I was aware of my own heartbeat, I could feel all my senses and all the sounds around me. I looked out the window and saw a few birds chasing each other around the branches of a tree. To the outward eye, it was a meaningless pursuit. Yet these birds were free and happy just to be in each other's presence. Its simplicity had a charm and it was beautiful.

"Charles," said Hannah, suddenly putting a halt on my thoughts, "Mike and I can take care of the rest. Why don't you go home?"

"I don't mind staying here and helping."

"No really, I insist," Hannah told me. "There is not much left to do. Thank you so much for coming."

"No really it's not a problem." I actually didn't want to fight hard to stay. I was too excited and wanted to go home to Sarah and Charlie. Technically, Charlie was home. Unfortunately, Hannah didn't fight as much as I thought she would with her offer.

"Well, if you'd like to stay, then sure. There are still boxes we have to unpack."

Sarah was asleep when I finally arrived back. I too was tired and went straight to bed.

The next day when I went to work, I wanted make certain to secure the specimen I had left in the storage. I wasn't too worried because it was hidden in a safe spot that only I had access to.

I went to my office early, straight to the lab and opened the specimen storage door where I had left it. I couldn't believe my eyes—it was gone! My heart was thumping and I was beginning to sweat. I scanned and searched, up and down, in and around, where I had placed it, hoping it had just accidently fallen, but no, it wasn't there.

I was left with two dilemmas: Who do I ask? And was it truly Charlie that Sarah was impregnated with? I didn't even know where to begin without raising suspicion. That's when John walked into my office.

"How are you doing, Charles?"

"Good, John, nice to see you."

"You're sweating. What's wrong? Are you looking for something?" he said, eating his apple.

That's when I knew John was involved. When you've grown up with someone since the age of three, went to the same schools and played in the yard with them every day— you know their jokes, their sarcasms, and when they are telling you they know something. John was speaking all of those dialects right now.

I went and closed the office door so we could have some privacy and quietly asked, "John, don't play with me. What do you know?"

"What do you mean?" he said, shrugging his shoulders, taking another bite.

"By God, I'm going to lose it, tell me where it is? I know you're up to something."

"Charles, are you crazy to just leave that there?"

"I don't know what you're talking about, John."

"Oh okay; ten seconds ago you were about to lose it—so now you even don't know what I'm talking about?"

"Just say what you have to say," I said.

"Charles, look at me—it's me you're talking to. We've been best friends since we were three. I know what you're thinking before you even think it! You said that yourself. You don't suppose I know what's going on here?"

126

"How did you find out?"

John stood with his hands on his waist and said, "Dr. Li had asked all the specimen storages to be checked. I didn't know what he was searching for; he just gave me the specimen number. I had no clue you and Sarah were doing this."

"What was he looking for? Did something tip him off?" I asked.

"Did something tip him off? Are you kidding me? You might as well have called the GSA. Charles, you had a fertilized egg in this specimen."

"What do you mean? We had seventy-two hours. Besides, I didn't have a choice."

"I bet you didn't!"

"John, why were you looking for the specimen in here?"

"Charles, you were the only person who had access to this storage and since you were away, I had the back-up keys you had provided me. We checked everywhere."

I was grasping my temple in disbelief. "I'm almost afraid to ask: what did you do with it?"

"What exactly were you thinking?" John said, shaking his head.

"What did you do?" I repeated almost aghast to hear the answer.

"Nothing," he said. "When I first looked I didn't see anything so I had nothing to report. It wasn't until after I saw Sarah in the hospital that I started to put it together. She was here. You had taken a day off without explanation. You came into work on a Sunday and we all know you never work on Sundays! I knew you were up to something when I saw you wearing your baseball cap in the hospital. That's when it all hit me. I went back to check and looked a bit harder and there it was."

"Oh God, what did Dr. Li do?" I asked, anxiously rubbing my forehead.

"He didn't do anything. He thought it was probably the mistake of the lab technician and as far as I know he went ahead as planned."

"So the sample he used was the one he had?"

"Yes, Charles. Have you gone mad?"

"I don't know what you're talking about."

"Don't play this game with me again. We both know what I'm talking about! Charles, I know how tough this is on you. I'm like your brother. When you suffered, I suffered with you."

"John, I know you mean well, but you have no clue what I went through."

"You're wrong. I do know."

"What's that? Is this about you losing your dog when you were twelve?"

"Hey, I hurt for a long time when Pepper died, and no, for your information, that's not what I was referring to. Did we have to bring him into this?"

"Sorry, I didn't mean to open up old wounds," I told him. "I take back what I said about Pepper."

"Charles, I understand your pain. I have wept with you every step of the way," he said, shaking his head before completing, "But this isn't how you make things right. This is not how you bring him back."

"So, how do I bring him back?"

John silently stared at me, and he had one of those concerned looks on his face that I was all too familiar with. He just replied, "You don't!"

There was a quiet pause and I knew where he was going

with this; I just wasn't sure if I wanted to hear it. "Where is the specimen now?" I asked.

"It's in the storage where you left it."

"I just checked; it wasn't there."

John went to the storage, opened the door, and pointed to it in a compartment below that I hadn't looked carefully at and said, "I put it down here. I'll leave this here for you."

"Thank you."

Then John asked me, "Does Sarah know about this?"

I didn't say anything; I sure didn't want to get into that conversation. I stood there frozen.

John just shook his head and said, "Charles."

The next few months we kept quiet about the pregnancy. No one knew outside of Sarah, myself and, of course now, John. There is always that small risk of incompatibility and a possible poor response with these procedures. I wasn't convinced we were in the clear until we went for an ultrasound. I could see Charlie's heart beating.

"Would you like to know the gender?" Dr. Li asked.

I didn't say anything even though he was looking straight at me when he raised the question. Sarah quickly responded, "I'd like to know."

"But I thought you'd always wanted to keep that a surprise until the final day. Are you sure?" I said, as that's what she had always wanted.

"I know, but I want to know this time. Aren't you curious?" she asked.

"I am. I guess we're going to find out then," I said, turning to Dr. Li.

He looked at us and said, "It's a boy, and he looks healthy."

I am not very good at lying, and definitely not much of an

actor, but I probably deserved an award for putting on a good show of surprise that day. "Wow, that's amazing. I would have never thought that. I knew the probability was 50/50 and everything, but a girl would have been great too. This is just amazing."

Dr. Li shook hands with each of us and said, "Congratulations to both of you."

XVI

On our drive over to the MacKinnon cottage for our next family gathering, Sarah asked me, "Charles, maybe it's time we tell everyone."

"Sure, if you're ready. I'm okay with it."

Sarah said, "I told Hannah earlier today. She is excited. If Hannah knows, we can't keep this a secret much longer."

I laughed, "That's for sure. The family probably already knows then."

"And you know how these things work. There is an order for how you tell people this news, who finds out first and so forth. Otherwise, they will all get offended. We can tell everyone at once tonight."

"That's true. It's a great idea!" I said, pondering how this would play out with the family. When dinnertime arrived, I thought it would be a good opportunity to announce it, as they would all be there together in one place.

Uncle Stewart was finishing his story with the children about Kenneth MacKinnon IX and describing his statue outside the small town where he worked. He had been a physician in the 1800s, and was heroic when smallpox had been an endemic disease in England. He worked fearlessly saving thousands of lives and was instrumental in bringing the vaccine and ultimately saving the village.

After Uncle Stewart's story, Sarah came beside me and wanted us to share our news. I knew this wouldn't be easy so I was happy to let her take charge. She said, "Everyone, we have an announcement to make!"

The entire family was there and they stopped eating to watch, wondering what this could possibly be. Sarah then looked at me to take the baton and run with it. I really didn't want to but everyone was staring at me to say something grand, and that's when I just said the first thought that came to mind. "We're pregnant. Well, I should say, Sarah is pregnant. We're going to have a child."

After a second of silence, the room erupted with a cheer and everyone started conveying their congratulations and joy. During all the chatter and hugs, Margaret asked, "How far along are you?"

"Three months!" replied Sarah.

"Wow, three months. Do you know the gender?" Margaret had a curious look on her face and everyone was listening intently for the response.

I really didn't feel comfortable answering that one, but Sarah responded swiftly, "It's a boy. We had the ultrasound this week."

There was deafening silence in the room as everyone was doing the simple math in their heads as to what the name of our boy was going to be. The silence was sure uncomfortable and that's when Blair, who would have been around nine years old at that time, shouted, "It will be named Charles!"

No one said anything. You could hear a pin drop. I heard a few whispers behind me—I ignored it. I knew they were thinking about how strange it would be for the family to adjust to us having another child named Charlie. That is why I had avoided the subject of her pregnancy until Sarah had brought it up earlier. The silence finally ended when Uncle Stewart walked over to embrace us. He put his arms around me and said, "I'm very excited for you. You've made us all very happy." He then hugged Sarah, "I can't tell you how thrilled I am for the two of you."

That pretty much cleared the tension in the room. The stillness slowly turned to a quiet cheer. Everyone then walked up to us, one by one, to offer their well wishes. I knew this would not be easy; it was certainly nice to have it out of the way.

Sarah's maternity was moving along smoothly and John never brought up the subject of her pregnancy again. We didn't attend the next family campout either. Everything was unfolding according to plan until I received a phone call from Uncle Stewart a few weeks later. He had wanted to share some good news.

"I know how hard it would have been for you to have another son with the same name as Charlie, so I thought you'd be happy to know that Margaret is having a girl."

Margaret and Harris had another ultrasound and it was

clear that their baby was a girl, not a boy.

"Thanks, Uncle Stew; that's great," I said with a straight face, hiding the frustration I was feeling. I honestly didn't know how to feel about this. This was a colossal disaster. I was about to have a son that was essentially Charlie—his genes, his flesh and his blood, in every way his identity—yet he wasn't going to be the bearer of his own name.

"Clyde is a beautiful name, Charles. We've had many great Clydes in our family history," Uncle Stewart told me.

We sure had, but I just couldn't see myself adjusting to calling Charlie, Clyde now. This just felt wrong, but there was no way for me to remedy this. The rules were the rules. As one would expect, I didn't sleep that night or the night after.

What didn't make it any easier was everything about this pregnancy reminded me of Charlie. One time Sarah commented as she was holding her abdomen, "Did you feel that?"

"Feel what?" I asked.

"Nothing, I was just thinking out loud," she said, looking down and feeling her tummy.

"Anything to be worried about?" I queried.

"No. Not that. Clyde just kicks the same way Charlie did."

"What do you mean? A kick is a kick, isn't it?"

"I guess, but it just has the same pattern. There's nothing, total silence, and then it's like he wakes up and he's kicking to a rhythm letting me know he's there." Sarah then went over to the stereo, turned up the volume and said, "Watch this!" She felt her belly and laughed, "Too funny. Charlie did this too. It's like he's dancing."

I went over and she grabbed hold of my hand, "Feel this!" He sure was a kicker and she was right, there was a definite rhythm to it. I said, "I'm sure lots of kids do that."

"Maybe; you might be right," Sarah told me.

When we went for our next ultrasound, we discovered that he was a breech baby just as Charlie had been. Dr. Li was telling us the reasons this could happen. We were all too familiar with this process; for me it was a pleasant reminder of Charlie.

At the following family outing, Scott and Catherine made their announcement that they too were having a baby. To make matters worse, it was also a boy.

"He is going to be named Charles!" said Uncle Stewart.

I had to hold myself back from crying. It was difficult seeing someone else taking the identity of my child, especially knowing the baby Sarah was carrying was my Charlie. I would look at Sarah's abdomen as though I was looking directly at Charlie. *What could I do?* I'd ask him silently in my thoughts. There was nothing that could be done. Everyone was excited for both Scott and Catherine.

I was going crazy. I had to talk to someone so I discussed it the next day with John.

"How do you feel about it?" John asked.

"I've tried to make peace with myself."

"...and how is that going so far?"

"I'm working on it!"

"Oh really," John said with a smile.

"I am resigned to having a Clyde. My attachment was never to the name, it was to the person that Charlie had been."

"No attachment to names? I'm going to disagree with that one, Charles. Your family has had the same name three times now from your father down to Charlie. If that's not attachment, I don't know what is?"

"That was chance. We didn't control that."

"Still, everything in your family is about names."

"It's tradition, John," I said with a frustrated tone.

"Sorry, I didn't mean it that way, but how many times did you want to hit the lottery on this? Did you even think about that?"

"I honestly thought it was destiny!"

"Destiny was your dad, yourself, and when Charlie was born. You planted this one. We both know that. This was you—not destiny. Don't kid yourself."

He had a valid point, which is why I didn't like how this was evolving. "Are you saying this is karma for what I did? It is, isn't it?"

"Charles, you know I'm on your side. I just think, maybe this might be a good thing. This child should have its own identity. The world did you a favor on this one. You should embrace it."

John was right. If this is a new start, I'll accept it. At the very least, he would have the same initials as Charlie. I guess when a man is hungry—he's looking for anything to call food.

We watched Harris and Margaret have their baby girl, Isla. There hadn't been a girl in the family for almost sixteen years. There was excitement and joy. As for us, everyone knew that we had been through a difficult time and genuinely wished for our happiness. They were also equally anticipating the birth of the next Charles so they were looking forward to Scott and Catherine's delivery with high hopes as well.

I had mentioned that every Charles had become a neurosurgeon and had ultimately achieved great distinction for our family. No one spoke of this, but I knew they were thinking the streak was finally broken when my Charlie had died. There were some in our circles who also looked at me as having failed for marrying Sarah, who never quite measured up to their standards.

What added to the disappointment was that my father and I were the first father and son to be named Charles in MacKinnon history; it also marked the first time two family members named Charles were alive at the same time. Everyone thought this had to be a sign—they just weren't certain what; but that sure didn't stop them from speculating.

Now you can imagine how much that anticipation was heightened when my Charlie was born. It only added fuel to the fire: three generations, one family, this was simply unheard of. My father's discovery of GEMA and Charlie's brilliance at such a young age had everyone believing we were on the doorsteps of an epic-changing destiny in MacKinnon history.

The universe had opened its arms and then simply turned its back. With my father's unfortunate death and Charlie's untimely passing, it left a few family members disillusioned. A premature death can defeat the hopes of even the strongest, and make them forgetful of all the good that had been achieved. Unfulfilled potential was what they imagined; strange, considering that MacKinnon history welcomed challenge as a catalyst for every triumph. I guess we all have our breaking point. It's probably fair to say they were eager to start a new chapter with a new Charles, and although they meant well, they were happy we didn't inherit the name. My family had that distinction for three generations, and I knew that deep in their hearts they wanted a new heir.

XVII

The winter came and passed and I decided not to go to the family outings anymore. Well, at least not until after the delivery. Sarah didn't ask but understood how I felt. Listening to everyone talking about the next Charles and it not being our son was too difficult and something I wasn't ready to hear.

Uncle Stewart would call from time to time to see how we were doing and why we hadn't come to the family gatherings. I'd tell him about work and the cold winter, but I think he knew.

However, I couldn't avoid the chance encounter with Catherine in the elevators and corridors at Genomica where she'd come for her obstetrical appointments. It was a MacKinnon tradition for every child in the family to be born at the same facility when possible. That distinction had been bestowed to Genomica when my father had built this hospital.

As for our son's breech presentation, just like our Charlie, he was stubborn and didn't make a turn. This time, however, unlike the last time he was scheduled for a caesarean section. Dr. Li didn't want to take any chances with the delivery.

The C-section was scheduled in five days on May 6th. Charlie or Clyde, this was my son and I was excited for his birth. I remember all too well when Charlie was born. The connection I felt as I held him in my arms that first time. That moment is something that I will savor forever and looked forward to reliving. I replayed that moment in my mind repeatedly and wondered how it would feel seeing it once more.

I knew if I were to start fresh, I would have to part with at least some of the painful memories. If there were ever a time to turn the page on certain chapters of my life this was it. I listened to Charlie's voicemail message one last time and did what I didn't think I would ever do: I erased the message.

I also went inside Charlie's room, something I rarely did, as it would bring back painful memories. Everything in his room was exactly as he had left it. Sarah had arranged for the new baby's room to be beside ours. We had five bedrooms so it wasn't an issue. She reasoned that the adjacent room made the most sense for a newborn, but I knew part of it was that she understood I needed the time to heal.

I looked around and realized that in a few days we would be starting a new chapter. In my heart, I said my goodbyes and picked up some of my fondest items to put inside a small wooden treasure chest. Sitting on Charlie's desk was the gold envelope with the photo I had given him. It was my last gift to Charlie—an unfulfilled gift in many ways. The photo was partially sticking out so I knew Charlie had been looking at it the night before he had passed away. I viewed the photo before pushing it back in its envelope. It was a tight fit, so I looked inside carefully to adjust it nicely.

I then placed the envelope at the bottom of the treasure chest, and added six other items that had a very strong connection for me to Charlie: his baseball hat and jersey, the first journal he ever read, several disks of videos and photos, his first research publication, and a sample of Charlie's hair that I had carefully covered inside a plastic wrap.

I then went downstairs to our basement to the same room where Sarah had once put a treasure chest of Jesse's items. I shelved it directly across from it. As I stood there and looked at these two wooden treasure chests, one on each side, I couldn't help but think again, it should be the children to part with their parents in this world and not the other way around. I guess my hope for this next child would be that he would, at the very least, outlive his parents.

On May 5th, I received a call from Sarah on my way home at 6:38pm. "Charles, I think it is happening."

"What's that?"

"I'm having contractions."

"Are you sure, Sarah?"

"I'm positive. I've timed it, and these are definitely—" she screeched as she felt another one.

"Okay, hang on. I'm coming home. I'm just a couple of minutes away."

I picked up Sarah, and we quickly arrive at the hospital. Unfortunately, while they had attempted to contact Dr. Li, they weren't able to reach him. Sarah was being promptly prepared by the on-call physician to go to the operating room for a C-section when suddenly, like the winds changing direction, I could feel the hand of karma offering me a glimmer of hope. Catherine and Scott had just come in as her water had broken. She was thirty-three weeks pregnant.

When I saw this, I looked at the physician and asked, "Has Dr. Li called back yet?"

"No. Not yet."

"If it's okay, let's wait a little. We still have some time, no?"

The doctor looked at me, then glanced at Sarah and wasn't sure what to say. He was confused as to why the hesitation. Sarah said, "I feel fine." The contractions at that time were about fifteen to twenty minutes apart.

I decided to go over and say hello to Scott and Catherine. Their room was directly adjacent to ours.

"Hey, what brings you two here?"

"Her water broke," said a disappointed Scott. "She's not having contractions yet but as a precaution they asked us to come in."

I won't lie, I was praying for Catherine to go into labor. It took all but twenty-seven minutes, and at 7:42pm that night my prayers were answered. Catherine had started having contractions. Just one problem: Sarah's contractions were picking up as well and Dr. Li had arrived and was insisting we go to the operating room right at that moment.

"Can we try turning the baby?" I asked. I needed to buy time.

"I'd feel more comfortable doing a C-section." The fetal

monitor was showing decompensation of the fetus as Dr. Li explained.

"Can we try once?"

"I don't think that's a good idea," he said.

"Please, I have a feeling this might work?" I had more than a feeling—I had been through the dress rehearsal once before.

"Dr. MacKinnon, I really don't…"

"Please try. It will work," I pleaded.

I could hear the sounds of Catherine's labor pains in the other room.

"Trust me," I said, "it will work."

Dr. Li didn't look comfortable doing this. "The last time I did this was twenty years ago," he said. He wrapped his hands around Sarah's uterus and made a few attempts. "I don't think this is working. We need to go to the operating room soon." The fetal monitor was showing further decompensation.

"Can I try?" I asked.

Dr. Li looked at me dumbfounded and just shrugged his shoulders. I remembered every event from Charlie's birth including this. Charlie's obstetrician was Dr. Lewis, an old school physician. The last I heard, he was now ninety years old and retired some ten years ago. I did everything as I remembered it. Shortly after I was done, the fetal monitor went back to normal. Dr. Li grabbed the ultrasound probe and started scanning.

"Well, I can't believe it."

"How is everything?" I asked.

"I think we're all good now," he said, shaking his head. "The baby is right side up."

That's when I heard Catherine's loud scream that

probably could be heard a few blocks away. The race, if I can call it that, was officially on.

I soon discovered it wasn't just me peeking to see what was happening on the other end. Scott was equally curious. I saw him on more than one occasion coming out of his room to see how things were progressing in ours; and that's when we both stepped out at the same time and bumped into each other in the hallway.

After an instant of surprised silence, "How are things?" I asked.

Scott had a blank look on his face before saying, "Oh, great! Looks like we'll be here all night; the baby doesn't look like he wants to come out."

"I know; ours too. I guess it's a MacKinnon trait. Isn't that funny?"

We had both apparently stepped out for a glass of water even though there was plenty in our rooms. As we each drank, I could see Scott carefully eyeing my every movement as I was his—each trying to measure up and gauge the other person. Neither of us wanted to look hurried but after a few slow steps back, we both hustled to our respective rooms.

We jockeyed back and forth like a horse race. I could see our baby's head and I could hear the obstetrician in Catherine's room yelling, "You're doing great. I'm seeing the head."

That's when I turned to Sarah and said,

"Here, close your eyes. Breathe with me slowly—in and out."

I gently massaged her neck and upper back, "Just relax. Breathe through your nose and out through the mouth."

That's when I heard the sweetest sound next to the sound of Charlie being born. I heard the cry of Clyde as Catherine had just delivered. I have to tell you, I have never been more excited for Scott and Catherine—ecstatic actually. This was also the first time in my life I was happy not to finish first.

I then leaned over and whispered to Sarah, "Okay, let's get this baby out of here."

Charles MacKinnon XIII was officially born on May 5th at 9:33pm. The recorded time of Clyde's birth was 9:32pm. I could have sworn it was more than a minute difference. Of course, did it really matter? It was all the same. Charlie was Charlie; Clyde was now Clyde.

The nurses finally prepared Charlie and put him in Sarah's lap. This was the moment I had been waiting for. Sarah held Charlie for a short time, then looked at me and smiled before saying, "Would you like to hold him?" and proceeded to put Charlie in my arms.

Those searching eyes were the same eyes I remembered in Charlie. He then stared at me and just as before you could see he was reading my thoughts. This was definitely my Charlie. He had the same look and feel as when he was born the first time.

I was overwhelmed with many feelings and couldn't fight back the tears. It was a beautiful moment that I was blessed to experience twice in my life, but seeing Charlie was also a painful reminder of the Charlie I had lost. It was that last part I wasn't expecting and hadn't given much thought to.

Soon the painful memories turned to happy ones. I've seen many parents say they have the perfect child. I do understand where they are coming from, but when they talk about what is particularly unique regarding their children it paled in comparison to what my Charlie had. Here was the difference: Charlie actually was the perfect child. He was the quintessence of a parent's dream. He was cute, funny, well behaved, and had a beautiful heart; then there were his creative and intellectual abilities that as far as I was concerned were unmatched by even the greatest MacKinnons. Life was always good with Charlie as he was always good to life. There was never a dull moment.

Many family members came to see us at the hospital with flowers and gifts. When John came for a visit, I knew something was troubling him.

"Congratulations. I'm very happy for you," he said.

"Thank you, John, it means a lot for you to come," said Sarah.

"He's really cute. He looks just like," he stalled before completing, "...both of you."

"Thank you," we said, but I knew something was troubling him. So when John left I told him I'd accompany him to the elevator. On the way, I asked, "You didn't seem yourself. Is everything okay?"

"I'm fine. It's nothing."

"Tell me, is there something about all this that's bothering you?"

That's when John realized he needed to explain what was weighing on him. "No, no, Charles. I'm very happy for you. It's work. I just didn't think today was the right time to talk about this; I didn't want to disturb you on your big day. We'll talk about it another time."

"Nothing work related can make me sad today. You might as well tell me."

John looked at me and finally said, "Well, I've been running some numbers on the patients we've treated the last few years. After six months their growth factors start declining, and their neuromuscular function starts regressing monthly after that."

"They're declining?" I remembered Charlie telling me about that, "0.52% decline," I said thinking aloud.

"Wow, you knew that? This is what I love about you. You're always two steps ahead of everyone. Here I thought I'd discovered something everyone had missed."

"Well, no. I can't entirely take credit for that one, I'll explain later, but tell me, how are the patients doing right now?"

"That's just the thing, Charles; I've called and followed up on all the initial trials we tested. They are all regressing to the point where it's now noticeable."

"Really, how much?"

"They can walk; just not as comfortably as they used to. What I don't know is where we'll be in six months."

"Let me look into it," I told him. "We'll figure something out."

All I could think about was that Charlie had told me this would happen. He had mentioned it just a few nights before he had passed away. I just wish I would have taken his comments more seriously and talked to him about his thoughts. I remember him telling me he had the solution for it.

That's when John said, "Sorry, I shouldn't have brought this up. Go have fun with your family and don't concern yourself with work today."

"Not to worry. It's okay," I reassured him.

John gave me a big hug before leaving. "Congratulations, buddy. I can't tell you how excited I am for you."

I was far too happy and nothing could put a blemish on my day. I wasn't concerned with John's dilemma either. This problem was minor and it would take only a couple of months for us to resolve. John and I would put our heads together and easily solve this. Charlie himself had told me the solution was very simple.

XVIII

Charlie grew up much like the Charlie of old, bringing back many happy memories and discovering new ones. There was, however, one notable exception: Charlie had long hair this time around. My prior Charlie preferred his hair shorter as it was the trend during those times, and after his unfortunate accident, it was simply more convenient. I for one wasn't going to discourage the longer hair, if for no other reason than I wanted him to appear a little different from my last Charlie.

To be frank, no one ever commented that this Charlie looked the same as the last. It's possible they were being polite. What I can say is this much: even as Charlie's father, my memories of what he had looked like in his childhood had faded somewhat. I mostly remembered him as when he was fifteen years old. With the new look it was almost like having a different child altogether. We don't often think of hair as changing the persona of an individual, but I can tell you this: the look, feel, and even personality of Charlie felt very different than the last by just those few inches of hair, which incidentally were also the impetus for what provided Charlie his new life, so it probably shouldn't come as a surprise. One thing was for sure: my career as Charlie's hairdresser was up for debate.

When Charlie turned two, Sarah decided it was time for her to return to school part-time to finish her degree. I welcomed the suggestion and thought this was something that would be good for her. She had stopped going to university right in the middle of her degree after Charlie's accident many years ago. I guess neither of us had given consideration to this as we were busy living our lives, but she had some untapped potential and I fully supported her desire to pursue her education. Sarah played the cello, and she was working toward her degree in music. The timing was right and this was obviously something important to her.

Life by all standards was great, and it had been many years since I enjoyed this peace and comfort. The birthdays seemed to be passing by faster this time around. Maybe it was because I was older, or maybe I just knew what to expect. In any case, it was around the time when Charlie was three years old when he met Chloe. They had connected right away.

Sarah told me she had met a nice man named Hunter in the park nearby our home. She didn't know much about what he did other than he had been married and his wife had recently died. He hadn't been working since his wife's passing. Hunter had one daughter named Chloe who was the same age as Charlie. Sarah wanted Charlie to maintain his friendship so she would arrange with Hunter to go to the park every day.

Sarah came home that first day when Charlie had met Chloe with a smile on her face. "I think our Charlie found a best friend similar to your version of John."

"Great, what's his name? I'd like to meet him."

"Meet her," Sarah said. "Her name is Chloe."

"Oh," and *oh* it was. This was something completely unexpected. The Charlie I knew didn't have too many friends let alone friends of the opposite gender. I had to gather my thoughts on this before asking, "What makes you think he's my version of John? Is it because they're friends at the age of three? I met other friends that age that didn't necessarily stick around. I even remember their names. Armando—that's a name I won't forget; I was just as close to him as I was to John. He was gone after two years. John and I were more than best friends; we also grew up to be colleagues and work together."

"Charlie is already gathering all his favorite toys to give to Chloe," Sarah told me.

Well, one thing was certain: if Charlie liked someone he'd want to give them everything he owned; my last Charlie was the same way.

"Call it mother's intuition, I guess," Sarah said. "I might be wrong. We'll see." And that's where she left it with a grin on her face.

"Where did you meet this Chloe?" I asked as this had clearly piqued my interest.

"I met her with her father, Hunter, at the park. She's going to be enrolled in the same pre-school program as Charlie this fall."

"Is she nice?"

"Charles, she's three years old. Of course she's nice."

"What about her parents?"

"It's just Hunter. His wife died about six months ago."

"That's terrible. What the poor fellow must be going through." I sure could relate to his pain.

Sarah described Hunter as a man of rough exterior but nice on the inside. He was a single father who had lost his wife to a sudden cardiac death from a known heart condition only six months before. I never inquired about the specifics of his wife's passing from Sarah. The timing was just very unfortunate as we had the technology at Genomica to cure almost any heart disease.

That was, of course, before it was banned by the GSA. The official explanation for the ban was that this "needs to be further studied before it is deemed safe," but I knew the real reason was that they were concerned about the public health and economical implications if everyone was to live to, say, 180. What would happen to social security? Who would pay for this if everyone were to retire before seventy? Already people's lifespans were well past the century mark with standard therapies. What would this new development do to the world's population? These were questions they weren't ready to answer so it was easier to halt the entire process rather than move forward.

Unfortunately for Hunter, his wife Beth went into cardiac arrest prior to seeking any treatment from us. Hunter would continually speak to Sarah of her sacrificial nature in life and also in her death. Beth had apparently always spoken about wanting to have her organs donated to serve others. Her last wish and final act in life was to help someone else, which was a source of pride for Hunter. I certainly could relate to his thinking as we had also donated Charlie's umbilical cord samples after his passing.

Sarah would mention Hunter every now and then mostly in the context of Charlie spending time with his friend Chloe. I hadn't met Hunter but I suppose he found a friend in Sarah who had also lost someone. I also figured he probably wanted Sarah to be a mother figure to his child. I didn't mind. I knew too well the pain of loss of a loved one and was more than happy for them to be helped and compensated in any way possible.

As for Genomica, the problem of treatment regression became a growing concern slowly over time. A few of our treated patients were starting to walk with canes and walkers. John and I had tried many different treatment algorithms—none of them worked. Fortunately, the only diseases that this regression had affected were ones related to neuromuscular injury. The other illnesses weren't affected to the same extent, and had a much slower regression rate that was not as noticeable. The degree of regression also correlated with their age, with the younger patients tending to regress slower. In any case, having any of these complications was starting to cast a doubt on the entire program. Thankfully, the media so far had not taken note of these deficiencies, otherwise all our work would be questioned in the court of public opinion.

To be sure, I went back to Charlie's room and searched to see if he had left the solution for this somewhere. Finding answers to these sorts of hurdles was Charlie's gift. He enjoyed it and absolutely relished these challenges. One could spend all day and marvel at him solving these problems. He was able to connect the dots whereas others just couldn't see the dots even existed. I remember vividly how he pointed to his wonderful mind, referring to the solution and said, "It's safer up here."

I looked and searched, and impatiently lamented, "Come on, Charlie, help me—please tell me you wrote it down." He had an entire closet and a desk full of files. As I searched, I only wished I hadn't taken his words so lightly and been more persistent in asking him to record it somewhere. I even remember betting he was wrong as a way to cheer him. One thing was for sure: Charlie had won the bet, and this wouldn't be the first time.

I had no luck finding anything. He hadn't written it down and in part I was to blame. One would think if he had stored the answer in his head, it would be straightforward. He himself had said it was "simple." Unfortunately, "simple" for Charlie was not simple by any other person's standards. That could mean anywhere from a one-page explanation to an entire textbook. He had a photographic memory and could store a thousand pages of information in his head if he had wanted to. I didn't know where this would leave me. The only thing that made me feel optimistic was that I had Charlie back again, and with him by my side, no obstacle seemed insurmountable.

When Charlie turned five, we planned a large party for him. To me this was an important day. I don't have to remind you what happened when my Charlie turned five the last time; well, technically he was in a coma and never actually saw his birthday. That fateful afternoon changed the course of our family's fortunes and Charlie's destiny.

I was adamant that I wanted it to be different this time around. I desired for this milestone to be reached on a different note—a happy one. Somewhere in the back of my mind, I wanted the record to be set straight and our destiny to be realigned with its intended purpose. It wasn't just a day of celebration for Charlie's birthday, but for all the difficulties we had endured. This was a day to look forward to a new future for Charlie, a destiny that had been robbed of him the first time.

Sarah instantly sensed why I cared about this birthday. There are certain days that are set in your mind until eternity. She never mentioned anything because she knew how painful that day was for me. This was also the same day that I had lost my father.

The day prior to Charlie's birthday, Sarah and I were both quiet, though neither of us wanted to say why. We both realized this was a symbolic anniversary of that tragic date, only I knew it was more than just a symbolic anniversary as this was the same Charlie, genetically speaking. Sarah was relaxing playing the piano, something she often did when she was stressed. She had been performing Beethoven's *Moonlight Sonata*, one of her favorites; then as she was playing, the unexpected happened.

I had mentioned before that every gifted neurosurgeon in my family had exhibited signs of creativity at an early age. Charlie's creativity, as I already knew, had no bounds. I had actually been waiting for this Charlie to show some sign, something that would reveal the same creative magic as our previous Charlie had shown when he built that three-dimensional model of a city. Then it came. As Sarah was playing the piano, Charlie came over and sat beside her. He watched her hand movements and then slowly reached to start playing along her side. Sarah froze watching him continue to play alone, and moments later, her eyes filled with tears.

"Mommy, are you okay?" he asked, slowly removing his hands from the keyboard.

"Of course, Charlie," she said, and wiped her eyes.

"Then why are you crying?"

"You played so beautifully, that's why," Sarah told him as she was trying to smile.

I was a little amused by Sarah's tears myself. Sarah is always a happy, positive, and strong person. One of her best strengths is finding hope where there is none—seeing positive when there is only negative. Watching her cry was definitely not a usual sight. I waited for her to walk over to the kitchen for a glass of water before asking her, "Is everything okay?" I was curious as to what had just transpired.

"Yes. I'm fine."

"Do you want to talk about it?"

"It's nothing. It just brought back some memories."

"What memories?" I asked. "Talk to me."

"I just had a flashback to the day when our last Charlie got into a car accident."

"Why is that? Is it because of Charlie's fifth birthday tomorrow?"

"No, it's not that," she explained. "On the day of his accident, just prior to your father picking him up, I was playing the piano, and Charlie came and started playing just like he did today." Sarah wiped her tears before continuing, "Then of course, the doorbell rang and he ran to answer the door; your father was here, and they left for the baseball game."

"Wow! I didn't know that." This was the first time Sarah had mentioned this. It was a surprise to me too.

"I had actually forgotten all about it," Sarah said. "I really hadn't thought about that episode until now. When Charlie left home that day the next time our phone rang, he was in the ICU and we spent all those months in the hospital."

Sarah was a little perturbed by this. I too was stirred by the coincidence, but praying she wouldn't read anything into the similarity of events. I embraced her, but all I could think about was that my Charlie was simply remarkable. Every great surgeon shows an ability to work with their hands early in their lives, and my Charlie's ability as I had correctly presumed had no bounds. He watched her hand movements and was able to replicate the motions. *What can I say, that's my boy!*

I woke up on the day of Charlie's birthday with anticipation. There aren't too many times in life you are able to turn back the clock and move forward from that point. My inner psyche was determined to correct the path that had deviated from us so long ago. If the clock had been broken, this is where it would be fixed. We had invited over one hundred children, family, and guests for the birthday party. Sarah had asked Hunter to bring Chloe a little earlier so she could play with Charlie. I too was excited to be finally meeting Hunter. I heard so much about him; it was as though he was already a friend.

It was a beautiful Saturday morning in May. The party was scheduled to start at noon. At 10am Sarah asked me if I could go pick up the cake for the event. It was to take no more than thirty minutes. Unfortunately, when I reached the store they were still working on writing "Happy 5th Birthday Charlie" on the cake. It was during this time that Hunter had arrived with Chloe at our home.

XVIII

This was what I was able to gather from that encounter years later. Hunter came with Chloe straight from the airport. He had been on a brief holiday. When he arrived, Hunter had admired the residence and its deep tradition, and mulled over the paintings and the photographs on the walls. He had curiously made it over to my study room while Sarah went to bring him a drink.

"Sarah, you look much younger in this photo. Who is this boy?"

"That was my son when he was four. He passed away a few years ago."

"I'm very sorry to hear that. I can relate to how difficult it is to lose a loved one. I'm still struggling with the loss of Beth."

"I know," said Sarah.

"What did he pass away from, if I may ask?"

"He had asthma. One winter day he had trouble breathing. He had a number of these episodes in the past but this time it was different. He had pneumonia. We went to the hospital and they did everything they could, he just never made it out."

"That's unfortunate. I'm sorry for your loss," Hunter said as he continued to examine all the photos sitting on my desk and the fireplace counter. "Your son looks so much like Charlie, don't you think?"

"You'll meet my sister later today. When people look at each of our childhood photos from the same age, they can't tell us apart."

"Still? The similarity is striking," Hunter said.

"You see that picture. That was my father-in-law in his younger days. When you meet my husband later today you'll see how much they look alike."

Hunter mulled over the picture. "Your husband looks like him?"

"Yes, very much so," said Sarah.

Hunter paused before saying, "Well you're right in that siblings sure can look alike. If I may ask, what did you say your husband does for a living?"

"He's a neurosurgeon working at Genomica. Have you heard of them?"

"Yes. I actually have." Hunter continued staring at the picture before saying, "This is interesting."

"What's interesting?" Sarah asked.

"You had mentioned that you had lost your son to asthma. Asthma can be inherited; you know you could have screened and had that genetically cured this time around with Charlie?"

"Yes, and we did!"

"Hmmm—you did? Really?"

Sarah smiled. "Why, what do you mean when you say hmmm?"

"No, nothing. I'm just playing devil's advocate."

"Then just say it. Say what you're thinking."

"Well, on a purely speculative premise, considering your husband works at a genetic company, you don't worry that maybe the genetic sample may have been tampered with?"

Sarah looked surprised and giggled, "For your information my husband wasn't even in town when any of this happened."

"Really?" said Hunter. "So it would only be you then." he said, laughing at his own humor.

"Yes just me—that great geneticist—that brilliant scientific mind of mine."

"So hypothetically you wouldn't have any trouble

testifying in court that you didn't plan anything illegal?" Hunter said jokingly, waiting a moment before saying, "I'm being facetious of course."

"You're funny, no, I wouldn't have any trouble testifying. What are you, the judge?" Sarah said laughing. "Here, let me give you a tour."

Hunter toured the entire house and admired the ornaments, furniture, and displays throughout the home. For a first-time visitor this is usually a nice treat. Anyone exploring the home would feel like they've gone back a few hundred years and coursed through history.

Charlie and Chloe were playing outside. We had also hired some helpers and they were in the yard making the final preparations for the party.

"Who is this?" Hunter asked, pointing to the portrait.

"That's Charles I. He would be Charles's great-great-grandfather from the 1500s. He's highly regarded in the family. They even say his name with a special reverence."

"That's a big painting, don't you think?" Hunter mused.

Sarah smiled, "It actually was life size before half of it was lost to fire. Every Charles in the family ultimately inherits this original portrait."

Sarah then turned to Hunter and said, "Come—help me get the balloons while the kids are outside. We stored them downstairs. Charlie likes popping all of them so we wanted to hide them from view until the right time."

Sarah walked to the lower floor with Hunter, and went inside the storage room where all the balloons were kept. Hunter had stood outside the door but it would have been impossible for him not to have seen the treasure chest labeled Charles XII. When Sarah opened the door to the left, it was the first thing in view on the shelf on the right side.

Sarah came out and said, "Grab the strings from the bottom here. They've all been nicely tied together. We'll untie them later." When they came upstairs, the balloons were all taken to the party room where the children were expected to arrive shortly.

Hunter then received a phone call and said he had to leave. "I wish I could stay, but I just got a call from the dog sitter. I have to pick up my dog; the sitter has to attend a family matter."

"Oh, sorry, I didn't know. Why don't you bring your dog here?"

"Are you sure? It's not a problem?"

"Of course it's not!"

"I'm so sorry for this."

"No, don't worry. These things happen," Sarah told him.

"What time will the party be done?"

"It will be finished by 5pm. You'll be back before then, no?"

"I'll try my best."

Unfortunately, when I arrived Hunter had left and Sarah was busy directing our helpers and making the last-minute preparations.

"How does the cake look?" she asked me.

"I haven't tasted it yet, but there's enough chocolate that I think will keep these kids running through the entire night."

The guests were slowly arriving with their children. The day was unfolding exactly as I had hoped. This was the birthday I had always wanted for Charlie to have. We had hired children entertainers to play games, sing, and for the children to watch their shows. A part of me couldn't help but reflect on how things might have turned out if Charlie had this birthday the first time.

Scott and Catherine were there and enjoying the festivities.

"Congratulations, it's Clyde's birthday too!" I told them.

They said, "Thank you!"

"You know, I totally forgot to put his name on the cake. I'm so sorry!"

"No, don't be. It's okay."

"Let me see if I can add it."

"Charles, it's okay. Really, you don't have to," said Scott. "He's been celebrating his birthday all week at school and at home. We don't mind the break."

That's when Uncle Stewart came from behind to wrap his arms around me in a bear hug.

"Fabulous party, Charles—the kids love it, and I love it too."

Well, I was also having the time of my life. I didn't think anything could spoil the evening. That's when the unanticipated event happened and what felt like an atomic bomb dropping on my lap.

Sarah came over and tapped me on the back. "Charles, I would like for you to meet Chloe's father, Hunter."

When I turned, my face froze. I could not believe it. Standing in front of me, right in my home, was none other than Hunter Dawson!

"This is Hunter?" I asked, looking like I just saw a bird drop dead from the sky.

"It's nice to see you, Dr. MacKinnon."

"You two have met?" asked Sarah.

"You could say that," I replied. "What are you doing here?"

He didn't have a chance to reply. That's when I noticed his bulldog barking and aiming straight toward Charlie. My instinct at that moment was to run in an attempt to stop it. "Charlie doesn't like dogs," I muttered, leaping in its direction. That's when Charlie and Chloe ran toward the dog and started patting and playing with it.

Dawson walked over and said, "It looks like he's doing quite well. I don't think you know your son; he's quite the dog person if you ask me." He had a smirk on his face as he continued, "Charlie, do you like dogs?" Charlie nodded his head in agreement.

Then Dawson looked back at me and said, "His name is Buster."

I was amazed and yet confused seeing Charlie playing with the dog. This was something I had never seen before. I had never given much thought to this, but it made perfect sense. Our first experience with anything is always the most powerful especially when it's during our childhood when our senses and perceptions have the deepest impact in routing our neural connections. I guess I had just assumed that Charlie's fear of dogs was something that was part of his character. Even though the logic was clear, it was still a strange sight watching him play with it. Although, in that moment I didn't care for the logic as much as I cared about the fact that Dawson was in my own home and had just denigrated me in front of my family.

I think both Uncle Stewart and John knew something was about to erupt and that's when they both quickly walked over. John had his hand on my shoulder. "It's okay, Charles, come back here. Let it go."

While they were all playing with the dog, I asked Sarah if I could speak to her alone. We walked back up the steps inside the house.

"What is he doing here?" I asked.

"What do you mean, he's Chloe's father. You knew that!"

"What I knew was that Hunter was her father. I didn't know he was the same man who single-handedly killed our son Charlie."

"That's a little dramatic, don't you think? How was I supposed to know? You never told me his first name was Hunter."

"And you never told me his last name is Dawson."

Sarah then pleaded, "How could I have known it's the same person? I thought the Dawson you spoke of was his first name."

"Do you mean to tell me you never asked what he did for a living?"

"He has been off work recovering, remember?" Sarah then shook her head before saying, "Charles, can we talk about this another time?"

I just looked down in complete disbelief and realized she was probably right; this wasn't the appropriate time to argue about this. People outside were starting to watch and it didn't look good.

If you ask me if I gleaned any joy from that moment onward, the answer is I didn't. Do I remember anything else from the party that day? No, not a moment. Everything was a fog. I spoke to some guests. I exchanged some pleasantries. My mind was on autopilot and giving standard automatic responses, but my emotions were blunted. The clock stopped again when Dawson arrived. After the guests left, I approached Sarah to discuss the matter further and the answer was an abrupt "I don't want to talk about it," as she went upstairs.

That's the same answer I received the next day and the day after. We didn't discuss this until three months later.

Sarah had been friends with Dawson for two years; she agreed not to bring him to our home again, but for Charlie's sake, his friendship with Chloe was something she didn't want to disrupt. I agreed. As much as I disliked Dawson, Chloe was a good friend to Charlie. I could only hope she had her mother's genes.

XIX

Except for the setback on Charlie's birthday, everything was otherwise well. There was a normalcy to life I hadn't enjoyed in decades. My work had its challenges but we had time, and I had Charlie back. With Charlie, the impossible was simply now possible. It also wouldn't take as long this time for him to reach the level he was at before. Charlie spent the better part of his childhood going in and out of hospitals and rehabilitation; this was either for his asthma or related to his accident. In many ways that held him back and hindered his development, as ridiculous as that may sound given his brilliance. That wasn't happening this time—not on my watch. We would see his progress unrestrained, and for Charlie the sky was the limit.

I understood Charlie and had the perfect roadmap for his development, and knew which shortcuts we could take this time. By my estimation—I had gone over the math on this a few times—with the proper guidance and navigation, we could see Charlie close to his previous level at almost twice the speed. So you could say I was confident we could find a way around our problems at Genomica sooner rather than later. It was also a relief that Dawson and the GSA were not a thorn in our side as they had been for so many years. This was despite the fact that Dawson had been recently promoted to the head of the GSA.

Sarah was continuing her education, and in many ways, things were back to normal for her as well. On one occasion when she was playing the piano, Charlie arrived once again to watch her. She could see what he desired with his eager eyes and posture.

"Did you want to learn how to play, Charlie?" Sarah asked warmly.

Charlie nodded and moved to sit next to her. He seemed enamored by the whole experience.

"Come, Charlie, sit right here with your back straight. Place your hands here a little curled like mine." Then Sarah pointed to her thumb and said, "This is your number one finger, this is you number two finger, this is…" Charlie was always a practical learner; he wasn't too interested in the lesson. He just wanted to play.

Sarah continued, "These are the high notes, and these are low notes on the left. Now put your fingers here, Charlie, and watch me. Don't slouch." Sarah repeated a few notes for Charlie to learn and then she started playing Beethoven's *Fur Elise*. Beethoven was one of Sarah's preferred composers and apparently now Charlie's too. He watched her for a few seconds before motioning his desire to play. He started to move his hands toward the piano and that's when Sarah said,

"Here, put your fingers right here beside mine and try to follow what I just showed you."

Charlie started playing as though he had learned piano in another life. He performed along with Sarah and then continued to play even after she had stopped to watch him. He knew the notes; maybe he had heard Sarah perform it before, maybe it was part intuition—I don't know, but he was playing as though he had done it many times before. Sarah had to pause and admire the moment: it was breathtaking. There were things she hadn't instructed Charlie in his style and technique that he was naturally doing on his own.

I came home one day and I couldn't believe what I saw. Charlie was sitting at the piano and performing like a concert pianist. I looked at Sarah and said, "When did this happen?"

"He started playing last week."

His long hair would flare back and forth, adding to the drama of the beautiful sonata. It simply looked charming given that he was five years old.

That was definitely my Charlie; like waiting for a giant to wake up, I had been preparing for such a sign. The Charlie I knew was able to do anything and mastered new skills with ease.

"That's great, Sarah." I continued to watch Charlie with amazement. I always knew he was creative; I knew he was smart. I also knew he had the acumen to be a neurosurgeon. What I never had the opportunity to see what his ability to use his hands other than that one time he made a three-dimensional city. To me, this was proof. Charlie would be the best neurosurgeon the MacKinnons had ever witnessed. I told Sarah, "Wow, this is just like Uncle Stewart. He'll love this."

"Why is that?" Sarah asked.

"My grandfather used to say the early sign of a great surgeon is in their ability to use their hands. Uncle Stewart apparently played the piano too. Charlie is just like him. He's a natural."

"He sure is," Sarah said with a smile as we both marveled at his performance.

I encouraged Sarah to teach him more. I knew he had all the other required skills and he would develop them in due time as he did before. This was, perhaps, the only element that was uncertain, as I had never seen the trajectory of my last Charlie's development in this arena.

"He's learning so much on his own," she said with a glow.

The next day Sarah took Charlie to the music store. She let him play with all the instruments. He tried the violin, the viola, and even the drums. Sarah would play a few notes just for Charlie to see the differences between the instruments. Then Charlie made his pick. It wasn't even close.

Sarah played the cello for Charlie and then had him play the same notes on a smaller cello for his size. Charlie didn't actually play the tune that Sarah had played for him; he closed his eyes and played his own notes. That's when Sarah knew he loved the cello.

"I want this one," he said softly.

"Just like mom," Sarah laughed as she kissed Charlie on the cheek.

He got his cello and started playing right away. It certainly helped that Chloe was also playing the violin. She had seen Charlie playing and wanted an instrument as well. If you want your children to adopt a skill, find a friend who will accompany them on their endeavor. Chloe choosing to do this was exactly the motivation Charlie needed.

Sarah started teaching both Charlie and Chloe every day.

This meant Chloe would come and stay with us until 5pm before Sarah would take her home. Of course, I was content with this arrangement, as I didn't want Dawson anywhere near our house.

This continued for about two years. That's when Sarah ultimately concluded she had nothing left to teach Charlie. This period also coincided with Sarah finally acquiring her music degree.

Charlie and I were both there on her graduation day. I was very proud of Sarah for completing her education and for being unrelenting in her efforts. She had always been looked down upon for never having finished her degree. No one really looked to the sacrifices she made as the reason for her academic setbacks.

After her graduation ceremony, I went to buy us some drinks. It was a hot day and being dressed in a suit wasn't the most comfortable experience. During the time that I was away, Sarah's professor, Mrs. McLeod, approached her.

"Congratulations, Sarah, we will miss you."

"Thank you. I'm enjoyed my time here and will cherish everything you have all done for me," she said warmly.

"You know how I feel. I can't convince you to do your Master's here with us?" Mrs. McLeod asked.

"I'm afraid I'm too old for that now. If I had been younger…"

"Oh, Sarah, age is just a matter of mind. Don't let that stop you."

"I know, but there is another personal matter I'd like to talk to you about."

"What's that?" Mrs. McLeod asked.

"It's my son Charlie." Sarah then called him to come forward to meet her professor.

"Charlie, this is Mrs. McLeod. She taught me everything I know about playing the cello."

He smiled and greeted her.

"Charlie also loves to play the cello," Sarah said.

"He does? That's wonderful. You're talented just like your mother," Mrs. McLeod said, and looked at Charlie with admiration.

"He actually plays better than I do," Sarah told her with a smile.

Mrs. McLeod replied, "That's impossible, you're our best student."

"No, he plays much better than I do," Sarah nodded and reaffirmed. "That's actually what I wanted to discuss with you."

Mrs. McLeod was starting to understand the scope of Sarah's thoughts. It was at this moment when I arrived with fruit punch for everyone.

Mrs. McLeod then said, "Why don't you come and meet me in my office tomorrow and we'll talk more about this."

After she parted I asked, "What did I miss?"

Sarah made her arrangements to meet the next day. Her discussion was about Charlie and if Mrs. McLeod could provide any direction for him. Sarah herself was not interested in taking on a master's degree and increasing her workload.

"Charlie, can you play for Mrs. McLeod what you were practicing yesterday?" Sarah asked him.

He nodded and played Bach's Suite No. 1 in G major. Charlie played it beautifully. Mrs. McLeod was lost for words.

"He did it perfectly. It was just like you played it on your exam. Was he practicing with you every day?" she asked.

"He actually played it for the first time yesterday."

XIX

Mrs. McLeod was starting to understand the complete picture as to why Sarah wanted to meet her.

"There is nothing left for me to teach him. I'm not sure where to go from here," Sarah said.

After some discussion, Mrs. McLeod agreed to provide Charlie instructional classes. Sarah offered to pay her privately for this, but she wouldn't accept any payment.

Charlie started classes with Mrs. McLeod the next week. There was only one problem: music was not fun without his best friend beside him. Charlie was often bored and not his usual happy self. So Sarah had to convince Mrs. McLeod into having Chloe join their classes as well. Chloe, though talented, was not quite at the same level as Charlie. Truth be told, nobody was.

I was happy for Charlie to attend these classes but I also wanted him to connect with some of the things I knew he had an inclination for, so I arranged for what I knew was a bulletproof plan: we were going to a baseball game.

It was a gorgeous sunny afternoon. I could have never asked for a more beautiful setting for Charlie to see his first game. I explained the rules as we watched it together. It had all the charm of the outdoors. We had hotdogs, fries, and anything we could get our hands on. I planned for Charlie to eat whatever he desired. He was getting a free pass on everything, and I wanted him to remember this experience for the rest of his life as something positive. The day was proceeding perfectly. Charlie was enjoying the festivities and we were pleasantly indulging in the event. So the next week I thought I would do a follow up and ask, "Hey, Charlie, do you want to watch the baseball game with me on TV? It's the same team we watched last week."

"I don't know, Dad; baseball is kind of boring," he said to

a surprised look on my face.

That's when Sarah stepped in and said, "Charlie, why don't you watch baseball with your dad? You can play music later."

We watched for a little while, but he wasn't engaged in the game the way I remember him being involved in every pitch and swing. After some time I said, "It's okay, son; you can go play music if you like."

He hugged me and said, "Thanks, Dad."

Charlie's music classes continued with Mrs. McLeod. I often came home late from work so I would only hear things in passing; for the most part, I wasn't too involved. I don't think I ever took note of how good Charlie had become until Mrs. McLeod had organized a concert at the university and had asked Sarah and Charlie to play a piece together for the closing act. Charlie was eight years old.

The concert was an annual gala held at the university as a fundraiser just prior to the winter break. This same event at one point used to raise funds for cancer research. Our company had found the cure for most cancers using gene therapy a few years ago, so they had decided to change their scope. They now donated their funds to the Valente Children's Foundation to purchase musical instruments for children who were unable to afford them.

Sarah had warned me to leave early; I did, but it was snowing that day. I could have taken the entire day off work; I still wasn't going to reach the venue on time with the winter traffic. I just knew Sarah was sitting there looking at my empty seat and wondering if I was able to arrive on schedule. Thankfully, Sarah and Charlie's performance was the last one.

I walked into the university's elegant concert hall that was well over a hundred years old with its beautiful high ceilings.

I could hear Mrs. McLeod's voice on the microphone as I was walking into the hallway searching for the doors for my section.

"...and for our last piece we have a special treat. We have a former special graduate of ours performing with her son, a very talented musician whom I've also had the pleasure to work closely with. Someone whom I also hope will be one of our future graduates." She looked over in their direction and said, "Introducing Sarah and Charlie MacKinnon."

I walked along the aisle just as everyone was clapping, and Sarah and Charlie were preparing to start their piece. Sarah's eyes caught mine as I was sitting and she offered me one of those smiles as if she was saying, "Didn't I tell you not to be late?"

What I heard next left me speechless. They played Antonio Vivaldi's "The Four Seasons Winter." Sarah was playing on the piano and Charlie on the cello. I think everyone in the audience was dazzled by their performance.

As much as I enjoyed it, I wasn't sure what to make of this. I had always assumed Charlie's creativity was a means to his ultimate destiny in becoming a neurosurgeon. A destiny in which I knew he would be successful. In a previous life, if I could think of it that way, he had over thirty publications in various journals. Some of these were landmark studies that were still being referenced today. He had received one of the highest awards in science, albeit posthumously; but what he accomplished at fifteen was what most of my colleagues took a lifetime to accomplish. My Uncle Stewart played the piano and he always said how much it benefitted him as a surgeon playing a musical instrument. Still, as much as I was pleased with him, I couldn't help but feel that maybe this musical hobby was distracting him from his true calling.

After their performance, Sarah and Charlie were the talk of the show. Every person in that room made a point of shaking their hands and congratulating them. I could hear the chorus of compliments.

"You must be so proud of him!"

"He's going to be a great musician."

And my personal favorite: "He looks exactly like his mother. They practically look like twins."

I have to admit, with Charlie's long hair he did look somewhat like Sarah—definitely not twins though as a few were suggesting.

The next day the winter break was beginning for Charlie. When he woke up in the morning, I asked him, "Hey, Charlie, how would you like to come to work with me?"

"Wow, can I, Dad?" He was certainly excited. That's the Charlie that I knew.

"Sure, son, I'll show you where I work and what I do. It will be fun."

It was the holiday season and there wasn't much scheduled at work. This was also the period when people at the office were more cheerful and happy. It was as good a time as any for him to come to the hospital for a visit. In my family, we just don't tell the next generation what they should do with their future; that's entirely up to them. However, we do bring them to work with us to watch what we do—and let the genes take care of the rest.

We walked around the entire facility. I showed him my

office and lab. Once the operating rooms had closed for the day, I showed him a small tour of this grand theater.

Charlie was enamored with the experience and in awe at what he was seeing. I believed everything to be proceeding quite smoothly; that was until I briefly left him alone with my secretary, Wendy, to attend a work matter. I didn't think I had stepped out for more than a few minutes. When I came back, he was fast asleep.

"Charlie?" I asked, walking back into the office. He was lying on my large arm swivel chair.

"I know it's a comfortable chair. You might have had a bit too much for your first day." I hugged him and carried him to the car. He slept the entire drive. When I arrived home, I felt optimistic that at the very least this was a good start.

The next day I asked Charlie if he wanted to come to work with me again. He didn't hesitate to tell me where his priorities were, "I can't today—Chloe is coming over."

"Well maybe Chloe might want to come too?" I suggested and Charlie happily didn't mind the proposal.

That day was our grand rounds at the hospital. All thirty-two neurosurgeons from the area would be meeting. With the exception of John, every neurosurgeon was a MacKinnon and John was like an uncle to Charlie, so I figured he might enjoy this event. It was a family reunion after all. Most importantly, Uncle Stewart would also be there and Charlie always looked forward to seeing him. It was also at these rounds when my last Charlie made his mark so I couldn't help but think that maybe this might be the little nudge to stir interest in Charlie's thoughts.

I took both Charlie and Chloe to this event. Other than chatting with Uncle Stewart for a few minutes, neither Charlie nor Chloe were engaged in what was being discussed. I tried to make it more entertaining for them by explaining it all in simple language; I would just receive a vacant stare in return.

Uncle Stewart started laughing.

"What's funny, Uncle Stew?" I asked, curious to know his thoughts.

"They are only kids, Charles, why don't you wait a few more years before bringing them here," he said as he continued his smile.

Sometimes people laugh with you, and sometimes they laugh at you. I think it was pretty safe to say Uncle Stewart was laughing at me on this occasion. He had a point, but a few more years and Charlie might be lost. I knew from past experience that Charlie had the acumen to grasp the content of these presentations at this age. I wasn't wrong in my logic.

Toward the end of the program, I was engaged in a discussion with the speaker, my cousin Scott. I looked beside me a short moment later, and both Charlie and Chloe had disappeared.

"Where did they go?" I anxiously asked.

"Where did who go?" said Uncle Stewart.

"Charlie and Chloe!" I replied as my eyes scanned across the auditorium.

"They were over there playing a few minutes ago. I don't know where they went," Uncle Stewart said, looking around.

I started searching everywhere, inside and outside—they were gone.

"Don't worry, Charles. They are smart; they haven't gone far," Uncle Stewart said to reassure me.

This is when panic starts to set in. I checked down the hall and around the corner. Then I ran inside the restroom calling out Charlie and Chloe's names; they weren't there.

I raced down the staircase, which led to the main lobby as

I saw a rush of people moving in that direction. I tried calling out their names. When I reached downstairs, the holiday music was so loud and the stampede of people was so congested that I panicked; how was I possibly going to find them in a crowd like this? There was a maze of people moving all around me. I felt overwhelmed and didn't know where to look. That's when suddenly I noticed an array of people fixated in the same general direction toward the central area. I turned to see what they were viewing when I noticed a band of musicians playing a song. I looked more closely and I saw what appeared to be the shape of two kids playing musical instruments with the band. I walked in their direction to have a better view and that's when I quite unexpectedly realized that Charlie and Chloe were performing with the ensemble our hospital had hired.

I'm not sure if I was disappointed or in complete admiration at what I was witnessing. They were both good. Charlie was outstanding; there was nothing he couldn't touch that wouldn't turn to gold. That part I always knew, and certainly, this was no exception. One thing was for sure: I was completely relieved they were both safe. Right above the band where Charlie had been standing hung the portrait of my father as the founder of the hospital. It was an interesting sight to say the least, seeing Charlie right beneath him.

After they were done playing, the band members shook their hands and the audience provided them a resounding applause. They both sprinted toward me in excitement.

"Son, you had me worried, why did you run off like that?"

"Sorry, Dad."

"Chloe are you okay?" I asked. She was smiling, and hugged me as did Charlie.

It took a moment for me to collect my thoughts before

asking: "Did you have fun? You both looked really good up there."

"It was amazing, Dad. Thanks," Charlie said before hugging me more tightly.

This was the most excitement Charlie had at the hospital in the few days he had been there. He asked me to bring him back the next day so he could play with the band again. Of course, I couldn't say no. I didn't mind spending the additional time with Charlie at the hospital; if this is what it took to get him there, well it certainly wouldn't be my first choice, but I would have to take it.

Charlie accompanied me to work all week. I'd entrust him to the care of the band and pick him up before I'd leave. Make no mistake—Charlie was the show.

"Thanks, Dr. MacKinnon; don't worry, he's in safe hands," Jimmy the pianist would say when I'd leave Charlie with him in the morning. In a strange way I felt Charlie was safe, not so much because of Jimmy, but because he was playing under the portrait of my father all day.

"If you need me, I'll be upstairs," I told Jimmy. "Don't work him too hard. I can't believe I'm paying you guys for this," I added jokingly.

"We'd love for him to be playing with us all the time," Jimmy remarked with a smile.

"Don't plan too far ahead; he's going back to school next week."

It was a special day. During his lunch break, Dr. Li saw Charlie playing and joined the band to play saxophone. I actually never knew Dr. Li played an instrument. It sure had Charlie excited to be playing with him. I would meet Charlie for lunch and during my breaks. The moments we had together were nice and brought back some nice memories of when I'd spend time with my last Charlie here many years ago.

The holiday season came to pass and Charlie returned to school. It was also time for him to apply to the Montgomery School for the Gifted. Their program for gifted students started at age nine. Sarah's worry was not so much about Charlie being admitted into the school as it was for Chloe. She wanted the two friends to stay together as much as possible. Sarah had spoken to Dawson and he was in favor of Chloe attending the school if she could be accepted. This was not an easy task. There were exams to be written, and they had their own methodology for testing the skills of the students. Being smart didn't qualify for being gifted, and neither did being nice.

Fortunately, three things worked in Chloe's favor. The first: the classes she had attended with Charlie with Mrs. McLeod had put her leap years ahead of the other students her own age. The second: the school had a category specifically for musically inclined students and these students could be accepted in that category alone irrespective of their scores in other disciplines; lastly, the MacKinnons had a long history with this school and Sarah was well liked by the principal, Mr. Jones, who hadn't changed in the last thirty years. If Sarah had hinted in any way that Charlie's admission hinged on Chloe's acceptance, they wouldn't take a chance to pass up a MacKinnon, especially someone with Charlie's skills.

In the end, Chloe was accepted on her own merit. Sarah said her performance exam at the school was perfect; as for Charlie, his scores were off the charts in every category. He had apparently tied another special MacKinnon before him. Sarah was very excited for both Charlie and Chloe to attend the school together. She insisted this time for Charlie to not be moved to a higher grade so they could stay at the same level. Sarah would take them to school every day before bringing them to Mrs. McLeod's lessons and then home again.

They continued attending these classes for a few years. However, contrary to my wishes, this also resulted in an increased involvement of Dawson and visits to his home. It also meant Sarah was spending more time with him. Although I never raised my disapproval on this, it was a prelude to another distraction I didn't need in my life.

Otherwise, I was very happy for Charlie. I couldn't believe how different things were this time around at the Montgomery School than for my last Charlie. Aside from having Chloe, he had several cousins attending the school with him this time, including Clyde and Isla.

Over the next few years, Charlie became not only the most talented but also the most popular student in his school. His prominence only grew with time as everyone tried to befriend him.

As for my work, things could not be advancing any worse; with the passage of time, many of our patients that were deemed stable were returning with a recurrence of their symptoms. John and I had tried everything we possibly could. I even turned to Uncle Stewart. He was semiretired and had been mostly working on his personal project of completing the MacKinnon history book. He had told me at last count he had 1,600 pages completed and was more than half finished. I needed his insight and wisdom to see if he could lend any thoughts on what we could do. The results were the same.

Uncle Stewart once looked at me and said, "I may not be as smart and quick on my feet as I once was, but I've seen my share of complications. I wish I could see a solution, but, Charles, there isn't one."

A frustrated John also lamented, "If this continues, they are going to shut us down. We can't go on like this."

"I know, John. I know," I said in a hopeless voice.

I couldn't help but feel defeated. What I needed more than anything at that moment was Charlie. I knew he could solve our dilemma if he had the inclination as he did before when he immersed himself into this field.

I went home that day and had time to think alone. Sarah was not yet home and had taken Charlie to his music classes. I was worried for Genomica, my father's legacy, and in many ways the Charlie legacy that our family endeared. I stood in front of the portrait of Charles I. I couldn't help but feel demoralized. I looked at him as I had done on many other occasions and just muttered, "I know, I've let you down." I was lost in my thoughts as I looked at the serenity of his look and the honor that he brought to our family. In my vexation I asked him, "Help me—help me out of this."

I stood there motionless trying to think of a solution when shortly after Sarah walked into the house with excitement. I did my best to hide my emotions so as not to alarm her. She, on the other hand, couldn't hide her enthusiasm as she was taking off her jacket and telling me about her day. "Charlie is doing so well at school. Mrs. McLeod is really pleased with his progress."

"That's great," I said.

"Which reminds me, what are you doing this Friday at 4pm?"

I usually leave work early on Fridays so I told her, "Nothing special. I'll be free around that time; did you need me to pick up the kids?"

"No, it's not that. The school called today and they want to meet with us, so I told them Friday at 4pm because I knew you would be available then."

"What's happened? Is there anything wrong? Is Charlie in trouble?" I asked.

"I don't think so. I actually don't know. The principal didn't sound too concerned but he was intentionally elusive in his answers so I didn't push. I figured we would find out on Friday anyway."

XX

Our arranged meeting for Friday finally arrived, and we sat in the office with the principal and Charlie's teachers. For me this was a bit of a déjà vu moment; I remembered this exact setting many years ago. Right now that felt like a different life and in many ways a different world. I started the discussion: "You have us both curious as to what this meeting is about. Is something wrong?"

"No," said Mr. Jones. "It is quite the contrary." He then proceeded, "First of all, let me thank you both for coming here on such short notice. I realize your time is valuable and I wouldn't ask you to come if it wasn't something of merit."

Sarah and I looked at Mr. Jones and a few of Charlie's teachers in attendance wondering what he was planning to say next.

"Charlie is exceptionally creative, maybe the most creative

we've ever seen at this school."

He paused to search for his next words so I interjected, "That's good, isn't it?"

"It is remarkable, actually," he said before pressing on. "Now, his teachers have taken the liberty to talk to me on this matter and I want to share with you some of our thoughts and see what you think."

"Sure, what is it?" Sarah asked.

"Here at the Montgomery School, if we see a child with a particular inclination we can modify their training and education to focus and provide particular attention to their talent. This, of course, would come at the expense of other areas of schooling."

I looked at Mr. Jones and wondered what he meant by all this.

"Charlie is exceptionally talented in playing the cello. All his teachers agree that it would be most productive if we decreased, say, some of his science classes in exchange for more time for him to receive additional instructions in music. He would certainly take the minimum course load for his science curriculum to qualify for our board's requirements, but it would be the absolute minimum."

I was silent and wasn't sure what to say. All the teachers were looking at us and nodding their heads in agreement with Mr. Jones. I turned to Sarah and she was looking at me for an answer. So I asked, "Mr. Jones, what were Charlie's scores in the sciences?"

He looked at the sheet in front of him. "He had A+ straight across the board."

"What was his percentile score?" I asked more specifically.

"He had the top score actually," Mr. Jones said,

somewhat surprised.

"Then why are we drifting him away from this?" I said with a concerned voice.

That is when his teacher Ms. Banks stepped up to say: "Charlie would probably excel at anything and be very talented at it. We just all feel music is where his inclinations are. It's simply the difference in level. Charlie may be better than other students in the sciences, but the margin is much wider in music."

I wasn't sure if I agreed with the logic and had to gather my thoughts before responding: "But don't you think that maybe he's inclined that way because he had been nurtured in that direction? There is nothing to say he couldn't become a famous scientist. He is, after all, the top of his class in the sciences at a gifted school."

They all paused to reflect before Mr. Jones said, "Perhaps you're right. Maybe then we should let Charlie decide?"

I looked at Sarah and we knew Charlie was sitting in the other room. Sarah then asked, "If you don't mind, is it possible for us to have a moment alone with Charlie?"

We walked over to the other room and Charlie was playing his cello. Ms. Banks called Chloe aside to her office so we could talk with Charlie in private.

"Hey, Charlie, your teachers are telling us you're doing very well at school," I said calmly.

"I am?" Charlie looked at us surprised.

"Yes," I said with a nod. "We're very proud of you, son.

They tell us you're doing well in all your subjects—so well that they think you might want to pick one and continue with that subject so you can get very good at it."

"Which subject is that?" Charlie asked.

"Well, that's what we wanted to talk to you about. Is there one you prefer to do? Or would you like to continue with all of them the way you are right now?"

"I don't know, Dad. Which one do you think I should pick?" he asked, looking at me intently for a clue.

"I think you should pick the option you like."

Charlie thought about it for a while and looked at both Sarah and me before saying, "I want to play the cello if that's okay."

I hugged Charlie and quietly said, "Of course that's okay." That was followed by Sarah embracing Charlie as well. We went back to the room where the principal and teachers were sitting. I asked Sarah on the walk back, "Are you comfortable with this?"

She said, "Yes, are you?"

"Yes," I responded.

Charlie was transferred into the accelerated music program the next week. Of the subjects they removed, which apparently wasn't required by the school board, was biology. He now spent additional time walking around those music halls; the same halls my last Charlie would seek refuge during his lunch hours nearly twelve years before. It was different now. Charlie was clearly the leader in those halls. He had the respect and admiration of everyone: younger, older, male and female, whether student or teacher. They all sensed he was perhaps the most talented student the school had ever seen.

It was around this time when I had one of my recurrent dreams. My father was on the baseball field throwing the ball and playing catch with Charlie. I always felt that my father wanted to speak to me. I had told Sarah about this some years ago and she suggested that perhaps I should ask him a question. I wanted to but I would wake up before I had the chance. On this night, I again wanted to speak to him.

Charlie was throwing the ball back and forth with my father on that beautiful field. Just as I was about to walk over to start my conversation, he threw the ball over Charlie's head, rolling in my direction, stopping at my feet. I felt as though he had intentionally thrown the ball high so Charlie would come to meet me. I actually wanted to speak to my father but it didn't happen that way, so I just went along with the circumstances.

I picked up the ball and placed it in Charlie's glove when he walked over. "Here, son; it's nice to see you so happy," I said.

"Thanks, Dad," he said with a serene smile.

"You know, Charlie, you don't have to play baseball if you don't want to."

"What do you mean, Dad? I love baseball." He looked at me baffled, and that's when I woke up.

It's hard to explain but it was nice to speak to Charlie. Maybe that's what my dad desired, or maybe, just maybe, that's what my subconscious wanted. If that is what my subconscious mind was yearning for, then I needed to ask myself why. Why now? And was it trying to tell me?

Maybe I had erred. Maybe the Charlie I had known was his true potential; perhaps this was what it was hoping to advise me. More than anything, I needed Charlie's brilliance to save Genomica and my father's legacy. Genomica was in rapid decline and we were surprised the GSA hadn't yet shut us down.

I would look at the painting of Charles I every day and ask him, "Please, just give me a sign—any sign!" There were days when I almost felt a premonition of a response, and at other times I wasn't so sure. I couldn't help but admire the beautiful carved frame that contained this noble portrait. Charles III had handmade this elegant frame. It was custom built in a Renaissance style to reflect its original feel with the acanthus leaves protruding and covering the burned areas within the edges of the portrait.

I decided to speak to John about my dream the next day. "What do you make of this, John?"

"Well you know what I think. I think our brain just filters whatever waste it has produced during the day in our dreams at night. It's the way it relieves itself. If you're stressed, you see more and filter more. That's all."

"I don't know. It was comforting. It actually felt like they were there."

"Charles, you know this better than anyone. That's just your neo-cortex."

"I know, but it felt so real," I pleaded. John didn't look convinced and was having a hard time holding back what he wanted to say.

"What?"

"Nothing," said John as he was restraining himself from speaking.

"Just say it. It's okay."

He paused before saying, "Look, as you said, maybe this is something important for your subconscious to resolve; I don't know. The subconscious influence on dreams is certainly well documented. What I do know is that sometimes our brain looks for its own placebo and its own way out of a problem. You give a child a teddy bear and tell them they will sleep better at night—what happens? They sleep better."

I knew where John was heading with this and it did make a lot of sense.

John continued, "Charles, I just think as we get older our minds get more sophisticated in creating their own antidote. That's all. We perceive and dream what we want to see and hear to feel better. We look for signs that just aren't there."

I nodded silently in agreement before lamenting, "Maybe you're right, John. Maybe you're right."

"But I have to tell you, Charles," he went on, "God bless the brain. I'm all for the placebo. If you can convince someone that giving them something will take away all their problems, I say give it to them."

John was probably right. My mind was playing games with me.

XXI

As time went on Chloe was finding it increasingly difficult to keep up with Charlie at Mrs. McLeod's classes. Mrs. McLeod came to visit us one day at our home. Sarah thought it was to discuss Chloe and her challenges in maintaining pace. I could see she was worried that maybe Mrs. McLeod no longer felt it was appropriate for Chloe to attend her lessons and all its implications, so it was a curious moment when we found out that Mrs. McLeod had actually come to speak to both of us regarding another reason.

"Dr. MacKinnon, Sarah, there is something I wanted to discuss with you about Charlie."

"Is everything okay?" Sarah asked.

"Everything is fine. It's too fine." She paused before continuing, "I have been involved in the music industry for more than sixty years now. I have seen gifted students come and go. I have mentored some of the greatest musicians this country has ever seen."

Sarah and I were wondering what the concern was then.

She continued, "A gifted musician is one who perfectly repeats what has been taught. I have seen my share of those. It's actually a very specific skill set." She looked at us more intently now. "That is not what Charlie has."

"I'm not sure I understand," I said, looking at Mrs. McLeod.

"Charlie doesn't just repeat what he has been taught. He has now reached a level where he creates." She looked at us, paused and then continued, "I really shouldn't be surprised. When I look back, he has always been composing; they were just simple and didn't draw particular attention. His compositions now have reached a level of complexity that is absolutely unmatched for his age." She then raised her voice and slowly said: "He is not just gifted; he is a prodigy. Being gifted is a limited skill set; what he has is boundless."

We were silent before Sarah told her, "Thank you. I am speechless; I'm not sure what to say."

Mrs. McLeod was not here just to pass a compliment. She pressed on, "In all the years I've been in this field I have never seen or heard of a child with his skills. I don't feel I'm exaggerating when I say this: we witness a child of this ability maybe once every few hundred years."

We both stared blankly at Mrs. McLeod as we were listening, and that's when Sarah said, "So where does that leave us?"

"Well, for starters, I'm not sure I have anything left to teach him; he has superseded me in every way."

"So what do we do now?" Sarah asked.

Mrs. McLeod looked at us and said, "You let him create."

I was too aware of Charlie's prolific ability to create even before he was born. I also knew his ability to create wasn't just limited to music. Charlie had his fingerprints all over many of the breakthroughs we had at Genomica. Right now we were in the most difficult circumstance and if there had been a time in my life that I needed Charlie's creativity, this was it.

In my dilemma I just couldn't help but wonder if this was "the sign" I had asked for from Charles I; I was never more conflicted. A part of me looked for every means to reject this notion. The other part—well, like it or not, was simply resigned to its outcome.

Mrs. McLeod knew several world-famous orchestras in the area that had wanted Charlie as their lead soloist. However, she warned us that "this wouldn't be enough."

"Let him compose. Let him write his music," she appealed.

Composing music was exactly what Charlie did. His music was on a scale and creativity that quickly captured local, national, and ultimately global attention. Charlie was twelve years old.

Charlie's music was what is known as modern classical. Although in many ways his preferred taste was still very much traditional classical; he drew inspiration from Mozart, Vivaldi, Bach and his absolute favorite, Beethoven.

His first concert was right here in Chicago. We came with Mrs. McLeod, her husband, and Chloe. I'd like to say Charlie was nervous. After all, he was only twelve years old. I was very worried as was Sarah. He had never played in front of an audience this large; he never played music that belonged to him; he had always played compositions written by others. Charlie never had to worry about validating other people's approval. This was an entirely new challenge. Mrs. McLeod had suggested that perhaps only one of his compositions be released on his first concert as a start. We gladly agreed.

Well, as I mentioned, I'd like to say that he'd be anxious as he was just like any other child; but like a baseball pitcher pitching in his first game, Charlie simply went out and pitched a no-hitter. He was marvelous! The audience was speechless, and Charlie didn't break a sweat. On that stage, he appeared more comfortable than I'd ever seen him on any other stage, including with me in the lab at Genomica. What made me most proud was the humility with which he bowed when he received a standing ovation at the end of the concert.

The press and media wanted to talk to him and ask him everything there was to know about him. What he'd like to eat? What he did in his spare time? What his hobbies were? That's when I realized we needed to shelter him. My father had always taught me, "Your humility is your strength; don't let anyone tell you otherwise. If they think it's a weakness, it's their weakness, not yours." Of course, that advice was much easier when you're in a small world of a few friends and colleagues. This was on a scale I don't think even my father could have imagined. I wasn't sure what to do. There is no training manual for this and no MacKinnon protocol. All I knew was that I wasn't about to lose my Charlie to the world.

XXII

The next weekend we went to the MacKinnon cottage. I was hoping that seeing family would provide me with new insight on my dilemma. Everyone was staying for the weekend this time, so we had packed the car with everything we required. One of Sarah's favorite containers for travel was a large plastic box. She loved it for its size and sturdiness. It was not only convenient for packing clothes but for many other items as well. The container was pink with a few flowers drawn on it. I gently asked, "Can we take another box?"

"What's wrong with this one?" she questioned, looking at me with an inquisitive stare.

"Nothing I guess."

"Well then, that settles it," she said quickly as she sat in the car.

"Do we not have a blue or green one?" I mumbled.

"Oh, Charles, I can't believe you are hung up on that. You should know better than anyone that gender bias of colors is a man-made concept. Look at children, they can't tell which colors are for which gender. We create those biases."

"Sure," I whispered as I got into the car.

As we were leaving the driveway, Sarah then turned to the back seat of the car where Charlie was sitting, and pointed to her pink scarf and asked him, "Do you like this color, Charlie?"

Charlie replied, "Yes, Mom," nodding his head in approval.

Sarah then looked back at me and said, "See, they can't tell the difference. Why should we have a bias?"

I said in a low voice, "Okay, okay—I get it; you're right," and regretted bringing up the subject. The truth is, I didn't mind the color as much as I minded the fact that she made me carry the box every time we went anywhere with it.

We arrived at the MacKinnon cottage. Charlie and Sarah emptied all the items in the trunk with only one item left: I was left to carry the pink box with flowers on it.

I looked around, waited, and realized there was no way around this without causing a stir. I picked up the container and started walking gingerly toward the front door. As I came closer, I realized there were a few people standing inside; change of plans—I decided to take a quick detour and walk through the side door instead. It would be quieter and more private too. Just as I reached the side entrance Scott pushed open the door and stepped out. He turned back with a swift look and snapped, "Nice box, Charles; does it come with a matching shirt?"

"Very funny, Scott," I muttered without trying to look back.

"I'm just kidding with you," he said, laughing as he walked away.

Then I stepped into the house and saw Uncle Stewart who was about to take the same exit. He stopped and stared at me and said with his deep voice, "Nice box, Charles!"

In my frustration I pleaded, "Oh, Uncle Stewart, not you?" protesting his humor.

He smiled and said, "What? I think it's a nice box."

"Okay, sure."

As I continued to walk down the hallway, I passed by my cousins Alistair and Bruce, both of whom chirped, "Wow, where did you get that box?"

I wasn't planning to answer that and just kept walking. I finally made it to the staircase. I hadn't realized every female member of the family had been sitting in the living room in its close proximity. They all stared at me silently with a smile as I walked up the stairs. I said, "Go ahead, get it out of your system," as I reached the top step and could hear a burst of laughter in the background.

I unpacked in our usual designated room on the second floor and returned to see the rest of the family in the courtyard outside. My grandfather was present that weekend and had heard the news that Charlie had been taken out of the science program at the Montgomery School. He was a little silent when I greeted him, "How are you doing, Grandpa?"

"I'm fine, Charles. How are you?" he said with a stern voice.

"I'm well, thank you."

"Charles, I'll need to speak to you at some point this

weekend. Not now, but maybe later."

"Sure, Grandpa. Anytime is good."

I knew what he wanted to talk about, and to be honest, I was surprised it took this long before he approached me on the subject. Charlie had been playing his music for many years now and they hadn't raised any concerns over it, probably hoping not to interfere and allow nature to take its course and for the balance of things to realign; that's the way it always worked with the MacKinnons. They don't interfere but things always work out in the end as they had wanted. I think he realized the stakes were much higher now. Charlie was the most talented MacKinnon, which made it all the more difficult to accept; there was also the Charles legacy, which I didn't even want to think about at this time.

He approached me after dinner when I was quietly enjoying the view to myself sipping on my cup of tea and said, "Can I join you?"

I put my arm around his shoulder, "Of course."

"Charles, I heard Charlie has dropped out of the science program at the Montgomery School."

"He didn't technically drop out; he's just put more focus on the music side of things."

"They tell me he was the top student in the sciences, why would they do such a thing? Being the top student in sciences at the Montgomery is not an easy task. Three quarters of the people here couldn't accomplish that feat and yet they are top neurosurgeons and leaders at their respective hospitals."

"I know, Grandpa, but they feel his talents are greater in music."

"Who is 'they'? Forget 'they'! He has skills and talents built over many generations in that mind of his."

"I know, but this is also what Charlie wants."

"He's twelve years old. What does he know? You are his father. You must guide him." He paused a little and shook his head. "Charles, what would your father say to this?"

"I don't know, Grandpa. I really don't know," I said with a sunken voice.

"I'll tell you what I think he would say; while it's not in our nature to tell the next generation what to do with their life," he then softened his voice to put his hand on my shoulder before continuing, "this is what we do. This is our talent. This is what God created us for."

I didn't say anything to that because I agreed with it.

"You know the history of every Charles?" he asked me as a good reminder.

I nodded. "Yes."

"Your last Charlie didn't even make it to university and he had more publications and left a greater impact than most neurosurgeons do in their careers."

"I know, Grandpa," I said hesitantly, "but there were others in the family that had musical inclinations that later went on to become great neurosurgeons. Look at Uncle Stewart; he played the piano. Look how great he turned out?"

Grandpa gave me a long look and said, "Charles, your Uncle Stewart played the piano for six months when he was eight years old. Don't fool yourself." He took a deep breath before adding, "...and what is Charlie going to do with his life playing the cello? Is he going to play at birthday parties and corporate engagements?"

"He's actually quite good," I defended.

He shook his head and said, "Seven hundred years of tradition and he's going to be a good wedding singer."

"He doesn't actually sing," I said respectfully.

Grandpa looked at me in disbelief before saying, "Not yet

anyway."

"Singing is a little different than playing an instrument."

He shook his head again and told me, "What difference does it make?" He then softened his voice and finished with, "Look, Charles, in the end the choice is still Charlie's, but you're his father. I just hope you know what you're doing."

"I hope so too," I said quietly to myself as he left.

Uncle Stewart was concluding his story time with the children and their parents sitting in the periphery. He was speaking about Sinclair VI. I didn't want to hear that story on this night, which is why I had walked a few feet away to enjoy the view. Sinclair VI was the story they always told us as to what happens when you ignore your forebears and break with tradition. Needless to say, he didn't meet a good end. It was a good reminder of our fallibility and the effort required to avert the mistakes of the past.

I was hoping we'd wrap things up and go to bed when Scott asked, "Why don't we have Charlie play us something?" Charlie, of course, was more than happy to play anywhere. A few others also encouraged him and he promptly complied with their wishes.

He returned with his instrument and that's when Uncle Stewart told him what I wish he wouldn't have said on this evening.

"Play us that famous wedding song," he asked.

I quickly said, "No, no, he doesn't know that one."

Charlie himself replied, "I know that one. I know it well."

"Sure, if you want to, but you don't have to," I told him.

"I'd like to," he affirmed.

"But—"

Uncle Stewart then interrupted, "Charles, if the kid wants to play it, let him play it!"

I didn't say anything; I just knew Grandpa was watching me and I didn't want to make eye contact. I managed to keep my gaze focused on Charlie, but I could see Grandpa looking at me in the periphery of my vision.

If it hadn't been for our earlier conversation I would have enjoyed this moment. Charlie played "Pachelbel's Canon" beautifully, but all that was running through my head was my Grandpa's comment about the seven hundred years of tradition to make a good wedding singer.

I turned away as much as I could, but in the end, I couldn't hold my gaze much longer and finally succumbed to glance in my grandfather's direction, and there it was—that look. I knew that look. My father had that look. That was the look that any instant made you cry of guilt all on its own without a single word. It was that gentle nod with the eyebrows raised and lips softly pursed. The look that said, "I told you so."

Yes you did.

I couldn't sleep that night. My grandfather's words lay heavy on my heart. *Was I doing the right thing? What was the future going to hold?* Sometimes an idea seems good at the time, but history doesn't look back on it kindly. There are many well-wishers of mankind that after the passage of time are not remembered fondly. *When a number of generations have passed how will all this be remembered? Have I destroyed the Charlie legacy?* These were the questions I was struggling with as I tossed and turned in my bed that night.

I finally rolled out of bed and walked out of my room at what must have been around 3am. In the hallways, I could see a number of portraits including those of Charles II and Charles III as I walked toward the staircase. It was a beautiful full moon that night and the moonlight had lit the walls sufficiently through the window that I could see the fine details of their image on the portraits.

I just muttered to myself, "What have I done?" I stared at the paintings for a while longer before going downstairs to sit outside on the steps and look at the moon.

The truth is, everything else aside, I had no desire for Charlie to be a musical celebrity; there were many factors that worked against this being a good step. Aside from losing him to fame, it would also expose every element of Charlie's life: his family, his background, my circumstances at Genomica; with Dawson circling around my home like a carnivore, putting my family in the media spotlight would be exactly what he'd want to facilitate his evil machinations.

I was outside by myself for about ten minutes before I saw Sarah show up and sit beside me.

"What are you doing up so late?" I asked.

"I was going to ask you the same question," she responded. "I noticed you were missing when I got up and came looking for you."

"Oh, you didn't have to do that," I said.

"Any reason you couldn't sleep?"

"No," I told her, not really wanting to divulge the details. "I woke up and saw such a beautiful full moon. I figured I'd come out and have a better look."

"It's beautiful, isn't it?" Sarah said as she sat closer beside me.

"Our last Charlie loved the full moon."

"He sure did," Sarah said with a smile. "He'd stare at it sometimes until he'd fall asleep."

We both laughed. It was a nice and comforting moment reminiscing of those times.

"Well, our Charlie now loves the moon too," she told me.

"Really, I didn't know that?"

"Oh yes, it's not as obvious, but he's always looking at it when he has a chance."

"I must have missed that. I didn't know," I said, obviously surprised.

"His favorite song is *Moonlight Sonata* by Beethoven; surely you didn't miss that one. He gets all emotionally charged every time he plays it."

I laughed, "No, I hadn't thought of that, but yes, he used to play that song over and over again for a long time."

There was a pause before Sarah asked, "I was just wondering: are you worried about Charlie?"

"Now what makes you say that?"

"You were very quiet and serious when he was playing his cello this evening."

"I was just surprised, that's all. It was nice. I liked it," I answered, not wanting to admit my dilemma at the time.

"Are you sure?"

"Yes. Why?"

"Are you having second thoughts about Charlie and his direction with music?"

"Well," I said tilting my head away, "maybe a little bit."

"Go on," she said

"I don't know. How many child prodigies do you know who have lived a good life?"

"Hmmm, I hadn't thought of that," Sarah pondered.

"Well, let's name them. There is Mozart. He passed away

when he was thirty-five. Then there was Beethoven, he died when he was fifty-six. Slightly better I guess. When you go down the list there aren't many happy stories."

Sarah looked a little surprised and deep in thought. "Bach lived into his sixties."

"Yes, I guess that's not bad, but his fame came mostly after he had passed on." I continued, "What if I said, I didn't care if Charlie was famous. What if I just want him to be happy?"

Sarah had a pensive look on her face and slowly uttered, "I really hadn't thought of it that way."

"He's only twelve years old. I'm just not sure what we are getting him into? Are we helping him or overwhelming him?"

"Well, if Charlie had been a prodigy in the sciences would you have felt the same way?" she asked.

I laughed, "No, I wouldn't."

"What's the difference?" she said.

"The difference is they don't get the same attention—there is no media, there are no cameras. Your life is not exposed. They pretty much live a normal life."

"So the problem is the attention they receive and its effect on the development of Charlie's character?"

"Yes. I guess that's a big part of it."

"Well, we can always change that," she told me.

"How do we change that?"

"We allow Charlie to compose his music, but we let him live a normal life."

"That's as big a contradiction if there ever was one. How can you have a normal life after they've heard his music? They will all be buzzing around our home," I said, appealing to Sarah.

"We won't release any more of his compositions until he

has finished his schooling. We're his parents; that's the choice we make. He lives a normal life, completes his education, and then we leave it Charlie to decide his future."

"Huh, it's not a bad suggestion." I mulled it over for a few seconds before saying, "Let me sleep on that one."

We talked a while longer before Sarah finally put her hand on my shoulder and said, "Come, it's late, let's get some sleep."

XXIII

We decided in the coming months that the concert Charlie had in Chicago would be his last as a composer until he had finished his secondary education. After some time life resumed to its normal structure, not only for Charlie but for us as well.

The next winter Charlie came home one day from school, and I had noted he had a lingering cough.

"How long have you been coughing for?" I asked.

"I don't know—at least three weeks," he said.

"Do you have a cold?" I questioned before asking, "Why don't you go see your doctor?"

"It doesn't feel like a cold. I'm not sure how I got this."

"Come here, Charlie; try this." I took out a new puffer of mine that I had stored in the medicine cabinet and told him, "Tell me if this feels better."

I showed him how to use the inhaler and he took a couple of puffs and looked at me and asked, "That's your asthma puffer, isn't it, Dad?"

I nodded in agreement.

"Do you think I might have asthma?"

"I don't know. It's possible."

Then Charlie asked me, "Dad, how come you never cured your asthma? You have cures for this, don't you?"

I smiled. "Yes, but my asthma is not that bad. It's mostly triggered when I go jogging; I haven't jogged much since you were a baby."

He looked at me a few minutes after he had used the puffer and said, "You know, I do actually feel better."

I didn't know if I should be happy or terrified that Charlie's symptoms improved. I had thought that gene therapies prior to birth were safe from regression, but apparently not. Like a perfectly stitched suture slowly unraveling, everything now felt like it was coming undone, and I had no way of stopping it. At this rate, the GSA would come and close our facility in the near future. My father, his hospital, his legacy would all come to nothing.

The next day I went to Genomica and met with John. I had a plan.

"John, I think we should re-try the treatments."

"Are you crazy? Why would we do that?" he protested.

"Well, think about it. Our therapies may not be a cure but they can give you symptom relief for a few years. What's wrong with that?"

"What's wrong with that?" he said loudly.

"Yes; besides, it's possible they may need several treatments before their body adapts. It's also plausible they may be cured after a second treatment."

John laughed, "You may look at it that way. The GSA won't. By God, Charles, they could have closed us down two years ago. This is just the reason they would need. You can't provoke them like that."

"Maybe, or perhaps this buys us more time until we can figure things out," I said.

"I don't know, and for that matter neither do you. We have never done this before. What if their immune system responds differently the second time? You can completely derail whatever good we did with the first treatment."

"It won't, John," I said, "The animal studies never showed any negative consequences. What you're saying is a bit of a stretch."

"Maybe, but it didn't show a cure in the resistant cases either. If you're wrong on this, there will be no turning back. The GSA will eat us alive. We'll be closed for good."

"Don't worry. Will you trust me on this? We'll be fine," I said, pleading my case.

John was stressed, but he also recognized that despite the risks we didn't have another choice. As he described it, we could hear the footsteps of the GSA coming behind us, and those steps were getting louder and louder each day.

We started the second round of treatments and the initial response was excellent. For a few months there was peace and quiet at Genomica, and that was the relief I think we both needed. Then John asked me one day, "Charles, me and the guys are going to play baseball tonight. Would you like to join us?"

I paused and looked at him in surprise because it had been a long time since I had been asked to participate.

He appealed to me again, "I never mentioned anything before because you were always busy with Charlie, but I thought if you weren't doing anything tonight we could play some ball."

"Sure, John, that actually would be great. What time is the game?"

It had been many years since I had last participated and I hadn't exercised in a long time, so I wasn't sure how I would play. John was a few players ahead of me in the batting order and his game hadn't lost a step.

The pitcher had pitched John inside a few times to scare him a little. John wasn't the least bit flustered and just looked over at me and smiled. He then shifted his weight to his front foot, brought his hands inside and changed his posture to be more upright. I remember Charlie explaining this strategy to me a long time ago and saying, "This is when you make the pitcher pay for it." And pay for it he did. John hit a three-run homer with the next swing.

The guys were cheering and we all congratulated John; when he walked over to the bench to sit beside me I asked him, "That was great, where did you learn that move?"

"Actually, your father taught me that one."

I smiled and nodded, "Yep! That would be my dad."

The next batter hit a ground ball and was thrown out at first base to which John said, "It's your turn at bat, Charles."

Unfortunately, I didn't have the same success as John. As one would expect, my asthma was slightly exacerbated during this game being so out of shape. That was the least of my worries. The summary of my game was I struck out four times and dropped two fly balls. The team didn't look too happy, but John was laughing more than he was upset. I think if my old Charlie had been around he would have called my mistakes on the field before any of them had actually happened.

John approached me after the game with a smile. "You look a little rusty out there."

"It's been a while since I played," I said in a sunken voice.

I looked at the field and remembered how much Charlie had desired to play baseball. That seemed like a lifetime ago.

"How are Sarah and Charlie doing?" John asked, halting my thoughts.

"They are doing well. When the summer holidays start we'll be going to Europe; Charlie will be touring with an orchestra in a few European countries."

"That's great. You will have some memorable times ahead then."

Charlie had already composed over eighty works in the past two years. None of these additional compositions were released or known to anyone. I knew it would be unrealistic to expect Charlie to hide these from Chloe but I asked him to anyway. Any knowledge of his music would make him a prime target for Dawson. As for his tour, it was with the orchestra. Sarah thought it would be good practice for Charlie to continue playing in front of an audience.

Charlie was old enough now that he could travel to any place in town on his own. I no longer had control over his whereabouts. With his growing friendship with Chloe, he was spending increasingly more time at Dawson's place.

Regrettably, Dawson would use these moments to speak to Charlie about his ideologies, particularly regarding science and ethics. One day Charlie came home and said he was not going to eat any food that was genetically modified. He had dinner at Dawson's home the night before.

"That's great, Charlie, what inspired this?"

"I just think they reduce biodiversity and are harmful to our environment. From a societal and humanitarian perspective, we've evolved to the point where we can be more responsible about this."

"Okay, if that is what you prefer," I said.

I didn't mind and I always encouraged Charlie to have his own views. Although the Charlie I knew loved to eat anything, so I wondered where this inspiration came from. If not eating genetically-modified food was the limit of his concern then I'd have no problem with it, but I knew this was the start of something much larger, and Dawson was using a harmless angle as a point of entry.

A few months later as I was sitting in our living room with Sarah, Charlie started speaking to me about animal rights and the laboratory testing of animals for medicinal purposes. Charlie had a common cold and said he didn't want to consume any medications because of where these drugs came from.

"Thousands of animals are tortured, experimented on, and killed so that one child can benefit. Isn't that selfish of us humans? When did we become so self-righteous?"

I wondered again where this had transpired from. "Is everything okay, Charlie? Who said they torture animals?" I asked.

Charlie didn't say who had said it, but I knew. He then continued, raising his voice, "I just don't want to take anything unnatural. The body heals itself anyway. I don't want to lend support to an industry that is ruthless in its treatment trials."

I was reading a journal when he was speaking. I looked up, shrugged my shoulders and said, "Sure, son, it's just a cold after all."

Sarah was more adamant than I was about this subject, at least with respect to Charlie's behavior. "Charlie, lower your tone. Speaking louder doesn't make your point better heard."

I didn't mind Charlie's ideas in principle, if this information had been his own original thought, but I knew the inception of these strongly-held beliefs. Charlie was sounding more and more like Dawson.

There was a calculated sequence to any one of Dawson's tactics. It was like playing a chess match. You never knew what he was thinking or what he was planning. I never worried about the moves I understood. The harmless steps were the ones you needed to be concerned about; those particular moves were a setup for a much larger and more dangerous play three steps away. He was a mastermind in knowing how to catch you off guard. The original intention of any maneuver was always a mystery. This had me anxious not just for Charlie but also for Genomica. I worried that perhaps part of the reason the GSA hadn't shut us down yet was because Dawson was biding his time for something more substantial. He would wait and linger, circle his prey and when he finally had what he wanted—he would strike.

I heard about this next episode many years later, but it didn't surprise me. On an occasion when Charlie had been invited to Dawson's home for dinner, Dawson had brought up the subject of genetic engineering and its application to treat disease.

"Do you want to know why genetic engineering has failed?" asked Dawson.

Charlie and Chloe were at the table when he was speaking.

"Because it was never meant to be; this is not what the world had intended. Trying to engineer something unnatural is like manufacturing a fake rose. Every one of us has a special purpose here in this world. It's denying that person their right to their uniqueness and interfering with their distinctive purpose here on this planet."

Charlie and Chloe nodded their heads in agreement before he continued, "We privilege an exclusive few, the right to live longer and to procreate with an advantage. There are close to eight billion people on this planet right now; with genetic engineering this will grow to twelve billion after just one generation. In fifty years we'll be at twenty-four billion."

They were listening intently to Dawson's words. "Charlie, tell me if that is even sustainable?"

Charlie was shaking his head and said, "No, definitely not at twenty-four billion."

"We are simply creating our own extinction. That is what we're doing here!" Dawson said, raising his voice. "Just the thought that we can't be disciplined enough as a race—our greed for more, our indulgence for comforts, our hunger for the excesses of this planet—it disgusts me!"

Charlie had been influenced by these words as he listened to Dawson press on, "There are eight hundred million people on this planet that are starving, another 1.1 billion that don't have adequate water, and here we are trying to increase the world's population and find better ways to leverage our advantage over them. Tell me, who pays for this? Who pays for our vanity? They do. They pay for it! The poorest, the innocent, the voiceless amongst our people, they are the ones that are paying the cost. Is that fair?"

Charlie and Chloe watched an angry Dawson forge ahead, "This world as it exists right now can sustain a population of no more than ten billion people. What happens when you're at twelve billion or twenty-four billion? We only advocate widening the gap between the haves and the have-nots. Is that sensible? Not only is it reckless, but we make a choice to offer some a leg up on the competition by giving them better genes! That's not something that happens halfway around the world. What do you think is the number of homeless people that live in Chicago?" He shouted and pointed to the ground saying, "This, right here in our own town!"

Charlie shrugged his shoulders not knowing the answer.

Dawson intensely clamored, "One hundred and fifty thousand! Just think about that. Twenty-five thousand of them are students like you." He stared at Charlie before saying, "What exactly are we doing about them? Does anyone even care? Here we are looking for ways to serve ourselves with this happening in our own neighborhood!" He shook his head and paused before completing: "Tell me, would gene therapy serve them? Or does it serve us? Are we finding solutions for them, or are these solutions for us?"

That's when Chloe asked, "Then what do we do?"

Dawson responded, "We give them a voice. We speak for those who can't."

I believe that is when Dawson had started his plan—his plan for Charlie and Chloe. In retrospect I should have seen this coming but I was too naive to understand a mind as complex as Dawson's. To truly understand a villainous mind you have to have one, and to truly comprehend someone of this character you have become him. This wasn't a path I could ever tread so I had no choice but to deal with the consequences.

I didn't know at the time what exactly had happened but

there was a definite change in Charlie's behavior when he was fourteen. He'd come home and would speak little when we were together or sitting at the dinner table. He would ask to be excused and go to his room. He spent decreasingly less time with me.

As for our European trip, it was my plan to join them for two weeks of their six-week tour. Sarah traveled with Charlie for the entire journey. I called every night to see how they were doing. This was Sarah's first extended trip with Charlie without me accompanying them.

"Charles, I never knew Charlie had such a talent for languages," Sarah told me on the phone.

"Why is that? Did something happen?"

"He was speaking perfect German when we were in Austria, and is now speaking Spanish fluently right here in Barcelona."

"That's great," I said.

"Were you aware that he spoke French as well?"

"No, I wasn't, but when I join you in Paris, we'll put that to good use. He'll be a nice guide to have."

"It's really amazing watching him speak. Did you know he had such a capacity?"

"I did, Sarah." I paused before continuing, "Charlie is Charlie; he can do anything when he sets his mind to it."

Having Sarah and Charlie away for most of the summer was a blessing in disguise. The situation at Genomica was starting to show more deficiencies. The patients were regressing after the six months as expected. What we hadn't predicted was that the rate of drop-off was 7%, not the 0.52%, with the second round of treatment. We anticipated this decline to be even more accelerated with the passage of time. At this rate, we'd be back to where we started in the not too distant future. The unknown factor now was whether their condition would deteriorate beyond their baseline if we opted to do any additional treatments. There was no way to know how their immune system would respond. We couldn't chance it, which meant one thing: barring a miracle, one way or another, we were headed for a tide of calamities a year from now.

I was running out of time. I needed to search Charlie's room again on the off chance that he had left the solution I had missed seeing in my prior searches. Over the years, I had stored some of Charlie's work-related items in boxes and started to label and number them; I had become more systematic in my search. For the most part everything in the room had been kept exactly the same. Sarah had wanted to change the decoration some years ago; I asked her not to, and she complied and didn't raise the subject again. That room was my last connection to Charlie, and she knew when the time was right I would do it myself. I still hadn't.

I searched Charlie's room in an orderly fashion and tried to be more meticulous and thorough in my approach. I went through every drawer and paper file that I had methodically organized. Once again, I was hopeless. Charlie had not written the solution down. I felt aimless and didn't know where that would leave me.

XXIV

I packed my bags and joined Sarah and Charlie in France. Charlie performed in Paris with the National Royal Orchestra. His performance was immaculate. After the concert we all went out for dinner as a family. That's when Charlie talked to us about some of his plans for the future.

"Mom, Dad, I was thinking that maybe I should use my skills toward conveying a message of social justice."

"Sure, son, what did you have in mind?" I asked.

"I don't know yet. I thought perhaps I wasn't just created to play music, but rather to use it as an instrument for something greater."

I was personally indifferent to his suggestion. I've never been much of a talker and didn't trust people who speak too much. You don't see too many doctors or nurses going around the world preaching good wishes. They help by just doing good deeds. I'd rather let Charlie inspire through his music than his words. However, things weren't quite the same between me and Charlie; they hadn't been in a while so I wasn't planning on being the voice of opposition on this one—well, at least not that much—so I said, "Whatever you feel is your calling, you do it, as long as you do it right. Make sure it is something worthwhile and don't let your head get too big. Most people want to hear your music, not listen to speeches."

"I know. Let me think on this for a while," Charlie quietly said.

Then Sarah told him, "Why don't you do something with Chloe?"

Great! Of all the possible suggestions, that was the one I did not want to hear. That was pretty much the clincher; bringing Chloe into the equation meant Dawson was involved too. I was done. Any humanitarian involvement on Dawson's part essentially implied traveling back to the Stone Age and living in mud huts.

"Well, Sarah, I think Charlie thought of this idea on his own; it's his own personal project. He's mature and clear-headed; I think we should let him spearhead this as he wishes."

"Mom, I think that's a fantastic idea."

"But, Charlie, Chloe can't play like you do and isn't part of your orchestra. This won't be that easy. If you do this it has to ring true."

"I know, but there are a number of ways I can make it work."

"How so?" I asked.

"Well, I can do something separate with Chloe, it doesn't have to be part of the orchestra."

"But, Charlie, all the time you've put into this."

"Dad, it won't take any time away."

"What about your school?"

"I can manage," Charlie said.

"Will you have the time?"

"It's a piece of cake, Dad. Besides, Chloe is good at organizing these sorts of things so she probably will do most of the work."

"Well, we don't know yet if Chloe wants to do this," I appealed.

"I can find out. She'll do it if I ask her."

From that moment on it was hard for me to enjoy the rest of the trip. With things unraveling the way they were at work, that last thing I needed was to let Dawson right into the nucleus of my own home. Charlie had his mind made up and Sarah supporting it essentially meant I didn't stand a chance to negotiate out of this.

We went to Rome after Paris. Naturally, I was amused when I heard Charlie speaking Italian. I didn't want to ask how little time he had spent learning all these languages. Charlie's every capacity was now a painful reminder of what I had lost. Close to seven hundred years of tradition and talent packed into one person, and instead of all this aptitude being used to discover medical breakthroughs, it was now going to be utilized as a vehicle to disseminate Dawson's views.

Maybe this is what I deserved for what I did. Maybe this is my lot for not being entirely honest with Sarah about what I had contrived. Genes don't lie, and interestingly they always come back—and so does karma.

I called John to see how things were at the office. He was particularly elusive in his conversation, always finishing every sentence with, "Enjoy your trip, Charles; we'll worry about work when you get back."

"That doesn't sound too encouraging," I finally said.

John changed the subject, "How are Charlie and Sarah doing?"

"They are well. They're both in town doing sightseeing right now. Charlie has his concert tomorrow so they should be back soon."

"Send them my regards. We'll talk later then."

"Thank you. John, I was wondering if everything is—"

"Charles, we'll catch up when you come back. I have to go right now. Have a safe trip."

"Bye, John."

Charlie's concert the next night was another standout performance. I was preparing to travel home to what I knew was a nightmare awaiting me at work. As John had alluded, the number of cases with complications at Genomica had increased. Sarah and Charlie still had another two weeks of touring left. When they finally returned, they both came back with a cold.

"We must have caught a virus on the plane," Sarah said.

They were exhausted from their trip so I commented, "It didn't help that you were traveling every few days. It may have been a bit too much stress."

In any case, Sarah was feeling better after a couple of days, but Charlie's cough continued and he was feeling worse. A week later, Chloe and Charlie had already made their arrangements to work on a project together. As I suspected, the project was really Dawson's idea though it was never presented that way. I'm not even convinced Charlie really knew the full scale of his schemes.

Dawson had run the concept past Chloe who had suggested it to Charlie prior to his trip. Charlie had felt uneasy about the idea and decided to circle around the subject indirectly, hoping his mother would suggest it herself, which she did. He now figured he had our permission and chose to follow through on their plans.

What I hadn't expected was for the concert to be happening two weeks after Charlie had arrived from Europe. He hadn't mentioned anything to me or to Sarah and was planning to attend the concert all on his own. It wasn't until we saw him leaving the house with his signature tuxedo when Sarah asked him, "Where are you going?"

"I'm meeting some friends," he said.

"Wearing a tuxedo?" she asked.

I joked with Charlie, "You look good. Anything we should know?"

"We're just playing some music, that's all."

Sarah looked at him and knew he was up to something, and said, "Where are you playing?"

He hesitated at first but eventually responded, "At the Royal Concert Hall."

Sarah and I were speechless. "You're playing at the Royal Concert Hall and you weren't planning on telling us?" she said.

"It's really not a big deal this one."

I quickly suggested, "We're not doing anything tonight," and looked over at Sarah. "We'll take you there."

"No, it's okay, Dad, it's really no trouble. I can go there myself."

Sarah said, "That's it, we're coming. I don't want to miss this. Besides, I'm not going to let you come home late at night all by yourself."

"Mom, I have a ride, not to worry. I'm a bit late. If it's okay, I have to run; you won't be ready on time."

"Alright," she said, "you go ahead if you have to, but we'll see you there shortly and take you home after."

We both dressed and prepared ourselves and were perplexed that Charlie had not mentioned anything about this to us. I said, "He's probably testing his independence; all kids do that at his age."

Sarah wasn't convinced; she had just finished traveling with him and this was never mentioned. "You don't just find out you're playing at the Royal Concert Hall the day before the event."

Traffic was heavy that night, and unfortunately, the roads were blocked. I took a back road as a detour and found a pathway straight into the rear entrance of the underground garage. We took the elevators upstairs in a rush. The hallways were empty as everyone had already taken their seats. We went to the ticket counter and Sarah asked, "We'd like two tickets for tonight's event at 8pm."

John called me at this point. I answered the phone quickly to let him know where I was. "Hi, John, I can't really talk right now. I'm about to step into a concert where Charlie is performing; anything urgent?"

The attendant at the counter in front of me then pointed to a seating chart and said, "We only have five seats left and these are the only two that are together."

"Great. We'll take it," I said and completed my conversation. "John, if it's okay I'll speak to you after we're done here."

He did ask me what type of concert this was and what it was for.

"I don't know, we just found out about this an hour ago."

Sarah and I were hurrying to run inside after receiving our tickets. The program had already started, and the opening speech had just concluded as we took our seats. I looked around and something didn't feel right. We were receiving many long stares.

I whispered to Sarah, "I know we're late and everything but it's just five minutes; what's with these people. Look at their angry stares. They need to relax a little."

The looks didn't go away. We then saw Charlie and Chloe on stage with a small orchestra that was preparing to perform. Charlie was watching us carefully. Sarah and I were both smiling, and motioned a small wave in his direction to capture his attention and let him know we were there. I was so proud of him.

They played two compositions. I wanted to give them a standing ovation, but Sarah nudged me back down when she noticed I was the only one standing and quietly said, "These people are really uptight."

"Are they still upset we're late?" I wondered.

That's when Sarah asked me, "What does that sign up there mean?"

"What sign?"

She pointed. "That one over there."

I looked up and it said, "The TruNome Project." Below it there was also a statement: "Embracing your unique identity and not your genome."

"I have no clue," I whispered to Sarah, "but I don't have a good feeling about this."

Then we heard the next speaker being introduced. It was

Dr. Brian Wright. I recognized his name and immediately understood what this was concerning. He was long ago a strong advocate for gene therapy and had a plentitude of breakthrough research; a brilliant scientist who had therapies that at one time rivaled close to what we had at Genomica. Then years later, without any explanation or warning, he suddenly switched sides and became the voice against genetic research. We never understood why. It was always a mystery.

We listened to his speech and Charlie looked at us very concerned. I had seen that look on Charlie's face once before; it was when my previous Charlie was sitting in the principal's office when he had been caught with his comic books and his "super-hero" tools. Those days seemed so far away and the innocence of that time was long gone. I looked around the hall and I didn't see Dawson anywhere in the audience. He was not here. He had later claimed he didn't know anything about the event and even seemed puzzled when asked by Sarah.

Now the stares around me seemed to make sense and I was perhaps slightly more uncomfortable, but not enough that I was impelled to move. My father once told me, "Where there is truth, there is opposition." He repeated that often and emphatically uttered, "Charles, it's the ultimate sign you're doing something right. Don't let it disturb you, and don't allow it to sway you from your path."

My concern right now was only seeing my son on stage— on Dawson's stage. I'm not sure I heard a word Dr. Brian Wright said. I was fixated on Charlie whose eyes would drift from staring at the floor and glancing up occasionally to see us looking at him.

After Dr. Wright uttered his short speech, the orchestra performed a composition in which Charlie was to play a solo part. I don't know if the stress of the current moment had any effect; in retrospect, I probably shouldn't have shaken my head when I saw him move forward prior to playing the next piece. Charlie was looking at us more than he was concentrating on his instrument. As he started playing, he had a coughing bout that interrupted him for that segment; a minute later it happened again, except this time, the coughing continued and he had to stop playing all together. After his performance, he stood up and slowly bowed out exiting, holding his instrument in one hand and trying to hold back his cough with the other.

That's when Sarah turned to me and said, "Come, Charles, we should go." I followed Sarah and we walked backstage where she told Charlie in a stern voice, "Gather your things, we're leaving right now." Charlie didn't hesitate to move.

The car ride home was an animated one. Sarah started the discussion: "Charlie, what were you thinking? Have you lost your mind?"

He responded, "But I thought it was okay; they were just saying we're all unique."

Sarah retorted, "I am very disappointed in you. Who convinced you that it was a good idea to turn on your family?"

"I wasn't turning on my family," he said in a dejected voice.

"Every one of those people was speaking against your father and our company; a company that your grandfather built. A company your Uncle John works at," Sarah replied.

Charlie was quiet and looking out the window as I watched him in the rearview mirror.

Sarah asked, "Who put you up to this?"

I muttered, "Who do you think?"

Charlie didn't answer that question specifically but said, "I didn't know this is what it was all about until a few days ago."

"Then why didn't you say anything to us earlier?" Sarah asked him.

Charlie didn't have an answer to that. I actually do trust in that he probably didn't know what exactly the concert was for, but I also believe he suspected it was something we wouldn't approve of otherwise he would have mentioned it earlier.

He started coughing again in the car, and that's when Sarah finally told him, "I'm taking you to the doctor tomorrow."

When we came home I told Sarah, "That's it; I want that Dawson out of my life. If this means Chloe has to go too, so be it. We're not allowing wolves in our backyard."

Sarah didn't mention anything other than nodding in agreement before saying, "Okay, if that's how you feel."

I was expecting a good long argument and had a long list of things to say. She pretty much disarmed me by passively agreeing with everything I said, which shortened the conversation.

"You know it was Dawson who planted this?" I said sharply.

"Okay," she said with a gentle nod.

"You realize he is just finding ways to tear us apart."

"Okay," she said.

"I don't want you or Charlie anywhere close to that man again."

"Okay," she said.

"Okay" just didn't satisfy me. This was not the response I

was expecting and it forced me to restrain my feelings. I actually preferred Sarah to challenge me so I could really let loose on how I felt, but that didn't happen.

XXV

The next day Sarah took Charlie to his physician and he was prescribed antibiotics for a chest infection. He was required to miss the first week of school, as it was difficult for him to even carry a conversation without coughing.

Perhaps I should have been surprised and perhaps not, but when I picked up the newspaper that next morning, whose picture was on the front page? Well, at least they caught the photo in the few moments I was smiling. The title of the article was, "TruNome's New Advocate?"

If the long stares I received that night were not awkward enough, the stares I received at work the next day more or less completed my experience. John was waiting for me that morning in my office. He had a copy of the paper in his hand. When I walked in, he had a smile on his face, so you could guess I knew exactly what was coming.

"TruNome's New Advo—"

He actually couldn't finish the sentence; he was laughing so hard he was starting to cry. "Is it that amusing, John?" I asked as I walked toward my chair and dropped my briefcase. "Go ahead, get your kicks."

"And I was starting to wonder why you didn't call me back last night," John said with a grin.

I sat in my chair and just watched him. This was obviously a lot more humorous for him than it was for me. He started reading passages from the article aloud as he was wiping his tears.

"Dr. MacKinnon's appearance at TruNome marks a new chapter in the evolution of the genetic industry, its regression and subsequent backslide."

"This isn't good. Stop laughing."

John continued, "He was seen applauding and espousing so worthy a cause…" He couldn't finish that sentence fighting back his tears. Then he clamored, "Charles, could you at least not have looked this happy in the photo?"

His laugh was contagious and I have to admit, I did look somewhat goofy in the picture. I couldn't help but crack a smile after he planted the newspaper right in front of me on my desk.

"I'm going to assume you didn't know what you were about to walk into when I called last night?" John asked.

"Nope, it took us by surprise."

"How did you not know? Did they not have any signs?"

"They did, but it wasn't very clear and we were in a rush to sit down. I don't know, John."

"How did Charlie become involved in such a thing?"

I hesitated to answer right away. He looked at me and said, "It wasn't Dawson, was it?"

"Who else would it be?" I questioned.

"You have the worst luck; I bet he must have enjoyed watching you there."

"If he did, then it was from home. He wasn't actually there; not that I could see."

"He's probably reading the paper right now and relishing every second of this," John said.

"Yes, he probably is."

"What about Sarah?"

"She was surprised too," I said. "Thankfully she agrees with me in that we need to have this guy finally cut off."

John went quiet suddenly and said, "Huh."

"What are you thinking?"

"If Dawson set this up, don't you ask yourself why?" John remarked as he started pacing back and forth in my office. He mulled and murmured, "Why now?"

"I hadn't thought of it that way. I just assumed his venom knew no boundaries."

"No, Charles, he is much more calculating than that. There is meaning behind every one of his moves."

"Yes. I know, and there's even more meaning when he's quiet and you don't see a move."

"This isn't random, Charles. He's planning something."

"How hard can it be to see what he's planning? He's trying to turn my son against me and embarrass us in the media."

"There is more to it. We have to look past the obvious."

"I'm not sure I understand."

"Think about it, we've had enough setbacks for him to have shut us down several years ago. He hasn't. Why?" John asked before pausing to say, "…and now he comes out and embarrasses you?"

"What are you thinking? What do you suppose he's doing this for?"

"I don't know but this isn't a good sign. If he's publically humiliating you, he's planning his next move."

"And what would that be?" I asked.

"I hope I'm wrong on this, but he probably wants public support to create the momentum to shut us down. This would force the GSA's hand into closing you."

I started to think about what John was suggesting before completing his thought by saying, "What better way to do that than by first having you look incompetent; make it appear as though you have switched allegiances."

John nodded in agreement. "He is also hoping you'll be angry and do something irrational; you know how much the media loves that."

"Yes, he wants us to destroy our public relations," I said, finally starting to see where John was going with this.

"He also wants you off your game."

"What do you mean, John?"

"Well, I'm going to venture a guess you had a little fight with both Charlie and Sarah over this last night," he said, looking at me as I confirmed his assumption with a nod.

He continued, "What better way to throw you off your game than by bringing disruption into your home and driving a wedge between you and your family."

"So basically you're saying he wants me to go crazy?"

"Yes," he said, "that would be a correct assumption."

I grasped my forehead with my right hand trying to think this problem through as I asked John, "Then what do I do?"

"Look at the phone on your desk, Charles—all those messages."

John had been sitting in my chair prior to me arriving. I

suppose he had seen that I had forty-eight missed calls and twenty-seven new messages. He was probably assuming that most of those were from media sources wanting a quote or a response to my presence at the TruNome event last night. Interestingly, there weren't any media there that I was aware of, but I guess the one that did show up knew enough about me to capture that photo.

"Okay," I said to him, "I see a lot of messages. What do you think I should do?"

"Don't answer. You're upset right now. You'll make a mistake and they'll turn it against you. Let us sleep on it for a few days and then in good time we'll provide a composed response."

"I can live with that," I affirmed.

Then John said, "Now, this is important; don't fight with Sarah or Charlie over this anymore."

"What do you mean?"

"Charles, you'll have to trust me on this. That's exactly what he wants you to do."

"But, John, what he did was ridiculous!"

"I know that, you know that, but you're not going to play into his hands. He wants you to argue and look like the bad guy on this."

"So what do you suggest I do, say nothing?"

"Yes. That's exactly what I want you to do!" he said.

"Then you should know that I've said quite a bit to Charlie and Sarah about this already."

"That's fine. From this day forward, you don't bring up the subject again. Trust me."

"You should also know that Sarah's been very supportive and Charlie's been very remorseful."

"Wonderful. Let's leave it at that then. Remember those

things can change in an instant; that's what Dawson wants."

"Okay, if you say so."

I didn't answer the phone at the hospital all day, and I continued to receive additional messages for the next twenty-four hours. Most of them, as we had suspected, were from reporters. Dawson had successfully brought a lot of media attention to an event that otherwise had very little coverage, and had put the subject of our company back in the spotlight where he knew it wouldn't shine.

I went home later in the evening and as I promised John, I didn't bring up the topic with either Sarah or Charlie. The next day John arranged for a press release. He himself had prepared a statement for me to provide the media. He handed it over for me to review just before its release. The statement was short and to the point; it was to the effect that "at Genomica we're always encouraging an open dialogue with our patients as well as other associated organizations—even those whose opinions may differ from us. The only path to progress is a collaborative one with all the concerned parties. The more we seek to understand one another's concerns, the greater will be our mutual growth and development in this process."

The statement was well received and shifted the momentum for the time being. John asked me later that day, "Now that we've weathered the storm, do you want to play baseball with us this week? Jack will be leaving town and moving away this weekend. The guys would like you to join our team for the remainder of the season, if you're up for it."

I didn't have to think too long this time to answer, "Yes. That would be great."

When game day arrived the team had even brought me my own jersey as a welcome gift. To be sure, they also did it with a sense of humor. John presented the jersey with all the teammates around and announced, "Welcome to the team. I know you're not superstitious; just that we all thought you'd play better if you had your lucky number. We figured it would make you feel more at home."

I looked at the jersey before turning it to its backside, and there it was: they had my name "C. MacKinnon" written with my regnal number "XI" in roman numerals sewn underneath it.

I smiled and said, "Very funny, gentlemen," and paused briefly before completing, "I think I like it; this is really nice. Thank you!" I shook each of their hands as they all welcomed me one by one.

Well, lucky number or not, it did work. I played very well and I was certainly much better than I was the last time. Three base hits including a two-run homer, four RBIs, and I didn't make a single mistake catching the balls out in left field.

After the game, one of the players, Josh Gilbert, approached me and said, "That was some game out there. Congrats, buddy."

John looked at me and reiterated the sentiment, "You played awesome; great to have you back."

It was nice to be back. Meanwhile at home, Charlie's symptoms had improved from the antibiotics, but his cough was not entirely gone. Despite this, he returned to school. A month later while he was practicing his cello at home, I saw him coughing after playing a few notes. I watched him from a distance in the other room while reading the newspaper. After clearing his throat, he took a deep breath and started playing. He was doing well for a few seconds, but once he closed his eyes to play as he usually does, he started coughing again. He finally stood up and walked over to the medicine cabinet to take a puff from an inhaler. I hadn't realized he was using this, so I approached him and asked, "How long have you been using a puffer?" I was clearly surprised.

"My doctor prescribed it for me at the last visit," he said. "I've used it every day for the last four weeks."

"You've used it that long and you're still coughing?" I paused before questioning, "Has it even helped?"

"It seemed to work at first but I can't seem to shake off this cough. The inhaler isn't working like it used to."

I took a moment to reflect before saying, "I think we should see your doctor again. I'll call and make an appointment." I went and picked up the phone and called his physician, Dr. Edwin Clark, who was also a friend of mine, and arranged for him to be seen in a few days.

I accompanied Charlie to this appointment. I was concerned about his symptoms and wanted to know for myself what was happening. We discussed Charlie's lack of progress, and he reviewed his condition and told me what I already knew, hoping it wouldn't be true.

"Charles, we've run some tests and your son definitely has asthma."

Dr. Clark worked at a different hospital than Genomica and didn't have Charlie's records from before; he was unaware that he had received gene therapy for this prior to birth. We also had never mentioned anything to Charlie about it, mostly because we didn't need to. He never had any symptoms so the topic never came up.

Anyway, this didn't feel like the most appropriate time to bring up the subject so I didn't comment on it but I asked Dr. Clark to do a genetic confirmation of Charlie's asthma. He agreed and we met him a week later for the results. I met

XXV

Charlie after school and traveled with him to his physician's office.

Dr. Clark greeted us, and shortly after we sat down, he looked at me and said, "The genetic testing confirmed our initial suspicion. Charlie does have asthma."

"Are you sure?" I asked.

"Yes, absolutely. Charlie not only has asthma, but a severe form of it. I am actually surprised he hasn't had symptoms earlier."

I was quiet and Dr. Clark suspected I wasn't entirely convinced of what he was telling me so he said, "Here, you can look at the results yourself."

I reviewed it in detail; in short, whatever treatment we had done prior to Charlie's birth had become, so to speak, undone. Charlie's genes had in essence reverted to their original form.

When we left, Charlie asked me, "What does this all mean, Dad?"

"Nothing, you just have to use additional puffers and take some medications—that's all." I didn't want to talk about it anymore than that. When we came home, Charlie discussed all the details to his mother during dinner.

"Apparently, I have a severe form of it, Mom."

I was expecting Sarah to be surprised and mention something about his past genetic treatment but all she said was, "There are worse things people live with. It's not so bad."

"What if it happens during my performance?"

"You'll just have to make sure you take your treatments on time when you need it."

That's all Sarah said. She never made any eye contact with me to ask how this happened. She didn't express any shock, nor did she bring up the subject later. That was Sarah; she was very quick to recognize people's feelings, their emotions and social situations, and swiftly adjusted her behavior to accommodate for the circumstances. She was what you'd call, socially smart, and also had a kind heart.

I, on the other hand, was extremely disturbed as to why this had occurred and was scratching my head for answers. This was, in brief, a colossal disaster. I talked to John the next day and mentioned to him what had happened with Charlie regarding his new asthma diagnosis.

"That's impossible, Charles. He was cured prior to birth. Those patients are safe."

"Here, look for yourself. These are his test results."

John read the pages slowly, studying some of the finer points diligently; he then looked back at me, removing his glasses, and just shook his head and said, "I'm not sure what to say. You're right."

We both looked at each other and knew what this meant. Everything we had done, all the treatments, all the hope we had built, had ultimately come to nothing. There were now no therapies that could be considered safe, as we had believed some were. Every treatment, all the cures, would appear in the public eye as just a mirage.

In fairness, Charlie had avoided having asthma during some of the most formative years of his life. Asthma tends to be worse in childhood and improves as they reach their teenage years. To suggest he hadn't benefitted from this treatment would be a flawed argument. If provided with a choice I would still do it all over again. The concern here was the concept of selling more hope than what we ultimately delivered, as well as the optics of this in the public eye. It would be very easy for public opinion to be manipulated to make these treatments appear as absolute failures and ineffective. The social tide was not our side these days; their views were tainted. There was already an abundance of negative publicity on the news and talk shows. This recent finding was something that could add another weapon to their arsenal of arguments.

I went home later that day and went to search for the wooden treasure chest of Charlie's belongings that I had put in our basement. Inside I had a copy of the first journal Charlie had read as well as a copy of his first research publication. Both of these I had stored here. I observed carefully the dates of each of these. They were apart by exactly three years, three months, and sixteen days.

This time measure was my target if I were to have one in order to find a solution. I knew if my Charlie were to redirect his focus toward the neurosciences that would be the approximate length of time it would take for him to unravel our conundrum. Still, it seemed like an unrealistic dream. As much as I once believed it could be done faster, I wasn't so sure of that anymore. My last Charlie had the inspiration and drive of his own condition. This one didn't have that motivating factor; even his asthma wasn't too much of a concern for him. I guess I could tell him this is what I wanted him to do and speak to Sarah to also win her support. I know Sarah would stand behind me. That would solve my troubles in an instant.

Within these parameters lay my dilemma. While I could

do this, I couldn't help but feel this was all about me. Yes, one can justify that millions of people would also benefit. When we want something, our minds can trick us and find many ways to defend it. I'm all too familiar with that ploy. I needed to think about this. I wasn't sure if I could bring myself to take this shortcut. I'd be asking Charlie to part with his passion to serve my purpose.

My heart went back and forth on this. My relationship with Charlie had also taken a step back after his last concert. Charlie was losing his connection with his family, his history, and drifting more and more under Dawson's influence. The remedy for this needed more than my voice. That's when I decided I wanted Charlie to spend additional time with Uncle Stewart. You wouldn't be able to spend five minutes with him without hearing a story or two about our MacKinnon history. His stories were so animated and beautifully told that you would want to travel back in time instantly to relive it. If Charlie understood the MacKinnon legacy, if he connected with his own "Charlie legacy," then perhaps he would finally understand.

I spoke to Uncle Stewart and had to explain it without explaining it. I approached him at the next grand rounds and said, "Can I talk to you about something?"

"Sure, Charles; what's on your mind?"

"It's about Charlie."

"Is he okay?"

"He's fine, it's nothing like that; just that my Charlie grew up without a grandfather. He never really experienced what it was like to have a grandpa. He never had it from Sarah's side of the family either."

"I know, Charles; it's unfortunate. We all miss your father. I always looked up to him, you know. He was a man of great integrity."

"Thank you, Uncle Stewart."

"Well at least he's blessed to have Grandpa William," he said.

"I love Grandpa but he would be Charlie's great-grandfather so it's a slightly different connection and the generations are too far apart."

"You're probably right," Uncle Stewart said, smiling.

"Well, Uncle Stewart, I was wondering if Charlie could spend a little more time with you. I'm his father, he sees me differently. You and my dad were very close and alike in many ways. I just thought that maybe he needs a voice similar to yours to guide and speak to him in a way that I just can't."

"I'd love to, Charles. It would be my pleasure to spend time with Charlie. He is always welcome. Thank you for suggesting it and thinking of me."

Uncle Stewart lived with his wife Bonnie. They had one daughter, Skye, who was two years younger than I was. She had married and moved to New York with her husband more than twenty years ago. She would make the occasional visit, but for the most part, their communication was limited to telephone calls. Skye and her husband never had any children, and as far as I know, they never wanted any. Knowing Uncle Stewart and his love for kids, I know how hard that must have been for him. He never spoke about it and we never asked. That, by the way, was another MacKinnon protocol; if a subject is uncomfortable, you don't ask about it, not even indirectly. If the person wishes to discuss it, you let them speak on their terms, not yours. I never approached it from that angle but I had a feeling that Uncle Stewart would also welcome spending time with Charlie, and perhaps this was mutually beneficial.

I arranged to take Charlie to Uncle Stewart's home every Sunday morning. Convincing Charlie was the easy part of the equation. He loved seeing Uncle Stewart. They would have breakfast together near his house and enjoy a walk at the park across from the restaurant before returning in the late afternoon.

Every week I'd commute to Uncle Stewart's home to collect Charlie; on the drive back he would speak about a new story from our family history that Uncle Stewart had taught him.

Then one day Charlie asked me, "Dad, did you know the story of Charles I?"

"Yes. I thought you knew his story; I had told that story before."

"You did, but Uncle Stewart talked about it again today."

"Did you like Uncle Stewart's version better?" I asked. There was no contest, no one could tell a story like Uncle Stewart. You could have three people describe different versions of the same story, but when you heard Uncle Stewart speak, it was an entirely different experience: you were there, you'd feel every movement, every gesture and emotion.

Charlie paused before answering, "I liked your version too, Dad."

He had learned his mother's diplomacy in answering these questions. I didn't mind. "I liked Uncle Stewart's version better if it makes any difference."

Then Charlie asked me, "Do you think everyone in our family became a neurosurgeon because of him?"

"No. I don't think so. I think everyone has a certain talent and inclination. Some of those talents are genetic and some are acquired. Charles I may have been an inspiration, but more than anything I think we just inherited some of his genes so we're naturally inclined as he was."

"Uncle Stewart was telling me that every "Charles" in the family had gone on to push the limits of neurosurgery to new heights, is that true?"

Again, I had thought that Charlie knew all of this, and he did, so it was surprising that he was asking as though the information was new. I knew Uncle Stewart speaking to him had stirred a renewed interest. I said, "Yes, it's true."

"Do you think I'd have the talent to be a good neurosurgeon?"

I paused before answering, "Yes. I think you would be a great one."

"Really? How can you be so sure?"

Charlie looked at me, and he was waiting for me to follow through on that idea.

"I think you'd be good at anything you choose to focus on, but ultimately, you have to look at your inclinations and write your own destiny."

That comment put Charlie in a deep state of thought. I could see him weighing in on his talents and his history.

The next week when I picked Charlie up at Uncle Stewart's home, he was telling me the story of Charles II. The following week his enthusiasm was about Charles III and so on. This had been Charlie's request, and not motivated by Uncle Stewart. He had asked Uncle Stewart to tell him the story of every Charles.

Seeing Charlie enlivened, I felt the excitement as if it were my first time hearing those stories. I remember well when my father was telling me those same tales when I was young, the connection I felt to every one of my family members that came before me, and my sense of responsibility to uphold their legacy.

The next week when I went to Uncle Stewart's home to pick up Charlie, he invited me inside and said, "Come, I want to show you something."

I was curious what this was about; he took me to his workroom and said, "I needed someone with elegant handwriting to write the story of Charles I in the MacKinnon history book. I had left those pages blank until now. Here, take a look at this."

I peeked inside and there it was: the story of Charles I. As I looked more closely, my eyes widened, gazing at the beautiful handwriting. "This is unbelievable. It's the calligraphy of Charles II. Where did you find this?" I asked, completely amazed.

Uncle Stewart looked me and said, "Charlie wrote this."

"Charlie?" I asked. "My Charlie?" I repeated, looking over at him.

"This is incredible. Where did you learn to write like this?"

"Uncle Stewart taught me everything," he said shyly, holding back his smile.

Uncle Stewart looked at me, shaking his head. "No, he's being modest. I wish I had actually done much teaching." He then examined the page and said, "The resemblance is uncanny. It's the exact same penmanship as Charles II. You wouldn't be able to tell the difference."

On the way home, Charlie asked me about my father. Uncle Stewart had spent the last few weeks chronicling the highlights of his life. My dad and Uncle Stewart had been best friends. They were first cousins, one year apart in age and were inseparable all throughout school. They were very much alike. When you were in the company of one you felt you could hear the voice of the other. They spoke very similarly in that they had the same logic, used the same expressions, and had many of the same gestures.

Uncle Stewart probably knew more stories about my father than anyone did. Charlie asked me in the car that day, "Can you tell me about my grandpa?"

"Sure; anything in particular you want to know?"

"No," he said. He was deep in thought so I knew Uncle Stewart had touched on a nerve. So I spoke to him about everything I remembered. Where he was raised; how he met my mother; how much he was revered at work and by his friends. I told him about how he had trained my best friend, his Uncle John, during his residency years. All the awards he had won and how he came about to start his company Genomica.

Charlie listened and reflected in silence. Then he quietly said, "I wish I could have met him."

We were driving home when discussing this so I said, "Well, we can at least do the next best thing." I turned right at the next intersection, drove down to a flower store and picked up two flower arrangements, and had Charlie hold one of them. We then drove to Rockhill Cemetery. Sometimes you have a sense about something. I knew Charlie wanted to see this and I did too. We walked together to my father's burial site. Charlie laid the flowers there and looked very carefully at the inscription. I was filled with too much emotion to speak and my eyes were filled with tears. Charlie had come here a few times when he was younger, but I don't think he had quite grasped the significance of it all. We then walked over a few feet to where my other Charlie, Charles XII, had been laid to rest. I had a quiet conversation in my heart and put down the flowers I had been holding for him.

Charlie observed it all but didn't know what to say. He too was gripped by the emotions and was very quiet.

The next few weeks I didn't ask Charlie much about what he had learned. I assumed if Uncle Stewart had been counting back in sequence, he would be speaking about my Charlie who passed away close to sixteen years ago. I wanted Charlie to bring up the subject himself but he didn't, so I didn't ask.

The next week when I went to pick up Charlie at Uncle Stewart's home, I rang the doorbell and no one answered. The door was open so I walked inside. There was no Uncle Stewart and no Bonnie anywhere in sight. Charlie wasn't waiting in the living room as he always had in past visits. I called out their respective names and didn't hear a response. I treaded toward the staircase, and as I came closer, I could hear some sounds coming from the floor below.

I went down the stairs and there they were: both Charlie and Uncle Stewart sitting at the piano. They were playing together. I had mentioned that Uncle Stewart had played piano for a brief period when he was a child. Uncle Stewart saw me as I reached the bottom of the staircase. He smiled warmly and said, "Good afternoon, Charles. Sorry, we were so caught up that I just lost track of time."

"You look like you were both having fun," I said.

"Having fun? Were we having fun, Charlie?" Uncle Stewart asked, looking at him with a smile. "We are having a great time!"

Charlie hugged Uncle Stewart before leaving and said, "I can't wait until I see you next week."

The following week and every week after that, I learned to come downstairs in Uncle Stewart's home to the piano room to find Charlie. As Uncle Stewart pointed out, "I haven't had this much fun since I was eight years old." I hadn't given much thought to this, but Charlie had found a way to reawaken Uncle Stewart's passion for music.

XXVI

The following weekend there was the family retreat at the MacKinnon cottage. Charlie and Uncle Stewart had thought of a novel way for Uncle Stewart to tell his stories. Everyone had to come inside for this. Uncle Stewart usually enjoyed telling his stories outdoors, as he preferred the setting of the beautiful gardens and nature; but it was different this time. We had an elegant grand piano, which for many years was nothing more than a decorative item in a room that functioned essentially as storage. Uncle Stewart had it brought out and had placed in the living room. All the children were asked to come inside, gather around, and sit within close proximity to this piano.

Uncle Stewart then started narrating his story and Charlie would set the mood to a backdrop of his music. It caught the attention of everyone in the family. We all eventually migrated inside to see what was happening; we were sitting on the floor and along the stairway to have a better view. Watching Uncle Stewart's stories synchronized to a background melody brought a different dimension to the experience. Every heightened moment, every suspense, and every joy or sadness now had a beautiful tune to accompany it. He then told the story of Grandpa William's heroics in the war in the form of a poem to Charlie's music.

It was the time of World War II,
A dark and cold night in the winter of 1942.

Grandpa William was a young soldier at hand,
And this was the night for the battalion's last stand.

Sirens were sounding, soldiers were marching,
This was no ordinary night as explosions were launching.

Till the morning dawn Grandpa worked at his station,
Side by side with the heroes of our nation.

When that tireless night had ended and all was bleak,
A loud crash could be heard atop the mountain peak.

An aircraft was seen with fire and smoke,
Bearing our flag with passengers afloat.

Few were left to help with the injuries so many,
Alone he journeyed with courage so plenty.

He climbed to the top to see if anyone was alive,
It's impossible they cried; no one could survive.

He pushed and forced and up the mountain he went,
Reaching that summit he just wouldn't relent.

Into the blaze he stepped with power,
Forgetting his life and serving till the last hour.

They watched and waited and nothing transpired,
Could this be the end as time had expired?

Then he emerged with a soldier on his arm,
Safely carrying him away from harm.

With more passengers he stormed back into the fire,
The plane was exploding it was down to the wire.

Grandpa William saved the life of five armed forces,
And journeyed down the mountain with limited resources.

When the officers awoke and asked about their hero,
It was none other than soldier CS-901910.

On his return home there was a letter at his Manor,
Invitation to a ceremony for his Medallion of Valor.

I had to take a moment to appreciate what I was witnessing. The significance of this was more than the current performance. While Uncle Stewart was instrumental in connecting Charlie to his history, he wasn't nearly as successful as Charlie who had connected Uncle Stewart to his music. I just didn't think that was possible. There are some immovable fixtures in life that one becomes accustomed to. You wake up in the morning and the sun is there; when spring time comes you expect to hear birds singing; and then there is Uncle Stewart—speak to him for five minutes and he'll have you immersed in MacKinnon history as though you were there. Charlie apparently was the countermeasure to Uncle Stewart's magic. He had found a way to sway Uncle Stewart and reunite him with his music.

"Greatness cannot be stopped, nor can it be contained. Resist it and it will surge like a storm from the middle of the ocean." That was a line Charles II used in his manuscript of 1663 to describe the history of Charles I. I appreciated that line in a certain way with my last Charlie, and now I was appreciating it from a completely different perspective with this one. Any deviance and the universe will have its own corrective measures to neutralize the imbalance. History would ultimately remember you in one of two ways: either as the person who tried to stop it, or as the person who aided its process. I did not want to be on the wrong side of history no matter what the cost would be to me personally.

When they completed the story, everyone was looking at Grandpa William for a response. Finally Clyde asked him, "How did you like it?"

Grandpa didn't appear too happy, "First of all," he said, "I want to say thank you to Charlie for that beautiful music. I am grateful; it was wonderful." Then he looked over at Uncle Stewart and said, "Stewart, I'm not dead yet; why are you telling stories about me? Unless you're trying to tell me something?"

Uncle Stewart replied, "A good story is a good story, what difference does it make?"

Then Abigail asked Grandpa, "Can we see the medallion?"

Grandpa was uncomfortable with the entire situation and shook his head. "There is no medallion; it is just a story." He then stood up and said before leaving, "I'm an old man and need my rest; if you don't mind I will go to sleep now."

I don't think he liked the attention drawn to him. I had heard from my father many years ago that over the decades the families of each of those soldiers had visited at some point with their children and even with their grandchildren to express their gratitude.

We continued to encourage Charlie to compose his music. Sarah and I still agreed not to allow his compositions to be released until Charlie had the maturity to handle the implications. Sarah had asked Charlie to write his music down, and he had remarked by pointing to his head, "But they are safer up here."

The expression was all too familiar to me. I had been suffering from that ill-fated decision for many years now—too many to count!—which is why I insisted he write everything down and store his compositions safely in his room.

One time I arrived home from work and saw Charlie and Chloe playing their instruments in our living room. I don't think Charlie realized I was coming home early that day, so I quietly went to my study room. I tried to stay focused on my own work but I couldn't help but overhear them. Charlie was playing for Chloe one of his own compositions. Well, I guess you can say my son hadn't changed much since he was a little boy in wanting to share everything he owned with his favorite friends.

After he finished playing, Chloe said, "That's beautiful, Charlie. It's really amazing."

"Let's play it together," Charlie told her. "This piece goes very well with the violin. When I release it, I want you to play it with me."

"Sure, if I can actually do it," Chloe sighed.

"You can—don't worry."

She stopped shortly after playing and said, "I don't know if I can do this; it's too difficult."

"You can, trust me," he said, comforting her.

They tried again and well, she was right in that she couldn't actually play it. Chloe had trouble completing the piece, and that was when I heard Charlie playing the violin for the first time. He stepped in to show her step by step. He played beautifully; it was immaculate.

Well, at least I had discovered that my son would have been an equally great violin player; what I also knew was that he hadn't followed my advice on not sharing his music with anyone. I couldn't help but worry if Dawson would use that for another one of his humanitarian projects.

Later in the winter, Hannah and Michael came to visit us in Wilmette. Hannah was twenty-eight weeks pregnant with their third child and their delivery would not be until the spring. Their first two children, Amelia and Nicholas, were eleven and eight years old and they would need someone to take care of them if they were both in the hospital for the delivery.

Sarah had been there for Hannah for the birth of her previous children and promised to be there again. She was also Hannah's only remaining family that lived nearby. Their mother, Lynn, had remarried eighteen years ago and had moved to Australia. Despite keeping in touch with telephone calls, their contact had been significantly limited over the years.

After a few months, my relationship with Charlie eventually restored to where it had been prior to the setback of the concert last summer. I had Uncle Stewart to thank for that. I could see Charlie gradually reconnecting with his family roots.

Unfortunately, just as we were capable of making plans, so was Dawson. I had noticed Sarah was spending more time with him. I'm not sure what he had done to mend fences with her, but he had achieved it. Whatever agreement we had with respect to Dawson was apparently forgotten. They would spend afternoons together. I discovered all this one evening as I was driving home and happened to take a different turn and drove close to Dawson's home. I had to stop the car to confirm what I had just witnessed. It was Sarah and Dawson sitting on a park bench together. Sarah never brought up the subject, as she never mentioned Dawson's name in my presence. I decided that I wouldn't comment on the subject either; I was going to keep my promise to John and not instigate an argument.

Dawson also had his measures on influencing Charlie. While Charlie was bringing Chloe to our home less frequently in view of my feelings, I couldn't stop him from seeing Chloe at her own home. My concern with Chloe was not so much for herself to the degree that it was in relation to her father's influence.

As the seasons passed, Dawson began showing his true colors—unfiltered. I put together these details many years later, but one time Dawson had taken both Chloe and Charlie to a restaurant for a GSA event. He had escalated his distaste for the genetic industry and counseled both of them on how their efforts could change the fortunes of mankind. He pointed to Charlie and asked, "Who chose your name?"

Charlie began explaining the tradition of names in the MacKinnon family history, to which Dawson quickly interrupted, "So it was neither your choice nor your parents, was it, Charlie? Your destiny was picked for you."

Dawson looked at him more sternly before saying, "And who made that choice, someone in the 1500s?" Some of the agents from the GSA began laughing before receiving a cold stare from Dawson.

"Charlie, does that even make sense?" he said, raising his voice. "Everything that you are, and all that you do—your hopes, your aspirations, your identity, is predetermined many generations before you; a generation that history now looks back on as being archaic and clueless in their practices. Did anyone even stop to think what you want to be and what your choices are in this matter? No, they didn't, did they? And why not?"

"I hadn't thought of that," Charlie said as he started to ponder on what he was being told.

Dawson intensified his tone. "The genetic industry, as it is unfolding right now, does exactly that! We are robbing the next generation of their identity and the right to shape their own destiny. We want to choose everything: what they look like, how they think, their traits, their personality. We want to write the script and force an agenda even before they are born. Tell me, did that generation have any choice in this matter? We just gave ourselves the right to choose for them, didn't we? And why is that? This is as absurd as someone from five hundred years ago wanting to choose your destiny for you, right now!"

Dawson then softened his tone and amicably said:

"Charlie, I think you're unique! You are special! You are you, and there isn't another one like you. You have your own thoughts, your own hopes, and are entitled to your own opinions. You deserve the right to write your own script, determine your own future, and the power to choose your own destiny."

Dawson had been planning another event and had ultimately brought up the subject to ask Charlie to perform one of his compositions. Charlie had been tempted to, but ended up providing an excuse to decline in view of my strict instructions to avoid Dawson; of course, had he firmly adhered to my advice he would have never even entertained this discussion.

Then one day at Genomica we received a visit from Devon Jackson. He had come on his own initiative to let us know to expect an audit soon and hinted for us to have our affairs in order. In brief, he was telling us that a tsunami was coming. I knew this would be the final act of Dawson's schemes; the fact that it had taken this long made me suspicious about the scale of his plan.

I spoke to John that afternoon and let him know what Mr. Jackson had said. He wasn't surprised and told me, "Charles, even without the GSA not too many new patients are actually requesting our treatments anymore. They just don't trust it." Most of our patients, while they had some movement, were back in their wheelchairs.

He was right, but what I hadn't known was that John had already started working one day a week at the Richmond Hospital. This is the same hospital where Uncle Stewart was the chief of staff.

"Why don't you join us and work there for one day a week?" John asked.

My pride wouldn't allow me. "Thank you, but I'm okay for now."

"I'm on call for June 16th. Can you at least cover my call?" John and his wife Sandra wanted to fly to Boston to visit some relatives. I knew he was also asking this favor as a way of trying to encourage the opportunity for me to start looking elsewhere for employment.

"Sure, John, no problem. Send me the paperwork we need to arrange this." I had worked at the Richmond Hospital part-time many years ago when I had first graduated and still visited Uncle Stewart there from time to time.

Speaking to John made me realize we were running out of options. I had a few cancellations that afternoon so I went home at lunchtime for one last search of Charlie's room to see if I could find any clues he might have left for the solution. I realized that in my prior searches I had never moved any furniture or fixtures to see if it had fallen in and around it. I parked my car in the garage as I normally do and ran upstairs to his room. This time I didn't leave anything to the imagination.

I looked under his mattress even though I knew it was physically impossible for him to have left it there. Still, I had to check. Then I put my mobile phone on the bed as I searched underneath the headboard and behind each layer of the curtains in the off chance it may have slipped there too; there was no sign. I moved his table and looked behind it— still nothing. I went through all his files, page by page, and read every corner. I had checked all these before but sometimes our eyes miss the obvious, so it was worth a second look. Regrettably, it wasn't there. Charlie hadn't done it. I was not only desperate but clearly in denial and simply had to accept that fact and move on. More importantly, I now had to accept the fate of Genomica. As I sat there and was lost in my own thoughts, I heard the front door of our house open. It had to be Sarah.

I was about to call out and let her know I was home when I heard her speaking to someone. I walked closer to the edge of the door to listen when I heard Dawson's voice.

"Can I get you something to drink?" she asked him.

Dawson responded, "Do you have coffee?"

"Sure, I'll make you a fresh pot. How do you take it?"

"Black and two sugars."

To say I was surprised to hear his voice in my home was an understatement; this was a direct violation of the agreement I had with Sarah. How this person managed to squeeze back into my family's life was beyond the ken of my understanding. I came out of Charlie's bedroom to the edge of the staircase to see if I could obtain a better view of what was happening.

I really wanted to go downstairs and tell him off as well as Sarah, but all I kept hearing in my mind was John's voice telling me, "Don't fight with Sarah over Dawson." I painfully decided to take his advice.

After Sarah brought him his coffee, I sat down on the edge of the staircase to watch the theater in front of me. Dawson was smooth. I don't know what Sarah had seen in him to even allow him in her sphere of friends. He sure knew how to lead into any subject from an indirect path.

He asked her, "How long have you lived in this home?"

Sarah said, "We moved here about thirty years ago."

"Wow, you never thought about a change?" he asked.

I was annoyed at these questions. It was obvious where he was heading. *How could Sarah not see past this guy?*

"No, I hadn't really thought about it," she said.

"Have you heard of George Bernard Shaw?"

"No, I haven't heard of him—should I?"

"He won the Nobel Prize in Literature in 1925. One of the famous quotes he was known to have said was, 'Progress is impossible without change, and those who cannot change their minds cannot change anything.'"

Sarah was quietly making the connections to what Dawson was trying to tell her with his line of reasoning. She then said, "That's interesting."

"Sarah, look at how happy Chloe and Charlie are together. It is as though they were always meant to be siblings."

"I agree; I felt that the day they met," she said.

"I did too. They were so good together. It was as if it was destiny for them to meet. They had this unspoken connection," Dawson told her.

They both smiled while I was trying to tame my anxiety. Then Dawson made a move for his final play. "The connection you and I have is also something I've always cherished. It was also there from the time we met. There are certain things that are just meant to be. I just think we could all be a happy family: you, me, Chloe, and Charlie."

Sarah stood there and didn't say anything.

My heart felt as though it was racing at a million beats per minute. I was waiting for her response and I didn't know what offended me more, the fact that he had made a pass at my wife, or that he was doing it in my own home in front of the portraits of all my ancestors.

I could see Sarah's face but I couldn't figure out what was running through her mind. It disturbed me not knowing what she was thinking.

The phone rang—it might as well have. I wasn't ready to see this in my own home.

All I could hear Sarah say on the phone was, "No worries. I'll be there in time to pick up the kids from school and bring them to the hospital later." When Sarah hung up, she looked at Dawson and said, "I have to go. Hannah is in labor; her water has broken."

"We'll talk later," Dawson said as he finished his coffee.

"Yes. Yes, we will," Sarah replied, and helped Dawson to the door.

I saw her run downstairs to the basement, and after a few minutes she emerged with her favorite pink plastic box. I could see her running upstairs to gather her clothes.

I tiptoed back from the steps to Charlie's room, and watched through a small opening of the door. It would be somewhat awkward if she were to see me now.

Sarah went inside our bedroom and collected some of her clothes to put inside the container. She also took the gift she had prepared and placed it in the box and closed its lid. Sarah then picked up her cell phone, scrolled through it, and dialed a number. My mind was numb for a few seconds watching her calmly before immediately realizing, *my phone*, and anxiously looked at the bed I had left it on. I glanced back across and could see Sarah was waiting for the line to connect. I darted across the room to reach my mobile device and quickly switched the ringer to vibrate, just in time as the phone sounded.

Needless to say, I watched but didn't answer the call; Sarah left home shortly after. Fortunately, her car was parked outside the garage door so she hadn't seen my car inside the garage either. A few minutes after she drove, she decided to call me back again.

I answered this time, "Hello."

"Hi, Charles."

"Hi, Sarah."

"I just heard from Hannah. She is on route to the hospital and will probably deliver later tonight. I took some clothes with me in case it goes late into the evening."

"Sure. No problem, Sarah. Everything else okay?"

"Yes. It's all fine."

"Alright then; have a safe journey and send my love to everyone there."

"Thank you, Charles. I won't hold you; I know you're busy. We'll talk later?"

"Yes, for sure. Bye, Sarah."

Well, I guess it shouldn't have been unforeseen that Dawson had actually done this. However, I was surprised that he had waited twelve years to do it, which made me wonder what was next.

I received a call from Sarah that night just after midnight that Hannah had not gone into labor yet. They were planning on waiting until tomorrow before deciding if she would need a C-section.

I smiled, as it reminded me of when Charlie was born. *That was a special time*, I thought to myself. There was so much hope and optimism then that I hadn't felt in years.

Hannah had her C-section the next morning and delivered a beautiful baby girl: Scarlett Eleanor Delaney, 7lbs 2oz, born on June 7th at 9am.

XXVII

    Charlie left home early that morning so he hadn't heard of his cousin's birth. While I kept my promise to John with respect to not complaining about Dawson when I was with Sarah, I could not keep that same promise with Charlie.

    That morning I needed to clear my thoughts so I decided to take my car for a drive. I took the same route that had me course near Dawson's home. I have to admit, there was a curiosity I couldn't explain that made me want to pass there. Maybe I had a premonition, maybe it was a prompting of the soul, or maybe I just knew my son. In any case, a few miles into my drive I saw what I never could have imagined. It was Dawson and Charlie walking along the sidewalk. There was no Chloe or any other person—just the two of them together.

    I drove by initially and pretended I didn't see anything. I passed maybe 50 feet before stopping the car in the middle of the road. Fortunately, there were no cars behind me. I took a moment to gather my thoughts. Did I really want to do what I was thinking of doing?

I didn't have a choice. There is such a thing called self-respect. I wouldn't be able to respect myself if I pretended not to have seen anything. "Sorry, John," I said to myself, "I am not able to hold back on this one." I shifted the gear into reverse, drove back, and rolled down my window. My appearance probably caught Charlie's attention as he certainly recognized my car. He was stunned and had a worried look on his face.

"Charlie, get in the car!" I shouted.

He hesitated and stood motionless. "Now, Charlie. Inside!"

He begrudgingly treaded toward my vehicle. Dawson walked up slowly and with a smirk on his face said, "It's okay, Charlie. Go with your father. We'll talk later."

"Good day, Dr. MacKinnon," he said slyly with a smug smile. I wasn't going to validate his greeting with a response nor did I want to look at him. Charlie opened the door and sat inside. I rolled up my window with a push button to close it on Dawson's grin and simply drove off.

As I was driving, I could not hold back my frustration. "Did we or did we not agree that you weren't to spend any time with that man?"

He didn't answer.

"I asked you a question, Charlie."

He didn't respond.

I pulled the car to the side of the road about a mile down from where we had started and turned off the ignition. I repeated the question again, "Did we or did we not have an agreement?"

"Dad, I'm fifteen years old, I'm not a kid anymore. I can choose who I want to spend time with."

"If you're not a kid then stop acting like one; that man can't be trusted! I am your father. It's my responsibility to protect and guide you. That doesn't stop when you're fifteen or eighteen. Even if you're seventy, I'll still be your father. If I'm alive, I will still guide you. That's our tradition."

"That's your tradition. It's not mine," Charlie grumbled.

"Is that so?" I said, and paused to digest what I just heard. "I have given you the freedom to choose your path in life— your passions, your interests, your career. I have sacrificed everything so you could be happy. What I will not do is stand by and allow you to grow up to be an arrogant human being that doesn't understand anything about loyalty, respect, and courtesy. Do you understand?"

Charlie sat motionless. I wanted to collect my emotions before starting the car again. When I turned on the ignition, Charlie opened his door and walked out. I quickly stepped out and said, "Charlie, where are you going? Get back in the car!"

Charlie continued to walk away.

"Charlie!" I shouted. "Charlie!"

He then crossed the street and went into a park where I wouldn't be able to follow him.

I could have left my car there and just ran after him, but it didn't feel like the right thing to do. Chasing after him would have compromised my authority as his parent and validated his behavior; if I had pursued further discipline, it may also have done irreparable damage to our relationship.

So I came back inside the car and thought about it. The more I reflected, the more I felt helpless as there was nothing to do. Aggression has never been part of my character.

However, I couldn't resist slamming my steering wheel with the palm of my right hand. I realized after the third strike that I had hurt my wrist and grasped it quickly with my other arm. I was frustrated. I felt incapacitated to do anything. If this had been chess, this is where you'd call checkmate. Dawson's tactics were now finally unveiling like a grand show. I just placed my forehead on the steering wheel and felt completely powerless.

I started driving home and my mind was racing through a number of different thoughts; that's when I saw the sign for Gillson Park. It had been many years since I had come here. I parked my car to the side, walked toward the waters, and remembered the times I came here with Charlie prior to his untimely passing. I couldn't help but remember the happiness of those times, all our conversations, the hopes we had. I shared in his joys and his sorrows.

As I walked along the waters I came across the rock where we took our last picture as a family. I stared at it, remembering the bliss of that moment as though it were yesterday. I finally sat on that rock and asked myself question after question like a victim on a trial stand being interrogated by the prosecutor.

"Where exactly did I go wrong?"

There were many instances in the past where I had wondered if I had faulted somewhere, but this time I believed it. I always debated how it was that my previous Charlie disliked Dawson simply by looking at him, yet this Charlie espoused him like a father figure. Why was that? I didn't have a good answer.

The only explanation that I could think of was maybe children read off their parents' emotions. When Dawson walked into my office some twenty years ago, Charlie could feel the tension in my general interaction and automatically adjusted his emotions. My current Charlie didn't have the same introduction. Sarah and his best friend Chloe were very close to Dawson, so perhaps it was just an entirely different experience for him. I don't know.

Why was this Charlie a musical prodigy, but my last one brilliant in the neurosciences? Which one had it right?

I had thought about this since Charlie's first concert. Did I miss something the first time around? I had never encouraged my last Charlie toward neurosurgery; it was always motivated by his own inclinations and initiatives. I never questioned it either because he was simply exceptional—the best the MacKinnon family had ever seen; now I wondered, was it really a genuine interest or had it been because he was in search of his own cure. He had limited movements of his hands so you could say he never had the opportunity to express a musical interest even if he had one. If Charlie didn't have his accident would things have turned out differently? Again, I don't know.

Why had my first Charlie loved baseball so much, but this one could care less if the sport even existed?

I remember how much we enjoyed watching baseball games together. I still find this a mystery. The only explanation that comes to mind is that my father loved baseball and took Charlie to his first game, which incidentally was the last time he saw his grandfather. Charlie wore that hat as a memento and was intimately attached to it. He also felt deeply connected to my father and baseball just went with that. Sometimes those early associations create deeper bonds than we assume. Was this experience genuine interest or just an emotional connection? Once again, I don't know.

Why was this Charlie so close to his mother but the last

one so close to me?

I love both of my Charlies, but one had been my best friend and the other was on most days indifferent toward me. How is that even possible? The simple explanation would be, I connected with my Charlie over his medical condition and that provided us with a common goal. Though logical, I'm not sure I can accept that answer. I connected with Charlie since the day of his birth. What happened? Where did this path deviate?

Finally, if I could speak to my own father right now, what would he want me to do?

It had been almost twenty-seven years since my father passed away. I still feel the void that I never had a chance to say goodbye—not even at his funeral. The closest connection I have felt to my father since then has been through the recurrent dreams I have had for over twenty-seven years. Yet even in those dreams I never had the opportunity to speak to him before waking. Why will my father not speak to me?

The more I thought about all these scenarios, the more I came up with questions rather than answers. I started walking along the park and into the surrounding streets and scenery. I wondered if this was the universe's retribution for not being completely honest in what I had done, with Sarah and with myself. Did I use my love for Charlie as a sword and shield to justify every means to an end?

Of course, I could also be over-thinking this; that wouldn't be the first time. Maybe each person is nothing more than a pinball whose direction is changed by the chances and accidents of life. I don't know. What I did know was that I wished everything could be exactly as it was when I had Charlie the first time. I was happy then. I would take back the condition of those times even with its challenges.

I was immersed in these thoughts, but I knew I should head home to see if Charlie had returned. When I arrived, I walked inside the kitchen to see if he was there. He wasn't. I looked in all the rooms as well as his bedroom. "Charlie?" I called out. There was no response. No one was home.

I tried calling Sarah. She didn't answer, so I decided to dial Michael's number to find out where she was. Michael seemed surprised by my phone call. "The doctors were planning to keep Hannah in the hospital for a couple more days after they did the C-section. Sarah said she had to return to Wilmette to tie up a few loose ends before coming back. Didn't she tell you?"

"No, I've been occupied all day so she may have tried to reach me," I said, but I knew that wasn't the reason.

Michael then said, "Sarah left here in the morning, about five hours ago."

Rockford is only ninety minutes away. Even with bad traffic, it wouldn't take more than two to three hours. I waited and Sarah finally arrived home after another thirty minutes. I didn't tell her I had spoken to Michael. "How is Hannah doing?" I asked.

"She's well, but she's going to be kept in the hospital for a couple more days."

Sarah was a little rushed. She had come back to pick up her make-up bag that she had forgotten.

"That's all you came back for?" I asked.

"Yes. I want to look good in the photos. These pictures last a lifetime, you know that."

"Sure, no problem," I said. "How was traffic coming here?"

"Great. It was as smooth as I've ever seen it."

I silently nodded in acknowledgement.

XXVII

"Where is Charlie?" she asked.

"Not sure," I said. "Last I spoke to him he was going for a walk in the park."

Well, if Sarah had come back it certainly wasn't to see me or Charlie, and it wasn't just for her make-up kit. She had spent close to three hours elsewhere and I didn't want to ask where—I knew. It was neither the right time to talk about this nor about Charlie; I wouldn't be able to bring up either subject without arguing about Dawson. She spoke little and left moments later, hurrying to get back.

I was all alone so I went to Charlie's room and took off my jacket and waited for Charlie to come home; he didn't. I finally went downstairs to my study room where I reflected on my plight. The writing desk in front of me belonged to Charles III, and sitting on it was a black manual from my father, nicely enclosed in its case. He had written this manual to lay out the specifications for the design of GEMA; this reference book was one of the few mementos I had from my father in my home. I couldn't help but wonder if any of this even mattered anymore. I finally walked over to the living room and fell asleep on the couch while waiting for Charlie.

In the morning I heard a loud knock on the door. I woke up and mumbled, "It must be Charlie!" I rushed to open the door with anticipation, when suddenly, I saw seven men standing outside my front entrance in black suits. It was the GSA along with armed forces. There were another twelve men surrounding the premises.

"Dr. MacKinnon, we have a search warrant for your home."

"A search warrant? Why?" I asked, feeling my heart thumping.

The men stormed inside and searched every corner of the

house. There was no Dawson, but make no mistake, he was behind this entire operation. Several of the agents had an earpiece and I knew they were talking to someone on the other side with complete knowledge of my home.

"Downstairs to the right?" one of the agents was confirming as he was listening to his instructions.

I protested in panic, "You don't have a right to be here."

I tried to stop them, but they pushed me aside. They ignored my plea and several men intrusively rushed downstairs. They went specifically to the room where I had stored the wooden treasure chest of Charlie's items. The person at the other end of the earpiece was providing clear instructions on how to navigate, where to hunt, and what to take.

I saw one of their men leaving with the wooden chest that had "Charles XII" marked on it. Afterwards, the same agent, listening to his earphone, stopped and turned back, and said to the other agents standing, "We actually need to take everything in that room."

They then started clearing all the boxes and items one by one until the room was empty. That's when Devon Jackson walked into my home. Nobody was providing me with any clear answers, so I asked him, "What is going on here?"

"Sorry, Dr. MacKinnon, as of today GSA is auditing Genomica for unsafe medical practices. They have reason to believe that important company documents are also stored here at your home. That's why we are here."

I knew what they were after and it wasn't company documents. I watched a few men hurry upstairs to Charlie's room. That would be my current Charlie. I was downstairs speaking to Devon Jackson when this was all happening so I was distracted. They were walking down carrying several items. I could see the end of the hairbrush in one of the see-through containers. They knew exactly which rooms to search. This was a surgical strike. One of the agents stopped to listen to his earpiece. I asked Mr. Jackson, "That's Dawson, isn't it, he's talking to?"

He didn't answer my question but the glum look on his face confirmed my suspicion. Before leaving, Mr. Jackson came to speak to me once more. I could see he wasn't comfortable telling me what he was about to say next. "I have been advised to tell you," he said as he cleared his throat, "while your hospital may continue to treat its current patients, no new patients can be treated until we finish our investigation. That's coming straight from the top." That was his discrete way of saying straight from Dawson.

I received some calls from the office shortly after. The GSA had come there too. There was a lot of commotion and no one knew what to do or where to go. I was exhausted. I had slept little in the last few days. Things were already up in the air with Sarah and now my company was on the verge of being taken away from me. I could also face possible jail time if they discovered where Charlie's genes had come from. I was now witnessing Dawson's grand plan unfolding in full force. The tides were coming. Not only had he tried to steal my family, he was now putting me behind bars to perfectly remove me from the equation. There would be no ethical dilemmas for anyone if I were to be in prison. He had also conveniently removed himself from the equation so the bloodstains of this would not be on his hands. I didn't know who to turn to; my support system had been cut off. I wasn't going to call Sarah, not with what had happened. Who could I trust?

Then John called me. "Charles. They've come. The GSA

is here."

"I know, John. They were here too. I'll be coming shortly."

I prepared to depart and looked around for my key fob; I recalled leaving it in my jacket that I had left in Charlie's room last night. I ran upstairs and found it on his bed. It saddened me looking at his covers that had been neatly made, as it only confirmed that Charlie hadn't slept in his bed last night.

As I was hurrying downstairs toward the front door, I had to stop myself as I noticed something from the corner of my eye. I looked in the kitchen and there was Charlie's bowl sitting on the table next to an opened cereal box. That definitely was not there the night before. I felt reassured that at least he came home for breakfast though it was odd I had missed it.

I spent the day at the hospital putting out fires and trying to bring peace and normalcy to the worried staff. Just before the end of the day, John approached me. "I know this is a bad time, but are you still okay to cover my call? I'm flying out later tonight with Sandra. The hospital said they tried to reach you just now but there was no response."

I had completely forgotten that I was covering for John. I looked at my phone and there was a missed call. "Sorry, John. I will contact them right now. Have a safe journey and not to worry; everything will be taken care of."

"Thanks again for doing this for me, Charles."

"No thanks needed. Enjoy your vacation."

I walked to my car and called the hospital. It wasn't anything urgent but it did require me to come in. I stopped at my house on route to see if Charlie had finally arrived. There was no sign of him. I was worried but couldn't help but wonder if he was with Dawson.

I drove by Dawson's home and did what I never thought I would do. I stepped out of my car and started searching the perimeter. I was looking through every window to see if Charlie was with him. I started from the front and worked my way from the sides to the back. Charlie wasn't there and no one was home.

I went to the hospital and attended to the patient I was called for. I then decided to visit Uncle Stewart in his office. He was finishing his workday. I knocked on the door and asked, "Is it okay if I come in to speak with you about something?"

"Charles, I didn't know you were here tonight. Of course, please make yourself comfortable," he said as he was writing his notes.

I looked around the room as I waited for Uncle Stewart to finish. My eyes gravitated toward the medical history book he had on his desk. It was open to a page with a painting from the 1500s. It was depicting a person attempting a "Burr hole": a neurosurgical procedure drilling a hole to relieve pressure within the skull. This practice was occasionally misused amongst an ignorant few back in that era. They foolishly claimed it would help release evil spirits from people's heads. This unfortunately became the impetus to sabotage and justify the persecution of Charles I. Uncle Stewart finally appeared ready; he looked at me and said, "Tell me—how are you doing?"

"I'm well, thank you. I'm actually covering for John

tonight."

"That's right. It had slipped my mind. Where is John going again?"

"He has a family function to attend with his wife this weekend."

"That reminds me," Uncle Stewart said, "your grandparents' seventy-fifth anniversary is happening in two weeks."

"Wow, I didn't know that."

"We'll be having a big celebration at the MacKinnon cottage."

"I'll be looking forward to it then," I said.

"So what did you want to speak to me about?" Uncle Stewart asked.

"Oh nothing, I was just wondering if Charlie had called you in the last day."

Uncle Stewart seemed perplexed at the question. "Why? Is he not home?"

I shook my head and said, "No, he was a little upset last night; I thought maybe he may have called you."

"Anything we should be concerned about?" he asked.

"No, I don't think so. You know, just your typical teenage problems."

Uncle Stewart stood up to put on his suit jacket and said, "Well, I'm going to go home now. If I hear from him, I'll call you to let you know right away."

"Thanks, Uncle Stewart, I really appreciate it."

I stepped out of Uncle Stewart's office and went to eat dinner in the cafeteria, which was empty for the evening. While sitting there I decided to call Sarah with the hope that she might know something about Charlie. Fortunately, she picked up her phone right away. She was with Hannah and her newborn. They were all so excited for the birth of Scarlett that I didn't want to mention anything about the GSA or my concerns about Charlie. However, during the conversation I did ask her, "Did you have a chance to speak with Charlie after you left?"

"No, I haven't had time to call anyone," she said with an excited voice and the sound of Scarlett crying in the background.

That pretty much answered it. Sarah didn't know of Charlie's whereabouts. I couldn't bring myself to call him for fear that he might be with Dawson so I called home instead and no one picked up the phone. I waited a couple of hours and tried again, and still no response.

I started walking, looking at my cell phone, debating what to do; I finally decided to swallow my pride and call Charlie's mobile and see if he was okay. The sound of the phone dialing went on and on. Charlie didn't believe in voicemail so you could have the phone ringing for a long time before tiring to hang up. It continued dialing, and while thinking aloud, I complained, "Come on, Charlie, pick up the phone!"

As I passed by the backdoor of the emergency room, I could hear what felt like an echo from my dial. I looked at my phone and then in the direction of the ring and there was a definite synchrony. I ended the call and listened carefully: the ringing had stopped. I waited a few seconds, pondered, and decided to dial again; the ringing started once more and I could hear its faint sound in the distance.

I opened the door, stepped inside the emergency room and looked around, following the sound with my steps; a few moments later, the ringing suddenly ceased. I glanced at my phone—the call had also ended. I quickly started searching, walking toward the patient rooms, and peeking inside each one. Then I saw a figure in one room from a slight opening of the door; it looked like Charlie. I smiled and was about to walk in when I heard a plea from the nurse behind me. "Dr. MacKinnon, I'm glad you're here; we need your help in the trauma unit ASAP."

I started walking and following the nurse, but my thoughts were clearly with Charlie—looking back, eager to return. I stepped inside the trauma room and the team leader, Dr. Juliet Connor, was loudly speaking instructions to the trauma team with the patient on the bed.

"Can we re-check his pulse and blood pressure again?"

That's when Dr. Connor saw me on her right side and quickly walked over and said, "Dr. MacKinnon I'm glad you're here. We have a fifteen-year-old patient hit by a motor vehicle with obvious head and neck injuries. He's right now intubated, back-boarded, and collared. His Glasgow Coma Scale is five with a dilated pupil on the right…"

In brief, they were not only concerned about a neck and spinal cord injury; there was also bleeding between the skull and brain that required surgical evacuation of the blood to release the pressure. I was viewing the patient from behind and seeing only the top of the head. I walked closer and could hear the nurse yelling, "His blood pressure is 90/60, pulse of 120, and an oxygen saturation of 88 percent."

There was something unusual about this picture. When I reached the head of the bed and slowly started to see the features of the face—I was shocked and horror-struck. It was Charlie!

"Oh my God, Charlie!" I yelled. Everyone stopped and looked at me.

"Do you know this patient?" the nurse asked.

"Yes. This is my son," I replied. Their faces froze, and for about three seconds the commotion in that trauma room turned into absolute silence.

I looked at Charlie's wound; he was unconscious and bleeding from his head. I requested the nurse to bring me some gauze, panicking, and turned to Dr. Connor and asked, "Does he have any other injuries?"

She looked baffled, and stalled for a few seconds before uttering, "No, I don't believe so."

I replied, "We need to take him to the operating room right now."

"Dr. MacKinnon, I don't think it is a good idea for you to operate on a family member."

I was angry at the suggestion. "We don't have time. He needs to go to the operating room now."

"But, Dr. MacKinnon..." She was pleading her case once more.

"Look," I said, "if I don't do this surgery the next neurosurgeon that comes in will also be related to him. The neurosurgeon you call after that will be related to him as well, and so on. In fact, you'll have to go outside a 100-mile radius to find a neurosurgeon that won't be related to him." I looked at her more sternly and said, "We don't have time for these games."

I stared at Charlie's head; it was bleeding profusely, and I could see the innocence and helplessness in his face. Then I felt something strange occur that had never happened to me before. The sight of Charlie's blood was too much for me to bear. I can't remember what transpired next because I was told I had passed out.

When I woke up everything was a daze. I heard Dr. Connor speaking softly in the corner of the room. "How are you feeling?" she queried.

I was told later that I hit my head on the counter behind me when I fainted. "I'm well. Where's my son?" I asked trying to sit up from the stretcher.

"He's in the operating room. They should be done soon."

"I have to go upstairs then."

"I think you should rest. You had a pretty bad fall. We were all worried, and thought we had a second patient with a serious head injury following your incident."

I didn't follow her instructions again and ran upstairs. By the time I prepared, gowned and went inside, I saw John finishing his work; he looked over his shoulder in my direction and said with a smile, "How are you feeling, Charles?"

"John, you should be on the plane right now. I'm so sorry," I said apologetically.

"They called me just before I was about to board. Don't worry, it was actually the perfect excuse not to go," John said with a laugh.

"How is Charlie?" I asked as I walked up to see the medical records of what had been done.

"Well, we relieved the bleeding in his head. There should be no issues there," he cautiously stated before pausing to search for the right words for what he wanted to tell me next.

I looked at John and said, "What about his neck injury?"

John stalled to answer and motioned to speak before pausing again. He then said, "Let me show you the imaging." John brought me the scans, stood back silently, and left me alone to view it. He knew there was no easy way to tell me. I needed time to digest this on my own.

I studied it carefully and in brief, Charlie had fractures of several of his cervical vertebrae. He was lucky to be alive. His spinal cord was not severed, per se, but there was injury and quite a bit of swelling around it.

John put his hand on my shoulders and said, "We've stabilized the fractures, but we won't know the extent of the damage until after the swelling goes down and we assess him later."

I was silent and didn't have much to say to John's comments.

"Sorry, Charles, I know you've been through this before and how hard it was on you. All we can do now is pray."

Pray was an appropriate word to describe Charlie's circumstances. Even if we had wanted to treat him, with the current GSA's investigation we wouldn't practically be able to do it. It was a matter of hours before they came to take GEMA away from us.

I wanted to call Sarah, but it was past midnight and I knew she was asleep. This is the not the type of news you want to wake someone up with in the middle of the night, and truth be told, we didn't have the complete picture, which made it that much harder to discuss. I decided to call Sarah in the morning.

I can describe how I was feeling about this using a single word: devastated. The hardest part was the guilt I felt for having indirectly hoped for this just yesterday, wishing for everything to be as they were with my first Charlie. The universe hadn't listened to me in the last twenty-seven years and it decided to listen to me now? Why it chose to do so at this moment was beyond my scope of understanding.

My Charlie was now fifteen years old, the same age as when my last Charlie had passed away. I could neither understand nor comprehend the universe's logic. It was at this same age my last Charlie's dreams were shattered; it was at this same stage where all my hope in life was utterly abolished. After patient persistence passing through precipitous years—here we were at it again.

I slept in the hospital that night in a chair beside Charlie's bed in the ICU. I woke up in the morning to see John standing above me, looking at me with his face inches from mine. He was whispering, "Charles, what are you doing here? Go home and sleep on your bed."

I mumbled, "That's okay. I don't want to leave Charlie right now."

"I'm here, don't worry. I'll take care of him," he said with a concern.

John insisted I leave and I probably needed a change of clothes, so I left the hospital for a short while. I arrived home that morning and had a coffee while resting in my study room briefly admiring the pictures sitting on my desk and counter. I was appreciating the photo I had with my father when suddenly I heard the front door unlock and open. It was Sarah.

She walked in and noticed me standing, and for a few seconds there was a quiet stare. We were both surprised to see one another. She finally broke the silence with, "Hannah was discharged early this morning and I wanted to come home before the traffic."

"That's great," I said.

"Where is Charlie? I tried calling him last night, he wouldn't answer his phone."

She could see there was a quiet despondence to my posture. So she asked me, "Is everything okay, what's wrong?" she said with her tone clearly more worried.

"I'm not sure where to begin, maybe you should sit down for this," I said while pointing to the couch.

"Is everything okay with Charlie?" she asked again,

trembling, not wanting to sit.

It's not every day a person has to break bad news to their spouse. I have been through this before and I can tell you it never gets easier; it only becomes harder. Our patience grows thin and we become wearier of the randomness of the universe and the ill-fated chances of life. I looked at Sarah and gently said, "Charlie was in an accident last night."

I could immediately see the panic in her eyes. It's important to understand that I was speaking to her as her husband. I was not a doctor in this equation. As a physician I'm obligated to tell her the entire truth; as her husband I accommodate the rules to what I know works best for her. So it was my intention to communicate this bad news in phases. Hearing it all at once was too much for her to bear. She needed to digest it in small portions so the news had to be piecemealed.

I told her, "Before you worry, you should know that he's okay. I was with him last night and John is with him right now."

"Why? What's happened?" she asked in fright. I knew she would figure out that if a neurosurgeon was involved then it probably was not the best news.

"He was hit by a car last night. He was wearing dark clothing and the driver did not see him crossing the road. Charlie suffered head and neck injuries. His condition has been stabilized, and they'll be doing some further testing. We'll have more answers soon."

This was about as much disappointment as she could bear at that moment. I didn't want to tell her about the extent of the neck injuries and everything that was concerning me. It wasn't the right time.

"Why didn't you call me?" she demanded.

"It was very late; there was nothing you could do. Charlie was stable, and it wouldn't have been safe for you to drive late at night in this state of mind, so I left it until the morning."

Sarah wanted to go to the hospital right away.

"Wait, I'll take you," I told her as we prepared to leave.

We saw John on our arrival who eventually explained to Sarah the remainder of what I hadn't told her. We wouldn't know the extent of Charlie's injuries until later when the swelling had subsided and he regained consciousness. Likewise, we wouldn't know if Charlie could walk or have complete use of his limbs, and the extent to which the body would heal itself in the coming weeks.

Sarah was too familiar with this process. We had lived with that uncertainty for five months with our last Charlie. John assured her it "wouldn't be as bad this time." The extent of the damage on the spinal cord was not the same. We wouldn't be concerned about whether Charlie could breathe on his own volition. We weren't worried about complete loss of neuromuscular function.

I understood intimately what was running through Sarah's mind. First, she was concerned about Charlie's health, his life and his capacity to enjoy it and fulfill his dreams, but somewhere in the back of her mind, she was also worried if this meant the end of his musical career, though she would not want to discuss it at this time. I knew because those were the thoughts that went through my mind when our last Charlie had his accident. I too wondered if that was the end of any possible surgical career.

Sarah never once asked about using our treatments at Genomica for his condition. The news of our company being investigated was broadcasted last evening. She was at the hospital with Hannah for most of the night so she probably didn't hear about it until the morning. I presumed that was the reason she returned early to discuss this with me before hearing the news about Charlie.

Aside from the current challenges, I didn't know which future lay before me. Would I go to prison? If I did, was this part of Dawson's greater plan to fulfill his ambition for a family; or did I have this figured out all wrong, and was I simply leaving Sarah alone with all these obstacles to manage? Not knowing the answer put me in a dilemma as to whether I should feel guilty or not.

As far as going to prison was concerned, in some ways it was the least of my worries and in other ways the most. I had often seen patients on their last days of life; their concern was never for themselves but the suffering of the loved ones they were leaving. I always thought it was interesting that a person could become so altruistic in their final moments. I now had a gleaning of that experience though I was not dying.

Of course, if I were going to prison simply so Dawson could take my place, my time there would be a bitter one. I knew one thing: Dawson wouldn't love Charlie—not the way I did; not now and certainly not with Charlie having any challenges. This is not who he is. So it came as no surprise when later that afternoon we were informed that the GSA would not be taking GEMA today as had been previously scheduled.

Devon Jackson had stopped by earlier to inform John. I knew this sudden change of plans by the GSA was prompted by something and I knew exactly what it was. Shortly after John had provided a complete update to Sarah, she had called Chloe to let her know what had happened to Charlie. I was surprised at the detail with which she had shared of Charlie's condition. I didn't understand at that time the domino effect her news would set in motion. I was even disturbed at the involvement of others, particularly Dawson's daughter in this measure.

Chloe had predictably told Dawson, and he knew he would need GEMA for one more patient. That's why he left it for us knowing I would use it for Charlie. Even though the treatment would last in his case for about fifteen years, that would put Charlie in his thirties before his treatment failed. At that age he wouldn't be Dawson's problem anymore.

John approached me later in the afternoon to tell me about the new development. "I've got some great news regarding GEMA. There may be time for Charlie."

After he provided me with the full update, I asked for his thoughts. "Do you think GEMA would work without another surgical procedure beforehand?"

John mulled it over and said, "Good question. I did as much as I could when we had him in the operating room last night. His injuries are minor enough that it just might be enough. We would need a blood sample and also his stem cells."

I replied, "That's not a problem; we have his umbilical cord blood and tissue back at Genomica," and we could get his blood test done anytime. The more I thought about it the more I realized John could be right. Then again, there really was no another option; we'd have to allow the body an opportunity to heal before considering any surgical procedure. There wasn't enough time for that.

John added, "It's worth a try; if nothing else it buys us time and it will restore most of his function."

Now, we just had to wait for the swelling to come down so to have a clearer picture before assessing for the specific

GEMA treatment he would require. I knew one thing for certain: if nothing else, restoring Charlie's health would consolidate Dawson's plan. I was well aware that the finish line for Charlie also meant the finish line for me.

Although that was in the back of my thoughts, it was the least of my worries. However, I did talk to John about what had happened in my home yesterday with the GSA.

"John, they have both of my Charlie's hair samples. I haven't yet spoken to Sarah about this but I am letting you know, so you're aware of what is coming."

"Don't worry, Charles. We'll find a way through this, we always do."

I admired his confidence though I didn't share his conviction.

"Let's worry about Charlie right now," he said.

I agreed. Charlie was in a medically induced coma and would be kept in that state for at least another few days to allow the brain time to heal. The swelling around his brain had to subside before considering reducing his sedation.

XXVIII

Uncle Stewart came to the ICU later in the afternoon and was stunned to see Charlie's name on the patient list. He was the first to visit us that day. He embraced Sarah and me.

"I've spoken to John and reviewed the files. I promise you, we'll find a way through this."

"Thank you," said Sarah. "Your support means a lot."

Some people make promises they don't keep; others make promises they do keep. It's fair to say that Uncle Stewart was one who never made promises, but when he did, he kept them. He believed your actions speak louder than your words. My father was exactly the same way and came from the same school of thought. They liked telling stories of other people's good deeds and heroics, but they never spoke about themselves. My father would say, "Charles, be careful of the person who talks too much about themselves. They are hiding something and can't be trusted."

When my father had first met Sarah he instantly liked her and encouraged me to spend time with her. When I told Sarah about it later, she said, "That's impossible. When we met, I was quiet and hardly said anything about myself."

I replied, "I think that's why he liked you."

That was the MacKinnon way: don't talk about yourself and don't make promises you can't keep. So to see Uncle Stewart making a promise now was a rare sight; I knew how much Charlie meant to him.

The news of Charlie being in the hospital reached the rest of our relatives the next day; it was also broadcasted through the media. We were inundated with calls and support. My mother had contacted us and was planning to come as soon as she could.

Chloe also came by later that day after school. She had brought a get-well card signed from all of Charlie's classmates. She was in tears and crying when she sat next to Charlie. Her heartfelt emotions were genuine and I found her affection in some ways amusing. I watched her closely with interest. It was a mystery to see that something so sincere could actually come from Dawson. If genes don't lie, and somehow find their way to come back, then I could assume only one possible conclusion from this: Dawson's wife had to be a special person. Why she was interested in Dawson of course raised another set of questions. Then again, Sarah had befriended Dawson, so I'd probably be the last person to judge. I could only infer one thing from all this: that good people and good judgment were two separate concepts.

"Dr. MacKinnon, I am very sorry about Charlie," Chloe said with her face covered in tears. "If there is anything I can do to help, please let me know."

"Thank you, Chloe; I really appreciate that. It really means a lot to us that you came here for Charlie. I know it would mean a lot to him too." Then I decided to take a page from Sarah's playbook. Thankfully, Sarah had left the room to have coffee so she didn't see this.

"Don't worry, Chloe; we'll be doing some tests in a couple of days and treating him in a couple of weeks. Charlie will be running around after that."

I needed time, and more importantly, I needed to reach Dawson's ears so he could provide us that time. My father would always say, "I never lie, and when I do, it somehow comes true so it's technically not lying." I was praying for that same karma right now.

Dawson needed to hear that there was hope for Charlie; he would walk again, and everything would be back to normal. He needed to hear this so he could make adjustments for his own plans. I had every intention to provide Dawson that hope if it meant restoring Charlie's health. I also knew once Charlie's health was restored, all bets were off. The hyena would come out of his cage and aim straight for his prey.

The next day when I spoke to John, he told me, "The swelling in his brain hasn't come down yet." He was obviously concerned as to how long we'd have GEMA for. There would be risks in Charlie regaining consciousness too soon. We would need to continue to have him medically induced to allow time to heal. John was worried about GEMA being taken away, so he asked me, "Should we use his stem cells now while we still have GEMA?"

I told him, "We could, but I think I have bought us some time. They won't be coming for GEMA anytime soon. Don't worry."

XXVIII

There was a marginal benefit in waiting. For the average person that small difference might not mean much, but for a world-class cello player there was a divergence between having a career versus not having one. Of course, the fact that our treatments ultimately failed in the long run was a dilemma for another day. Right now, we wanted to provide Charlie with the most effective treatment before they took GEMA away, and that meant waiting until the swelling had subsided before running the tests.

The next day, we received more of the same news. The swelling had improved slightly but not enough to reduce his medication. I wasn't feeling optimistic that we'd be seeing the finish line anytime soon.

I realized as the days passed that I needed to have a conversation with Sarah at some point before the truth was made public. I would rather she hear it from me than the GSA or the media. If I was going to prison, it was important for me to let her know that I was sorry. I appreciated all that she had done for me, the life we had lived, and I was regretful of any grievance this would cause her.

I needed to find the right time for this. That night I couldn't sleep. I repeatedly tossed and turned. How exactly do you tell someone who has been your best friend since you were thirteen years old, the person whom you've trusted the most, that the child you've had for fifteen years was based on an entirely dishonest premise? It was always my plan to tell her at some future time. That's the way these things unravel; today becomes tomorrow, then next week and next month, and then you see the years go by and it reaches a juncture where it's just too late.

I couldn't find rest that night thinking about this. I finally stepped out of bed and came out of our bedroom. As I was standing in the hallway, I saw a glow coming from downstairs. I gravitated toward the light and wandered gently down the stairway. The light was from the basement room the GSA had evacuated; it was left on. I knew someone had been there and had seen the emptiness of this room. It was probably Sarah. I sat there on the floor with hands on my temples and thought about the future that was awaiting me until I finally fell asleep.

I had the same recurrent dream that night that I have had for almost twenty-seven years. My father was playing catch with Charlie on the baseball field. Everything was as I had remembered it—a beautiful spring day with a nice breeze. I admired their joy and the freedom with which they played. Even in my dream I wondered if my father was going to speak to me. I watched them smiling and laughing as they were throwing the ball back and forth.

This time I walked in the direction of my father and sat on the bench near where he was standing. I admired his strength, agility, and his upright posture while playing. He threw the ball high and Charlie wasn't able to catch it. My father then took a moment to come sit next to me.

I had my head slightly down and turned to the left as I watched Charlie chase after the baseball. I then slowly looked over my shoulder and asked, "Dad, where have I gone wrong with my sons?"

He gazed at me and said, "Charles, I'm not sure what you mean. I don't think anyone has loved their sons as much as you have."

I appreciated his kind words but I still needed to know. So I asked again, "But where did I go wrong? Which Charlie did I have it right with?"

He smiled and said, "You raised each one as you were

supposed to. Your two Charlies are as different as you and me."

I was quiet for a few seconds and mulled over his comment before telling him, "But we are not that different."

My father laughed, "No we're not, but we are still two completely different people."

"What about Sarah? Where did I go wrong with her? Everything that has happened, was it my retribution for hiding everything from her?"

My father smiled and laughed a little; then he stood up to walk back onto the field. He took a few steps while still smiling and paused to catch his thoughts. Then he slowly turned and said, "Charles, you're looking but you're not seeing," while shaking his head. He gazed at me once more and calmly said, "You don't think a mother can recognize her own son? Who do you think had been protecting you from Dawson all these years?"

I was stunned; the image in front of me started to fade as I watched him walk back onto the field. I could see the sun shining brightly behind him as he was waning into the background. As I slowly arose from my sleep state and the picture in front of me became clearer, I could start making out the image of the sun to be the light above me that was still on in the room. The home phone was ringing. I slowly stood up and started to walk upstairs half asleep to receive the call. It was John.

"Charles, I have some good news," he said. I slowly brought my mind up to speed from its somnolent state and listened to him continue, "The swelling has finally come down. If everything goes well, we could be looking at having Charlie conscious either later today or tomorrow. I'll be running some blood tests afterwards so we can prepare for

GEMA."

I rubbed my eyes and realized the magnitude of what he was telling me. "That's great, John, thanks for letting me know. What are you doing there so early?"

John was quiet. "I was waiting for all of this to pass before telling you; you haven't been at work lately so I didn't want to burden you with some of what's happened."

"What is it? Tell me; it's okay. Things can't get any worse than they have been."

"The GSA came by Genomica yesterday and asked for all our inpatients to be slowly transferred to other facilities. Since I also work here I've asked for all my patients to be sent to the Richmond Hospital."

This was a recent development; I was surprised and shook my head before saying, "Oh, I didn't know that. I thought we just weren't allowed to see new patients."

"I should probably mention that I also asked for all your patients to be transferred here as well so I could follow them for you while we work things out with Charlie."

I had to take a moment to absorb what he was telling me. "Thank you, John. You are a true friend. I appreciate it. We'll try and be there at the hospital shortly."

Sarah had come downstairs as I was concluding my conversation.

"It was John," I said, looking at her. "Charlie is doing much better. He thinks he might be up even as early as later today." That sure brought a nice glow to Sarah's face.

"Oh, thank God!" she said. "Are you sure?" needing another confirmation.

I nodded and said, "Yes."

She smiled in excitement and looked at me before saying, "Thank you, I can't wait to see him."

We both hurried to get ready to go to the hospital. John had been waiting for us. He came into Charlie's room and said, "Sarah, Charles, we're planning on slowly weaning him off some of his medications and see how he is doing when he wakes up."

"Thank you, John," an upbeat Sarah remarked, cautiously optimistic.

He looked at me and waited before saying, "Charles, I know you've done this a million times before."

I looked at him wondering why then he was saying this.

"I just want you to be prepared for what is coming. It's a different experience when it's your own family. We don't know what limitations Charlie will have once he is conscious. I just don't want you to feel blindsided by what we find out," he said with a concerned voice.

"Thanks, John; I understand."

Then he looked at Sarah and said, "When he wakes up, he won't be himself either. He may be agitated and aggressive. That's normal and it's the effect of the medication. Don't let that disturb you."

"Thank you. I appreciate it," Sarah replied.

John left the room, spoke to the nurses, and provided the instructions for Charlie to be tapered off his medications. I sat there the whole day looking at Charlie waiting for him to regain consciousness. The waking up from a medically induced coma can be anywhere from a few hours to a few days. I wondered what deficits he would have and how he'd cope with them while I was in prison. If we provided him any of our current treatments, its effect wouldn't be permanent; how would he manage without me being here to help him through this ordeal down the road?

I was alone in the room when they came to do blood tests and to remove the dressing around Charlie's head. You could see that his head had been partially shaved before surgery and he no longer had his usual long hair. The resemblance to my previous Charlie with his hair shorter was striking. I hadn't seen Charlie look like this in seventeen years, and I couldn't help but reminisce about those years and step back in time.

I knew once Sarah returned she would probably see the similarity too. The moment had arrived for me to have the conversation with Sarah that I always needed to have. With Charlie coming out of his coma soon, it would only be a matter of time before Dawson looked for his deathblow.

When Sarah returned she came and stood across from me on the other side of bed. She looked at Charlie and I wondered what was running through her mind. "Sarah," I said, "there is something I need to tell you."

She looked at me gently and said, "Sure. What is it, Charles?"

"The GSA came by our home when you were in Rockford with Hannah."

She looked at me curiously and asked, "Why is that?"

"They said they were searching for evidence related to their charges of Genomica."

"Did they find what they were looking for?" she asked.

"I think so," I said before pausing to continue. "I'm not sure how to tell you this so maybe I'll begin by apologizing first." I stopped to catch my breath before gathering my thoughts to say, "I'm sorry. I'm very sorry, Sarah. This is not the way I had intended for any of this to happen and for me to tell you."

She was looking at me affectionately waiting for my next word when we heard a knock on the door. It was Dawson.

I think he had assumed I would be at work in the afternoon so it would be just him and Sarah. Dawson looked surprised when he saw me. After greeting us he said, "I heard from Chloe what had happened to Charlie and my thoughts were with both of you and wanted to see how he's doing."

We stared at him, not certain what to say.

"I would have come earlier," he said, "but I've been away from work all week with a terrible cold and didn't want to visit Charlie with an infection."

Sarah nodded her head, listening to what he was saying. I couldn't bear to hear him speak anymore so I just shifted my gaze toward Charlie. He continued on, "I was shocked when I came to work today and found out they had come to search your home and everything they were doing to Genomica. I couldn't believe it. I had nothing to do with this."

Dawson was trying to distance himself from everything that had happened with regard to the search warrant and the investigation.

I maintained my posture of looking away at him and fixed it solely on Charlie; he was my concern now. I could see that Charlie's eyes beneath his eyelids were moving. This was the initial sign that he was waking up; for the first time I could feel the excitement, almost the same delight I felt as when he was born.

Dawson pressed ahead with his thoughts, "I don't know if it makes any difference but I brought you something they took and shouldn't have."

He was carrying the same large gold envelope that contained our family picture. I recognized it right away. It had been in Charlie's wooden treasure chest the GSA had taken. It was my last gift to Charlie seventeen years ago just before he had passed away—a final gift that went unfulfilled.

I knew what Dawson was attempting to do. He was mending fences with Sarah. He was trying to portray that he actually cared for her family. He also knew as well as anybody that once I was in prison it wouldn't make a difference if he had showed an affectionate sentiment toward her loved ones, so why not score the points.

He handed the envelope to Sarah and she pulled out the large photo and looked at it. It sure was a beautiful picture. The photograph was of the three of us by the waters on perhaps the happiest day of our lives. I briefly looked over and could see Sarah was emotional when she saw the photo with a few tears trickling down her cheeks.

She put the picture back in the envelope, wiped her tears, and said, "If this is what you came for, it's done. Thank you. Now please leave."

Dawson didn't quit, "But, Sarah, I had nothing to do with this..."

I could see Sarah was ready to roll up her sleeves; she put the envelope on Charlie's bed with its backside up directly in front of me before saying: "You crossed a line. Once you crossed that line there was no going back." She then raised her tone, "I told you this before: I want you out of my home, away from my son, and away from my family."

I was fixated on Charlie as she was saying all of this; I could see the increased rapidity of the eye movements under his eyelids. Then as my gaze drifted slowly toward Sarah's direction, I glanced to where she had placed the envelope on

Charlie's bed.

There were Chinese characters written on the backside of that envelope facing me. I was dumbfounded and speechless. I'd never seen this; it was Charlie's writing. My eyes were rapidly looking at every character and putting together its message. It was Charlie's code. I remembered it well.

I was completely lost in my thoughts as I was deciphering it; Sarah's conversation with Dawson faded into background noises. I can only remember her saying, "Dawson, you can show yourself out. I don't want you here!"

As I was putting together the code I realized this was it; this was the solution I had been searching for. Charlie must have written this down the night before he had passed away. I was stunned; how could I have missed this?

My mind was overwhelmed with excitement and yet puzzled trying to put it all together. I was still perplexed that I had not seen the backside of the envelope when I packed it at the bottom of the treasure chest. I was retracing my steps to when I had stored this; it was before John had approached me about the complications. I certainly wasn't looking for the solution then. I did open Charlie's wooden chest one other time, but I had neither seen this nor could I have imagined it being there.

I was lost in my joy and in these thoughts when suddenly I looked up and saw Dawson pointing his finger at me. I can't say I could even comprehend what he was saying, I was so elated.

He said sharply, "From now on, there will be no Chloe, and as for your husband, we'll have the test results soon. Tomorrow we'll be coming for you. Your company will be shut down, and you'll spend the rest of your life rotting in a prison cell!"

I was trying to read the code and listen to Dawson at the same time, so I had a dazed expression on my face as I looked up and muttered, "Sure, Dawson."

That's when Sarah raised her voice and gestured to the door, "Show some respect. My son is in a hospital bed here. As for Chloe, she will be old enough to make her own decisions in a few years. Please leave."

Dawson was stunned, as was I.

"Please leave," she repeated.

I had to take a moment to gather my thoughts. I was dizzy between reading the code that Charlie had left and unraveling what had just transpired between Sarah and Dawson.

When Dawson left the room, there was complete silence for a few seconds. Sarah was looking at me as I was at her. I was flabbergasted. I glanced at the code on the envelope that she had turned to its backside and placed in front of me. I knew she had no knowledge of what it represented and the mystery she had helped solve. Time was short and I needed to act on this. I looked back and hurried to walk over to her; I gave her a kiss on the cheeks and said, "Thank you!" before storming out the door.

I reached for the phone in my pocket as I was running out and called John. I also quickly grabbed the blood tests that had Charlie's name on it. It was sitting on the counter at the nursing station.

"John, it's me, where are you?" I asked. He was on the fifth floor and Uncle Stewart was with him.

I continued, "I don't have time to explain. They'll be coming for GEMA tomorrow." I was scurrying for the elevator as I was speaking, "John, I think I have figured a way around our treatment regression. I can't get into it right now but bring as many blood samples of any of the patients you have with you. I'll call the lab at Genomica for our remaining patients."

"Are you sure?" John asked.

"I'm more certain than I have been in the last fifteen years."

John waited before saying, "Charles, we've been down this road before."

"I know, but you'll have to trust me. It's different this time. Can you bring Uncle Stewart as well?"

"Okay," he said, "I will. See you then at Genomica."

I quickly ran down to my car and dialed my office on the way. I needed to arrange for a rapid thaw of the stem cells of all our active patients as well as other necessary preparations. Some of our patients would require a retreatment for this solution to work, but many of them did not; we needed to prepare for each and every circumstance where GEMA was concerned. The rest we could do later.

XXIX

When I arrived at Genomica, I was sitting in the lab deciphering and translating Charlie's code. It was magnificent. It was so simple and methodical, yet so precise in its detail. I then called over my secretary, Wendy, as there were Chinese characters I couldn't translate. I didn't know if they were Mandarin words or disguised filler words; I just knew they weren't one of our medical coded words.

Wendy looked at the writing and recognized Charlie's handwriting, then glanced back at me and laughed.

"What's funny?" I asked while she was giggling.

She said, "That's Charlie's name. You are able to read every word except this one."

Wendy then described for me the sound of each character. I just shook my head. I had to pause to marvel at it all. To be sure, Charlie had signed his name at the top and at the bottom. John and Uncle Stewart finally arrived and were beside me as I continued to decrypt the code.

The first part of the equation we already knew would work. John saw the second part and said, "Didn't we already try this?"

I quickly pointed to the chart, "Yes, but we didn't include this particular growth factor."

Uncle Stewart looked at the third part of the equation, "Charles, we tested this last year."

I looked and said, "Yes, at half the concentration of MSCs; notice the combination of progenitor cells here?"

As I was translating the rest of the code, John looked around and said, "Wait a minute, am I missing something here?" I stopped to see what John was referring to. He opened his arms looking confused and said in jest, "When did you learn Mandarin?"

I turned to watch the dazed look on John's face before he voiced, "Uncle Stewart was telling me on the way about Scotland; when did I miss the chapter about your migration to China?"

Uncle Stewart seemed baffled too. I smiled and said, "I'll explain that later." I was busy writing the rest of the equation down. Both John and Uncle Stewart were starting to see what I was seeing: it was perfect, magical actually.

John was thinking aloud, "Okay, this is really clever …nice, I like this too…interesting choice of DNA vectors." Then he pointed toward the end and said, "I don't know how that's going to work?"

Uncle Stewart looked at it intently and paused before saying, "It will, John; look at these chemokines and these markers right here."

"What about this segment here, I thought we knew the

patients couldn't tolerate this?" John remarked.

I reviewed it closely and said, "Look at the step that comes before and how perfectly it's balanced. We never tried it with these anti-inflammatory cytokines."

He mulled it over and softly whispered, "No, you're right."

We admired the synchrony of it all. There was a silence in the room as we collectively looked at the flowchart drawn. It was flawless.

Uncle Stewart nodded his head and said, "Charles, this is perfectly orchestrated. It's outstanding."

I quietly affirmed his comment, as I couldn't help but remember Charlie—his charm, his spirit, and the gift he had for solving these sorts of problems. That's when Uncle Stewart clasped his hands and said, "We have enough evidence to administer the first two parts. They are already approved; we still need to study the last five segments before administering them."

I said, "I know. I asked Wendy earlier to call the lab for the animal blood and stem cell samples before they were transferred to the Talbot Facility. We can store and freeze those remaining segments for testing later."

Uncle Stewart then clamored, "What are we waiting for then? Let's get started with GEMA!"

I glanced at my watch and said, "I've asked for a rapid thaw of our patients' stem cells. It should be ready by now. We should have their blood samples from the lab prepared as well."

John motioned to walk and said, "I have our inpatients' blood samples in the other room."

"Great. Let me help you with that," I said.

"I'll have GEMA ready," Uncle Stewart said.

As we walked together to the other room, John was still

in awe. He asked me, "Charles, this was absolutely brilliant. How did you come up with this?"

I paused to answer his question.

He asked, "Charlie?"

"Yes," I affirmed.

He smiled and gestured in agreement.

As we were walking back, John told me, "I went directly to the lab and was able to gather recent samples of most of our patients. I had them deliver it to us. It saved a lot of time."

We both knew our patients' conditions and histories from memory. We had so many failed attempts over the years that it was impossible not to remember.

There were many patients. It was a tedious process entering each person's blood sample, stem cells, and having GEMA prepare the treatment protocol customized to their condition. At midnight, I asked Uncle Stewart to head home to rest. He resisted but John helped me convince him.

"Thank you, Uncle Stewart, for coming tonight and for all your help; it meant a lot to us," I told him.

"I was glad to be here and help you boys," he said. That brought a smile to our faces. John and I didn't feel like boys anymore, but I guess in Uncle Stewart's eyes we'd always be boys. Then Uncle Stewart looked at John and said, "What are you doing on June 27th?"

John shook his head and told him, "I'm not sure; nothing planned yet."

Uncle Stewart said, "It is Charles's Grandparents seventy-fifth anniversary. We're having a big celebration at our cottage. I would like for you and Sandra to come." I agreed with Uncle Stewart, "We definitely would love to have you there, John; you're like family."

John nodded. "Thank you; that would be very nice."

Uncle Stewart shook hands with each of us and looked at me to reaffirm my attendance, "I will see you there too, Charles."

I wasn't sure how to answer that now as I didn't know what was waiting for me in the morning when the GSA was coming; so I compromised and said, "For sure. I'll try my best."

John and I worked until 5am and finished every sample that was left. I was helping him store all the specimens for transport to take with the company vehicle. As we were packing the remaining few, I handed him one more covered in a special case.

"What's this?" he asked.

"It's for Charlie," I said. "Let him know how much I love him."

John was puzzled. "Aren't you coming?"

"The GSA will be arriving in the morning. I'd like to be here when that happens."

John was looking at me, lost for words. "Charles, the building is practically empty. You don't have to be here."

I never understood why any captain would want to sink with their ship. The idea never really made much sense to me, but tonight I understood. "This is my father's company. I need to be present," I said. "Besides, I'd rather they take me from here than from my home." That was the other small detail. Our house was also the home of my wife and Charlie. If I wanted them to continue living there, it was important not to taint its memory. You could say me being taken from there to go to prison might blemish its luster.

John was quiet. "Okay, if that's your wish," he uttered before hugging me. "You take care of yourself," he said as he embraced me. "Have faith. Everything will work itself out. It always does."

"Thanks, John; I mean it. Thank you for everything. Thank you for your friendship. Thank you for all that you've done for Charlie. I don't know how to thank you enough; I'm not sure what I would have done without a friend like you in my life."

"Stop it; I'm getting all choked up," he said with a laugh as he wiped a tear from his eye.

We shook hands and I helped him to the elevator. I was alone in the hospital now. I prepared GEMA for a complete shutdown. I knew I only had a few hours before the GSA would come to take GEMA and close down Genomica. I couldn't help but reflect on the structure I was standing in. My father had built this; it was his legacy. I had spent almost my whole career here. Both my Charlies were born here. I walked and passed by the delivery rooms of each of my Charlies.

I paced down those halls and reminisced about my entire time at this hospital. There were too many memories to count. Each hallway, each room, had its own story. John was right: the hospital was empty. All the inpatients had been transferred to nearby facilities. There was no overnight staff either as there was no one in the hospital.

I finally strolled down to the main lobby and saw Phillip there at the security station. He was covering the overnight shift, and he had been the only other person who was still at the hospital. I looked at him and asked, "What time does you shift end?"

He said, "At 9am, sir."

I nodded and said, "Why don't you go home and get some sleep. I'll cover for you from here on."

Phillip was surprised at my suggestion.

"It's okay; this is on me," I told him.

He took out his notepad and started to wonder where to put all his work-related items.

"Don't worry," I said, "leave that all on the desk."

The time was 7:50am and I knew the GSA would be coming soon. I looked at the lobby and remembered all the memories—the first time my father brought me here, and the first time I came here with each of my Charlies. I couldn't help but smile at the week when Charlie had been suspended from school and came to work with me, and how it led to what culminated in today's final discovery. It all felt strange.

I knew they would be closing down Genomica today and yet I never felt prouder. After today's discovery I knew it was all worth it. We made a difference. It might take months, perhaps years, for everybody else to figure it out, but we completed what my father had always started out to do; and who better than for Charlie to place the final stamp.

I could hear the sirens now in the background. The GSA was near. I looked at the portrait of my father and remembered the times when Charlie played his cello here. As I gazed at the painting the siren sounds were becoming louder and louder to a rising echo.

I then walked to the wall and removed the portrait, grasped it in my arms, and walked back to sit down on the couch in the center of the lobby and waited. I watched as nearly forty men from the GSA and armed forces came through those front doors and started closing down the building. One of the agents came to read the verdict that Genomica would cease to exist as a medical facility. I could see a few men taking the elevator. I knew they were looking to find GEMA to remove it.

I finally stood up and watched Devon Jackson haplessly walk up to me and say, "Dr. MacKinnon, I'm afraid we'll have to close down the hospital." He went further to explain the GSA's position regarding our treatments' failures, their growing concern of further deterioration beyond the patients' baseline, and the unknown long-term side effects.

I was only listening for the punch line to see if there was any more to it that involved me personally.

"I understand, Mr. Jackson," and nodded as he appeared to have completed his instructions. He looked at me and sensed my concern. "We have a few of your items back at the station. We should have them ready for you in the next week or so, and you should be able to come pick them up."

I waited to see if there was anything more on that topic. He then said, "You're free to go otherwise."

I was confused, though I didn't want show that I was. I looked back at Mr. Jackson; he knew what was on my mind and then scanned around the lobby to make sure no one was listening. He quietly said, "I have to admit, the pictures of your two sons were strikingly similar. We ran the genetic testing three times simultaneously; I personally supervised all of the tests. They were very similar, definitely close, enough to be siblings, but they weren't the same."

I didn't know how to react. I just looked at him as though I wasn't surprised, holding back my every thought. I slowly reached out to shake his hand and said, "Thank you, Mr. Jackson. I appreciate it."

As I walked away with my father's portrait in hand, I wasn't sure what to think. Charlie wasn't Charlie. It certainly explained many of the inconsistencies over the years. How was this even possible?

When I reached the parking lot, Dawson was there. He had finally appeared and was standing imperiously, staring coldly in my direction. He was trying to portray a bold face but there was defeat written all over it.

"Dr. MacKinnon," he said, "You will never, ever be able to practice your genetic treatments again."

I shrugged my shoulders, "That's okay. If it's not me, there will be others."

"There will be no others; this isn't something that will change," Dawson asserted.

I paused before saying, "Well, you know what they say: 'Progress is impossible without change, and those who can't change their minds can't change anything.'"

Dawson had a forced smile on his face and didn't have a comment. I walked to my car and placed the portrait carefully in my vehicle before driving off. My mind was working at every angle trying to figure out what had happened and how my two sons were different. My father had mentioned in my dream that my two Charlies were as different as him and me. It made absolute sense now.

As my mind started connecting the dots, it became perfectly clear. It had to be John. He was there that day when it had all happened. He told me on many occasions that "he had to protect me from myself." He believed in providing a "placebo" if it resulted in solving the problem. Even over the last few days he was confident I wasn't going to prison, and reassuring me to "have faith. Everything will work itself out," and that "we'll find a way through this, we always do."

XXIX

My father once said, "The most powerful of good deeds are the ones that are done without your knowledge." Of course, I always reasoned that it would be powerful only once you found out. I realize now that it doesn't change the equation even if you don't. The universe has its own way to restore the balance. John is a good man, my best friend. Sixteen years ago, if I had found out John had done this, I would have been furious. John knew me better than I knew myself and protected me; I owe everything to him. I was tempted to call him, but I was also moved to show him the same quiet graciousness he had shown me for almost sixteen years and simply accept his kindness with the same silence he had shown.

I went back to the Richmond Hospital. I needed to see how Charlie was doing. When I walked into his room, Charlie's eyes were closed. I wasn't sure if he was still in a coma or if he was sleeping. I sat by his bed and waited. Then his eyes opened and he stared at me. I knew that penetrating look. I had seen it before. Those deep searching eyes had been firmly imprinted in my memory. It was the same look Charlie had when he was born. His hands reached over to mine and gripped it tightly. He wasn't going to let go and neither was I.

"You're going to be okay, son; we'll get through this."

Charlie continued his gaze with tears in his eyes.

"Everything will be okay," I repeated.

In the coming days, Charlie's condition improved rapidly. John administered the first part of his treatment to expedite his healing. There were some deficits in both his arms and legs, but the GEMA treatment needed time to work and we would provide the subsequent parts of the treatment at the appropriate time. I told him, "Don't worry, Charlie,

Uncle John will have you up and about in no time."

As for John, when I saw him the next time he did ask me what had eventually transpired with the GSA. I smiled and told him what he had always said to me, "I had faith, and things just worked out."

He pretended as if he didn't know what I was talking about. It was not in his nature to pry to obtain details. He finally shrugged his shoulders, accepted that answer, and didn't push to discuss it further.

After a few days, Charlie was finally ready to be discharged from the hospital. My mother had also come and was staying with us. Charlie needed time to heal so we brought him home in a wheelchair. Once we arrived, I searched and brought him the same robotic wheelchair that my previous Charlie once had. I had it stored in the basement closet of our "hideout." I said, "Here, try this. It belonged to your brother."

Charlie then slowly placed himself in the robotic wheelchair and looked at me and said, "It fits perfectly—well, almost." As he glanced back at me in amusement of his new toy, he then looked at the fingerprint sensors and asked, "What are these?"

I told him, "That's a fingerprint-activated control for this device."

Charlie then slowly placed all his fingers around the fingerprint activation. We both watched with anticipation as he gradually completed putting all his fingers on all the sensors. We waited a few seconds—nothing happened. "Of course it wouldn't," I said to myself.

"We need to reset this, Charlie. Here, let me help you." The reset button was at the bottom. I cleared it and helped Charlie set his own fingerprints on the device.

He then looked up at me and said, "Dad, there is something I need to tell you."

"What is it, Charlie?"

"I'm sorry for what I did."

"Sorry for what?" I asked.

"For everything that happened prior to my accident; all the things I said. I don't know what I was thinking and what got into me. I didn't mean it; not the way it came out."

"It's okay," I said with a nod. I accepted his apology. I had almost forgotten what had happened in the turbulence of the last few days. Charlie himself had no recollection of where he had been prior to his accident. The last thing he remembered was our final encounter in the car. Considering the extent of his head injury, this sort of retrograde amnesia was quite common.

As for the robotic wheelchair, Charlie found the device absolutely remarkable. I could see the same joy on his face as my previous Charlie had playing with it. With Charlie now beside me, there was one last item that I always wanted to do and wasn't quite sure how to do it. I brought my dad's portrait inside the home and asked him, "Where should we put this?"

"I think it belongs here, Dad," Charlie pointed to the center of our living room.

"I agree," I said, and liked his suggestion. It just felt right, so we hung the portrait there.

XXX

My grandparents' seventy-fifth anniversary party was coming up and Charlie wanted us to attend even though he had been recently released from hospital. We prepared and drove off to the anniversary party. When we arrived at the MacKinnon cottage, Charlie, Sarah, and my mother went to the courtyard while I retrieved a package from the trunk.

Then I saw Hannah and Michael arrive with their children: Amelia, Nicholas, and now beautiful Scarlett. I walked over to congratulate them and provide Michael a helping hand in pulling the carriage out of their luggage compartment. Hannah was holding Scarlett and had started to walk inside with the children.

As Michael was bringing out the carriage, I couldn't help but notice that they also had one of those pink boxes with flowers on it. I laughed, "Michael, you've got one of those too. We're officially brothers-in-law. Let me shake your hand. No explanation necessary."

Michael took out the pink box and said, "This isn't actually ours—it's yours," as he handed it to me. He then explained, "Sarah had left it at our place when Scarlett was born and forgot to take it back, so we brought it here to return it to you."

"Thanks, I guess."

I took the box to my car and Michael went to the courtyard with his carriage. As I placed the box carefully inside my trunk, the lid popped open. I tried to seal it back on but my eye caught something familiar within the container.

"What is Jesse's treasure chest doing here?" I whispered to myself, looking back inside the box.

I slowly opened the wooden chest and browsed inside it with interest. There were a number of items of memories and about fifty pictures. I looked through each one: pictures with Sarah in the hospital bed holding Jesse, pictures of the three of us together. It was a long time ago and yet looking at these photos, it all felt like yesterday. I searched curiously through some of the other items—his clothes, his head cover, and then I saw something that confused me.

"What's Charlie's hair doing here?" I mumbled.

I stood there silently mulling this over. "I thought it was still with the GSA?" I quietly said as I wondered what hair the GSA had in fact taken. I continued looking through the treasure chest and I couldn't find Jesse's hair. It was not there. There was only Charlie's hair. I had my hand on the back of my head trying to think this through. I was lost in the translation and its implications as to whose genes the GSA had actually tested when suddenly I saw Charlie come back on the front patio.

"Dad," he called out.

"Mom said there is a faster way to make this go up the stairs."

I looked at him and said, "There is, Charlie; it requires the fingerprints of both your hands on the levers on the back. Let me come and show you. We have to set it up."

Charlie then asked as I was closing the trunk door, "Why is everything on this fingerprint-activated?"

I laughed, "Your brother designed this. He did it for security reasons, so no one can control where you are going except for you. He liked controlling his own destiny; he was smart. He recognized that your fingerprint is one of the simplest and yet highest levels of identification a person can have—it's even stronger than your DNA."

Charlie looked up at me and said, "Why is that?"

"That's because your fingerprint doesn't start taking its final form until you are in the mother's womb. All those fetal movements—the shearing and compressive forces—can ultimately change the fingerprint's final form. You can have quadruplets all with the same DNA and yet they'll all come out with different fingerprints—because nobody's activity will be exactly the same within the womb."

"So, they'll all be different?"

"That's right, Charlie." I paused before telling him, "We all ultimately write our own script in life starting from conception, and it begins with our fingerprints. That's why this is so useful."

I showed Charlie where to put his hands on the levers for the fingerprint sensors. "This is it right here. It should work now."

"That's cool, Dad. So essentially it's effective because of its simplicity, not its complexity."

XXX

I stood back and smiled, admiring his comment before saying, "Yes, something like that."

Then Charlie looked at me and said, "You never talk about my brother much; what was he like?"

I thought about it a few seconds before answering, "He was a lot like you—just different."

We were both silent. I then smiled and reached to put my hand on his shoulder and said, "Come on, let's go in." I brought the gift we had for my grandparents and passed it to Charlie to present it to them. We went inside toward the courtyard. There were many guests, family, and friends alike; each and all were approaching my grandparents with congratulatory comments.

I watched as my grandparents hugged Sarah and Charlie, and when it was my turn, I embraced them too. My grandfather smiled and said, "I hope you'll have your seventy-fifth anniversary here with Sarah."

"Thank you, Grandpa, I hope so too. I just don't know with all the excitement in my life if I can live that long."

All my cousins were there and their children were playing. Clyde and Charlie, both birth mates, were trying to figure out how to fly their kites. Scott, Catherine, Margaret and Harris were sitting on a bench under a tree enjoying the beautiful summer breeze and laughing.

My mother was reconnecting with all the family and friends, and I could see how much she had missed every single one of them. Each family member for her had some memory that tied back to my father.

As for Sarah, we never finished the conversation we had started in the hospital that day. I realized with time it was neither my apology she was seeking nor a confession for that matter.

When did she figure out what I was up to? I can 't say for sure, but I suspect she sensed something from the very beginning. I think she always knew that I needed Charlie. She also realized that one day she might need to defend me for it. Dawson confirmed that the day of Charlie's fifth birthday party. Ensuring I was out of town for the conception and having no conscious knowledge of what I had done better positioned her to protect me. As she became more familiar with Dawson, I guess she probably figured I needed all the protecting I could get. She also knew from his last visit that his true ambitions would soon unveil itself, which is why she went to the basement to retrieve her pink box to place Jesse's treasure chest inside. There was just one notable exception: it wasn't Charlie's hair in the treasure chest she left behind.

As my first Charlie once told me, quoting Sarah, "Sometimes it's better to let the mouse know where the cheese is than to leave it to his imagination to find it." It was a way of leveling the playing field with someone like Dawson. Sarah was always a step ahead. Well, at least I can finally comprehend where Charlie received his exceptional genes from—and thank God for that.

I looked over and could see Sarah starting to play the piano along with Dr. Li on his saxophone. Dr. Li was there the day Charlie was born and was one of the few people who appreciated the talents of each of my Charlies and connected with them both.

Uncle Stewart then saw me and waved for me to

approach him. He was standing next to a table with John. He smiled and congratulated both John and me on all the work we had done, and assured us in the coming years our efforts would be recognized. We also thanked him for his kind words and his contributions to our historic night.

Then Uncle Stewart showed me the book he had been working on: the stories and tales of the MacKinnon family. This beautiful book was sitting on the table. It had an elegant ancient cover and design; it was more than three thousand pages with each chapter narrating a different MacKinnon or closely related accounts.

I knew how much time Uncle Stewart had exerted in writing these stories for our family and the priceless gift he was leaving us all. I thought about the men and women whose stories he had chronicled—their sacrifices, their courage, and their fortitude—who characterized every value I endeared.

I opened the pages and browsed through this classic book. Uncle Stewart had used roman numerals to number the sections within a chapter to reflect its historic feel, each with symbols to mark its beginning, middle, and end. I couldn't help but admire the particular respect he had paid to Charles I. His name, when referenced, was always written in a distinct style to reflect his esteemed rank in the family.

Uncle Stewart looked at me and said, "Charles, I have completed this book as much as I could. I have left space and would like for you to write your account with your two Charlies." Raising his two fingers he asked me, "Will you consider writing these two chapters for me one day?"

I looked at John; he smiled and shrugged his shoulders as though he was telling me, *it's up to you, Charles.*

Uncle Stewart sensed a hesitation in my silence, so he told

me, "I've taken the liberty and asked Charlie if he would write a few introductory pages for you, and he has agreed."

"You mean like a prologue?" I asked.

"Yes, exactly; Charlie has even accepted to do it in his beautiful calligraphy or, if you like, his elegant handwriting, whichever you prefer. He smiled before finishing, "Now, how can anyone say no to that?"

I agreed in principle, but I still had some reservations about his proposal.

Uncle Stewart collected his thoughts before continuing more persistently: "Our family needs the story of every Charles in its purest form—your thoughts, fears, and hopes. I can't emphasize how important this is; you'd be leaving us an indispensable legacy." He paused to gaze at Charlie before saying, "Charlie represents the thirteenth Charles. This concludes an important epoch in our family history. Charles I was born in 1513; we have thirteen names of each gender in our family tradition and now the thirteenth Charles." He then pointed gently to his book and said, "This first volume simply would not be complete without this."

I gently felt and moved my hand across the blank pages that Uncle Stewart wanted me to fill, and could see he had already marked its first page with a crown and a header: 𝒮cotland 1563.

Charlie's hallmark "𝒮" was used to signify its opening letter that looked like a musical G-clef. I wasn't quite sure what they had in mind.

I reflected while admiring Charlie, who had moved closer to watch Sarah play the piano, and fondly remembered the contributions of each of my sons as the driving force to where I was stationed in life today.

I looked back at Uncle Stewart, who was waiting

expectantly for my response. I nodded in acknowledgement. "Yes. I'll write the story of all my sons—one day—and help complete the final segment of this volume—but I may need three chapters."

THE END OF CHAPTER I

EPILOGUE

Scotland High Court

he guard slowly approached and circled Charles MacKinnon I, who was peacefully seated. He asked him to demonstrate the curse he had previously performed. The afflicted victim was brought inside the room as a subject for him to implement and reverse his spell. Charles calmly retorted that this was not devilry, but a procedure used for medicinal purposes, and politely declined their request. The official struck him in the face and asked why it was then that the sufferer could not move his left arm. 'Remove thy curse!' he commanded.

Charles MacKinnon paused to watch the agitated warden before patiently reiterating that the loss of function was related to his unfortunate accident and not the intervention performed. He then reminded them that were it not for his procedure, this mortal would not be alive.

319

Failing to obtain a confession, they tied his hands and removed his footwear: he was shown 'the boot.' The foot press was applied by the assisting guards, and the crank mechanism was tightened: at the rhythm of every turn they waited breathlessly for his confession. They watched with anticipation only to be defeated by their captive in a battle of wills.

Unsuccessful and fatigued in their attempts, a hot-pronged iron was unveiled within the chamber. The composed prisoner heeded the persuasive pitch of their hammering. They exposed his hands and the guard showed the array of tools he intended to use to remove his nails. Confess—you shall be set free, they unfaithfully vowed. Revoke thy witchery—your brothers shall be pardoned, they perfidiously pledged. Charles MacKinnon serenely declined without fear or despair to the trickery tone of every promise. They angrily punished him only to be vanquished once again to an unearthly resistance.

The officials then clustered in a private room to discuss their plan and revise their schemes: they were clearly distraught by the failure of their pursuit. Without a confession, their case was weak. The ambitious chant of the masses outside could be heard in synchrony, clamouring for justice, hastening the officials for closure.

Charles MacKinnon reflected his plight alone in the chamber, tied to his chair. It was at this time that his son, Duncan, crawled through the window in an attempt to save him. Charles advised him as he had aforetime, to leave at once with his mother towards the Northwest Highlands and begin anew. He refused to accompany them, for as long as he was free, they would not be safe.

The beat of the guards' footsteps could be heard in harmony, marching, returning once again: Duncan climbed back through the window from which he came and looked on fearfully at the pending fortune of his father.

The officials reappeared sneering as they had a devised plan: 'pricking' as they called it. A 'Devil's mark' was to not have pain to their 'pricks.' A professional pricker was brought inside the room to perform this act. They observed expectantly as the thick needles and pins pierced his skin throughout his body.

Charles MacKinnon was ever mindful that his son was watching tearfully through the window. He neither cringed nor showed any display of pain. They summoned the judge as their plot had finally been fulfilled. He possessed the 'Devil's mark!' they claimed. The witnessing officials confirmed their scandalous verdict at which moment the guard stepped out of the courthouse and screamed, 'Guilty!'

The mob of civilians cheered and waited impatiently for Charles MacKinnon to be carried out of the building. His hands and feet were bleeding as he was dragged. Once outside, a resounding burst of anger ensued as the enraged populace was ready to unleash their wrath. The first person to cast a stone was the patient whose life he had saved; multiple strikes then followed to the chorus of their contempt.

The commotion garnered momentum as every man, woman, and child gathered to witness this spectacle. Far off in the distance, at the centre of town, flames and smoke could be seen.

As Charles MacKinnon was steadily ushered, Duncan followed discretely, eager to intervene. Charles stopped to gaze at him once more, and gently nodded to remind his son to carry forward his duty and trust its destination—for until the future is written, before his fate is determined, destiny has more than one story.